LOST

A Novel

PRISCILLA AUDETTE

ISBN 978-1-64140-014-5 (paperback)
ISBN 978-1-64140-016-9 (hardcover)
ISBN 978-1-64140-015-2 (digital)

Christian Faith Publishing, Inc.
832 Park Avenue
Meadville, PA 16335
www.christianfaithpublishing.com

Printed in the United States of America

Not until we are lost do we begin to understand ourselves.
—Henry David Thoreau

Dedication

To the steadfast tortoise,
who may be slow, but who travels far,
symbolizing a mothering energy whose magic
joins heaven above and earth below.

PART I

Descending

***

Denial
Anger
Bargaining
Despair

DENIAL

Denial helps us pace our feelings of grief. There is grace in denial. It's nature's way of letting in only as much as we can handle.
—Elisabeth Kubler-Ross

CHAPTER 1

ON HER WAY TO THE dry cleaners, Faith Kincade sang along with the Burt Bacharach song on the oldies station, "LA is a great big freeway / Put a hundred down and buy a car / In a week, maybe two, they'll make you a star…" Pulling into the parking slot, she killed the engine, silencing Dionne Warwick. Faith stood next to her car and stretched.

A casual observer would have noticed a woman who, while deep in her middle years, was still a head turner. Her long legs were accentuated in snug leggings and short soft-suede boots. The bright multicolored scarf draped about her shoulders added just a touch of sophisticated elegance to the hip-long top she wore. Her shoulder-length blonde hair, possibly touched up but not noticeably so, floated around her face, thanks to a gentle breeze. Her makeup was understated, leaving the impression of a flawless complexion with only a few laugh lines around the eyes adding both character and authenticity to her face—a rarity in this culture full of women desperate to retain their vanishing youth. What one would see and admire when looking at Faith was a well-put-together woman who had chosen to age naturally and gracefully.

Faith's eyes traveled toward the backdrop of foothills behind the foreground of city buildings. There was no cloud in the sky, or a wisp of smog. Warm, but not too hot—a perfect spring day. She thought of the song about LA being a great big freeway and smirked at the irony that she (like so many other Southern Californians) would drive the six blocks to the dry cleaners instead of walking the distance on such a beautiful day. She only had three items to pick up, and it would have been no hardship to schlep them home again on foot. But Southern Californians loved their cars. Pulling her claim slip out of her purse, she turned toward the store that boasted 365-days-a-year-24-hours-a-day service.

This particular establishment has been Faith's home away from home for many years. She had owned a little boutique that sold gently used upscale clothing, and, of course, second-hand clothes often needed a nip or a tuck here or there before they could be put on the racks in the store. This place was always open and always had a seamstress and a tailor on the premise. But since she had sold her business a few months before, she only dropped off or picked up clothing here on the rare occasion. She wallowed in a moment of nostalgia while she thought of the shop she'd loved and had finally sold mostly because it hadn't been economically feasible to keep it any longer.

And, truth be told, for the past few months, she had enjoyed not having the constant obligations of the store. She and her husband were able to spend more quality time together; and, she had to admit, she liked the life of leisure. She spent more time doing things she rarely had time to do in the past, photography, for example. She had always enjoyed taking pictures when on vacation. Photographing nature was her specialty, and even though digital pictures had taken over for most people, she liked doing things the old fashion way. She discovered she enjoyed the whole process of photography—from snapping the picture to watching it develop. That feeling that filled her when she saw the image appear on a blank sheet of paper was close to awe. In the early years, she had experimented with developing her pictures at home in her bathroom. She kept the light out by shoving a towel under the door and putting blackout curtains over the window. But her daughter had complained about the chemical smells; and while her husband didn't say anything about the inconvenience, he did roll his eyes and shake his head a lot. And, she had to admit, it was a cramped and awkward space to work. She found a place in town where she could rent a darkroom when she wanted one and that made everybody happy. Lately, she'd been experimenting with some black-and-white expressions and felt very satisfied with the results.

In addition to photography, she also found time to indulge in her passion of gardening. Her front yard was a neighborhood show-place. But her backyard was her favorite spot, her own personal delight. Tending to the plants and weeding several times a week gave structure to her days while at the same time providing her with that special Zen time—a time when she went to that place of no time—where she allowed herself just to be. But a person could only do so much gardening. It wasn't like she had acres and acres of land. Houses in Burbank were mostly on fairly small plots, and the houses took up most of that square footage. Besides, she was starting to get itchy feet again. As much as she loved her life of leisure, she'd been thinking about going back to work. In fact, Clark had been encouraging her to do just that. Money was tight and the economy, contrary to what she'd hear on the evening news, was not getting better. It had been in the toilet for years and was still there. So, yes, it was time to start looking for some kind of job, time to be heading in a new direction, and time to start doing something else. But what? She hadn't figured that out yet. Shaking off those thoughts, she headed in to the store to get her items.

Returning home from the cleaners, Faith had the radio on but was not really hearing the song. Her mind was on her daughter's upcoming graduation from college. Emily, her baby. It brought a few tears of pride to her eyes knowing that her smart, capable daughter had reached that milestone and was ready to leap into life. Entering the intersection, Faith saw a flash in her peripheral vision.

The woman driving the oncoming car made a choice that would alter Faith's life forever. The woman decided to make an immediate (albeit illegal) U-turn. She rammed into Faith's car full-on broad-side—to use the vernacular: T-boning it.

In that very split second before the inevitable impact, Faith saw the other woman's face. Her eyes huge and round, her mouth opens in a perfect circle of shock. She also realized, in that split second, there was a complete absence of sound. She imagined that breaks were squealing and perhaps even she or the other woman was screaming, but she didn't hear a thing. She was immersed in a void of soundlessness. Then the impact occurred and the woman's air bag exploded instantaneously. Oddly enough, Faith's own airbag failed to expand. That was her only fleeting thought, then nothing for the next few moments.

The collision drove the door and frame into Faith's left side, impacting the side of her head and body. The rebound first propelled her away from the driver's side door and partway across the car in the direction of the passenger door, but the seatbelt held and the force of the impact snapped her back within nanoseconds, and once again, her head *cracked* into the window and frame on the driver's door. That crack was the first sound to penetrate the soundlessness. Whether it was her cranium, the window, or both, Faith didn't know. All she knew was she heard a sound that reverberated inside her head. *Crack!* The car spun in several circles, and, seatbelt notwithstanding, with each turn Faith's head, again, hit the frame of the door and window. In turn, her brain proceeded to bounce around in her cranium like a pinball in a machine hitting *tilt* again and again. The car finally came to a stop.

She may have been unconscious for a moment or two or three. She gained awareness to the sound of someone calling to her. "Lady, hey lady, are you okay?" Her eyes fluttered open and she saw a man in a hardhat trying to open her door. "It's stuck, lady, are you okay?"

"I don't know," Faith stammered. She looked to the passenger side of the car, which was slammed up against the wall and railing of the freeway overpass.

"I'll see if I can get a crowbar and get this door open. Don't go anywhere." The man took off with those silly words hanging in the air.

"Don't go anywhere," she said to herself. Stunned but slowly becoming cognizant of her situation, she picked up her phone and called her husband. "Clark, I've been in an accident." Her voice was breathy, shaky.

"Are you okay?"

"I don't know. I think so. I'm trapped in the car. I can't get out."

He could hear sirens through the phone. "Did someone call 911? Are those sirens for you?"

"I don't know. Yes, the police are here now. I can't get out of the car, Clark."

"Tell me where you are!"

It was only a few blocks from where they lived. Clark, who had just gotten home from work, jumped in his truck and was there in moments. When the Jaws of Life arrived, the rescue workers got going on Faith's car. Clark stood out of the way, listening to the woman from the other car talk to a police officer. She had blood splashed down the front of her blouse and she kept dabbing at her nose, although it was no longer bleeding. "I didn't see her. She wasn't there." Then defensively, "There's no '*No U-Turn*' sign!"

"Why didn't you see the car?" The policeman asked.

"I don't know." The woman was shaking her head in bewilderment. "It wasn't my fault. I'm sick. I left work early because I don't feel well." Then she reiterated, "*It's not my fault!*"

He made a notation to self to get the woman's phone and check to see if she was texting or talking while driving.

Clark then overheard one of the freeway construction workers talking to another police officer. "The car was right in the middle of the intersection when it was hit. The light was green. That other dame should have expected cars to be driving through the intersection on a green light. I don't know what she must have been thinking to attempt that U-turn like she did."

That cop finished writing something down in his notebook then scanned the surrounding area. The freeway ran diagonally under this particular intersection, and a new freeway onramp had been under construction for months. A couple of the construction workers had started moving some of the orange cones from where they had been placed to divert traffic while they worked. The officer stepped up to them. "Please don't touch anything. We need to leave the scene of the accident intact until further notice." One of the construction workers looked over toward a foreman who was standing a distance away. The worker shrugged and the foreman just shook his head.

Up until that moment, Clark had been like a fly on the wall just listening to and observing the goings-on. But after seeing the cop stop the workers from moving the cones, something told Clark to start taking pictures with his phone and that's what he did. He snapped the two smashed up cars, the broken glass, metal and fiberglass pieces in the street, the freeway construction, and, particularly, the orange cones that the workers had been trying to move before the cop stopped them. He took pictures from every possible direction and angle, instinctively trying to preserve the scene.

Stepping back and resting against a wall, Clark pressed a hand to his heart, which had started to race. "Calm down," he cautioned himself. "Don't give yourself a heart attack." He took a few deep breaths while watching the authorities deal with the accident. Clark had added a little girth to his frame in recent years and his knees had been starting to bother him more and more. Between that and the recent acid reflux he'd started popping antacids for, the heralds of aging were making themselves known. He had always been proud of the fact that there was no male-pattern baldness in his genes. His full head of hair had always been one of his vanities. But the telltale strands of gray that had started slowly making their appearance in his thirties and forties had suddenly begun a stampede as he cruised through his fifties and closed in on sixty. He was now much more salt than pepper. Like his wife, he had laugh crinkles around his eyes that deepened every year, but it was the twin goal posts of worry between his eyebrows that were becoming one of the most obvious features in an otherwise handsome face. And the worry was clearly evident as he watched and waited.

It took the Jaws of Life an hour to pry open Faith's car enough to get her out. She was shaken, stunned, but seemingly all of a piece. Her shoulder, elbow, hip, and ankle on her left side were sore, as was the side of her head; but there was no blood, no broken bones, and, therefore, she was not too worried. An ambulance had arrived and for precautionary measures, Faith was taken to the emergency room of the nearest hospital for observation and a check over, her husband following in his truck.

Apparently, this was a day for accidents. There had been some kind of a school bus disaster that resulted in an emergency room full of kids—some with cuts, some with broken bones—and frantic parents. As Faith had neither cuts nor broken bones, she was put at the end of the line.

After a long wait, the harried young emergency room doctor looked into Faith's eyes with a bright light, told her she was probably a little concussed but that he didn't anticipate any problems. He suggested she ice her sore spots and told her to go home and rest.

Clark interjected with a question, "Shouldn't you do some kind of tests or something to make sure she's okay to go home?"

The doctor made a gesture around the emergency room at the banged-up kids and their nearly hysterical parents. "Compared to them, she's had a day in the park. Some of them will be traumatized for life. Take her home. Put ice on what hurts. Rest." And they were dismissed.

So under doctor's orders, Faith did just that—rested. Clark got some Mexican takeout for dinner and they sat on the couch and ate while they watched TV, and that was that. Faith was chilly, odd as it was still warm outside, but she snuggled under a throw and was content just to veg in front of the television.

Nausea got her attention. Faith put her hand to her stomach and then acted. She tossed back the throw and made it to the bathroom just in time. *So much for the Mexican dinner,* she thought to herself.

Clark knocked on the bathroom door. "Honey, are you okay?"

"I'll be out in a minute." She turned on the tap and filled her cupped hands with water. After rinsing out her mouth a couple of times, she brushed her teeth.

When she went back into the family room Clark was looking at her with concern. "Dinner didn't sit too well?"

"Guess not."

"Better now?"

"I think so." She snuggled back down on the couch and pulled the throw over her again.

After staring at some mindless sitcom for the better part of a half hour, Faith picked up her phone and called her daughter.

"Hi, Mom."

"Hi, back at you. What you up to?"

"Going over notes. I've got my last final tomorrow."

"Yeah!"

"Chris and I were looking at apartments the other day. We found one we liked and we signed a lease."

"Yikes! Are you…are you sure you guys are…are ready to move in together?"

"Yes, Mom, we're sure. We've been together all through college. We're ready."

Faith sighed. Her baby was growing up so fast and so sure of herself. The summer before, Emily had an internship with Target and upon her completion of college, they offered her a position that she couldn't refuse. The money figure was great and she would be starting up the ladder, working her way into a corporate position. Life was good. Faith sighed again.

"Mom? You still there?"

"Yes, I was just thinking…of how fast you've…grown up. By the way, just wanted to tell you, I was…in a car accident today."

"What! Mom, are you okay?"

"Fine Emmy, just…fine. Bumps and bruises is all. The car's…a mess, probably totaled."

"Did you get the other person's insurance information?

"A…I think…I think the cops got all that. They were there… the cops. It was quite the ordeal. Took over an hour…to get me out of the car."

Emily thought about that for a moment. "Wow, are you sure you're okay? Whiplash? You might be able to sue."

"Honey, I don't think…it will come to that. Accidents…happen. I'll be fine."

Clark signaled that he wanted to talk to Emily too. "I'm going to pass you off to Dad now. Bye, I love you."

"Love you too, Mom."

"Hi, princess."

"Tell me, is Mom really okay?"

Clark looked at Faith and winked at her. "She's fine. You know your mom, doesn't let anything get her down." They chatted for a few more moments and then said their good-byes.

When Clark handed the phone back to Faith, her next call was to her sister. Hope answered with a, "What's up?"

"I was in a car accident today."

"Oh, my Goodness! Are you all right?"

"Yes, fine. Just a…a little shaken up…at the time."

"What happened?"

"Some woman…she made a U-turn…right into…a…into my car as I was going through an intersection. It just…happened so fast. It took…over an hour…to get me out of the car."

"That doesn't sound good. It must have been quite the impact."

Faith rested her hand on the side of her aching head. "Yeah, it was…a heck of an impact. I'm a little…battered and bruised… and I guess I'm still a little shocky. We had…Mexican take out…for dinner. I just puked all that up. But other than that, I'm okay…you know me…I'm a survivor."

"Are you sure you're okay? You sound, I don't know, a little spacey."

"Well, guess I'm…entitled. Anyway…, I called just…to let you…know.

"I'm glad you did. How's the person in the other car?"

"I think her…airbag broke her nose. She had a lot of…blood on her. There was no…blood on my end. Oh yeah, and my…airbag… didn't…didn't…"

"Inflate? Your airbag didn't inflate? I told you that car you drive was a piece of junk."

"Well…it's now…a totaled…piece of…of junk."

"Do you want Cliff and me to head home?"

"No. No. Where…are…you anyway?"

Hope laughed. "We're at the OhKay Casino in New Mexico. I just hit a little jackpot, so cashed out, and am now basking by the pool with a long, cool drink."

"Of course…you did. How…much?"

"Well, not the biggest I've ever hit, but a nice chunk of change. Eleven hundred dollars."

"You are…always so…lucky. What was…it? The…Blazing 7s slot…machine like…like that time in…in Vegas?"

"That was Mesquite. No, this time it was the Electric Storm slot machine."

"Pennies?"

"Nickels."

"I guess eleven hundred dollars...is a lot...of nickels. As I... said...you sure are the...lucky one."

"Sometimes. But I also stick to my rules and never go over the limit I allot myself when I gamble. That's why I'm lucky more often than not. But, speaking of luck, sure sounds like you weren't so lucky today."

"No. Guess...I wasn't."

"Really, Faith, we can head out first thing in the morning and be back home before you know it."

"I'm...fine..., sis. I just need...a good night's...rest."

"Okay, then."

"So you...going to be staying at the...casino for a while?"

"No, you know me, hit and run with casinos. We heard of a hot springs spa kind of place that's located east and north of where we are. We'll probably go check that out."

"Sounds...fun." Faith yawned hugely.

"And it sounds like it's bedtime for you. I'll touch base with you tomorrow."

"Okay. Talk to you then."

CHAPTER 2

The next day, Faith was sore all over, but that was to be expected. She still felt a little queasy so had only a piece of toast for breakfast. She didn't really feel better after the toast, but no worse either. She couldn't decide which was more annoying, the queasiness or the headache that still lingered from the night before. So ignoring her head, her stomach, and her stiff and sore muscles and joints, she did some weeding in the backyard during the morning hours. She was a little dizzy when she stood up after weeding, but the sun had been beating down on her for a while. Shaking the dizziness off, she went indoors and gulped down a glass of tap water. Then, feeling sleepy, she lay down on the couch, tossed a throw over herself, and didn't awaken until Clark arrived home from the building site, wondering what was for dinner.

"Wh-what?" She was so groggy from the hours-long nap she couldn't think straight. "D-dinner?"

"Never mind, sweetheart, I'll go get us some In and Out burgers. Or do you want something else. Is your stomach okay?"

"I-I'm f-fine. In…and Out's o-okay."

They got through dinner and Faith was grateful there was no resultant nausea. Not being able to concentrate on the television news with her aching head throbbing away and feeling tired to boot, she excused herself and headed on up to bed.

When Hope called to check in, Clark answered Faith's phone. "Hi Hope, she's sleeping. But it's really too early for bedtime, I'll wake her up."

"No. Don't. Let her sleep. I just wanted to know how today went. I'll bet she's sore."

"Yes, sore and a little confused too. And very tired. Is that normal?"

"I don't know. Maybe."

"I guess sleep is the best medicine at this point."

"Well, promise to keep me in the loop."

"Will do."

***

Two days after the accident, Faith was talking to the neighbor over the little split rail fence between the two properties as she watered the front lawn. After a moment, Faith paused and stared at her friend. "Wh-why are y-y-you loo-looking at m-me li-like I ha-have ta-ta-two h-h-heads?" she asked.

Meghan cleared her throat then said, "Did you hear what you were saying? No, not what you were saying, but how you were talking?"

Confused, Faith shook her head, "Wh-wh-what ar-are you ta-ta-talking a-a-about?"

"You're stuttering. I've never heard you stutter before in my life."

"Wh-what? I-I-I am?"

Meghan stepped over the low fence and rubbed Faith's arm. "I think you need to go back to the hospital and talk to that doctor again. Is Clark home?"

"N-n-no. He-he-he's at th-th-the s-s-site. O-O-ooh d-dear G-G-God, I-I-I am st-st-stut-te-erring!"

"Come on." Meghan took the hose from her and turned it off. "Let me drive you back to the hospital and let that guy have another look at you."

***

And so the nightmare began.

"When a person sustains a head injury," the doctor was explaining to Faith, "particularly in a car accident where there is a lot of bouncing around, the brain sloshes around inside the cranium. There are little bony protuberances inside the cranium and the brain smashes up against them and it gets bruised, and sometimes, there is internal bleeding that causes swelling. So it looks like that might be what has happened inside your head."

"And you didn't know that two days ago when she was in here?" Meghan got right to the point. "Maybe she should have been given a heads-up as to what kind of symptoms to expect from this head injury."

The doctor sighed. "She just needs to rest and let the swelling in the brain subside. And that takes time."

Faith, uncharacteristically, just sat in silence while the two conversed.

"Is there a reason you didn't order a CAT scan when she was in here last time?" Meghan wanted to know.

"Look, there was no fracture…"

"How do you know that? Isn't it possible some fractures are so small that you can't see them with the naked eye?"

"She was fine when I saw her. There was no fracture. She wasn't stuttering then."

"Even I know that symptoms from head injuries can be delayed for days. Even I know that when the brain is injured that the pathways the brain uses to send messages back and forth can be messed up. Which is what has happened. Hence the stuttering."

"I've gotten a CAT scan ordered now. Get that done and find her a neurologist. There is no more we can do for her here. This is an emergency room. She is no longer an emergency."

On the way back home, Meghan had to stop fast to avoid a person who made a left turn in front of her. Faith threw her hands up over her face and barely held back a yelp. "It's okay, Faith. That idiot was just in a hurry. Didn't want to wait for me even though I had the right of way."

Faith's response was to cross her arms and rub both her upper arms with her hands as if she had a chill, and her breath started coming faster and faster.

"Come on, stop breathing like that. You're going to end up hyperventilating. Don't worry. I'll get you home in one piece."

Faith concentrated on slowing down her breathing while Meghan drove more conscientiously. "Sorry about slamming on the brakes like that, but it was better than the alternative."

"N-n-no ki-ki-kidding."

Meghan pulled into her driveway and turned off the key. "There, safe and sound."

Faith, took a couple of breathes. "I d-don't th-think I want t-t-to go an-anywhere in a ca-car again f-f-for a wh-wh-while."

"Understandable."

Just as they were getting out of the car, Clark arrived home. Meghan walked next door with Faith and greeted Clark. "Hi, neighbor, I just took you wife on a little joyride to the hospital."

"What? Honey, are you okay?"

"I-I-I don't kn-know."

Meghan took Faith by the arm and started steering her toward the front door. "Why don't we go inside and I'll fill you in."

Faith lay down on the couch, pulled the throw over her, and immediately fell into sleep. Clark and Meghan stood in the kitchen, talking in low tones.

"What happened?" Clark wanted to know.

"She was stuttering, I mean really stuttering. Now, I know that Brian is the psychologist in the family, but I've picked up a few things over the years and I think what's going on with Faith is serious, very serious. At any rate, I wanted to get her back to the doctor who first saw her to see if he could give us some insight into what's going on. He was not much help at all. He did order a CAT scan and recommended we find her a good neurologist. That's was the extent of his help. He basically dismissed us as rudely as possible. 'Here's your hat, what's your hurry.'"

Clark shook his head. "I asked him about taking some tests when we were there. He said it wasn't necessary. Or maybe he didn't exactly say that, I don't remember. What I do remember is that they were busy with a bunch of banged-up kids from a school bus accident. They were his priority, and Faith apparently got the short end of the stick."

"Well, what's done is done, but she needs help now."

"Okay, then, I guess we'll get her to a neurologist."

"Yeah. And, just a thought, maybe you need to start documenting what you remember from when you got to the scene of the accident, when you were in the emergency room, etc. Get the record down while it's fresh in your mind."

"Because?"

"Because you never know."

Clark pulled open the fridge, popped the top off a beer and offered it to Meghan. She shook her head, so he took a swig. "Then, what? I mean, other than getting her to a doctor. I don't really know what to do for her. She's been sleeping a lot these past couple of days since the accident."

"Well, the sooner you get her to the neurologist the better."

"Is Brian around? Maybe he could give me some insight here."

"He left for Sacramento this morning. Won't be home for a few days."

"Okay. Well, at least you were here and noticed that Faith needed help. You guys have been such great neighbors. I hated to see that 'for sale' sign go up on your lawn the other day."

"Would you believe we already have an offer?"

"That was fast! Did you accept it?"

"Counteroffered. You know Brain. Loves a good haggle."

"And if they take the counteroffer, then what? Off to Sacramento? For good?"

"Yep."

"Don't know what we're going to do without you next door." He looked through the doorway to his sleeping wife. "Especially now. You guys have always been there in a pinch."

Meghan smiled at the compliment but shook a finger in Clark's face. "I think you need to get Emily to move back home after she goes through graduation this weekend."

"You think? I don't know. Faith has really been enjoying her empty nest after Emily moved into the dorms. Only child notwithstanding, we always had a houseful of kids and teenagers while she was growing up, and, the fact is, the peace and quiet has been great. A whole new experience."

"Well, it's reality check time. Faith has had a severe bonk on the head and has sustained a brain injury. We don't know the extent of that injury, but, well, my father always used to say, 'Hope for the best, expect the worst, and take what you get.' So I think it's time to start planning for the worst and then hope it isn't that bad."

Clark took a long swallow of beer. "You're starting to scare me, Meghan."

"Good! Now get on the horn and start talking to that daughter of yours."

"Graduation is Saturday. I'll talk to her then, face to face."

Meghan looked through the doorway at Faith who was as still as a corpse. "It's a long drive to Long Beach and back."

"Not that long."

"With her in this condition? Yeah, it's long. Just driving her home from the hospital was a challenge. She doesn't want to spend any more time in a car than she has to. And who can blame her?"

"Well, she's not going to want to miss the graduation ceremony. That's not going to be an option. And we have a big dinner planned afterward with Emmy's boyfriend and his folks. I mean, that's all in stone."

"Then drive down Friday night and get a motel. But wait until after the traffic lightens up. You don't want to be stuck in any gridlock. That way she will be rested for the ceremony on Saturday and not exhausted from the trip down. And you'll probably want to go back to the motel after the celebration dinner. She'll be too tired to drive home after the graduation and all that."

Clark just looked at her, set his empty beer can on the counter, and crossed his arms over his chest as he leaned back against the sink.

"Yeah, I know, I'm bossy. I'm also right."

"Yes, I suppose you are." He walked her to the front door. "Thanks again, Meghan." He gave her a hug and closed the door behind her.

He looked in on his wife, then went into the office, booted up the computer, and proceeded to make a reservation at the Best Western he knew was near the university. That accomplished, he sat back and looked at the framed photograph of his wife that had the place of honor on his desk for nearly twenty-five years. She was as beautiful now as she had been then: a statuesque natural blonde whose green eyes were the exact same shade as his. In the photo she was laughing, head tossed back, her long hair flowing in a breeze. He smiled recalling the day he'd snapped that photo. They were newly engaged and had been talking about the family they dreamed of having. She had wanted lots of kids. Unfortunately, they were only able to have the one. But at the time the photo was taken, they didn't know that would be the case. He sighed, remembering the curve ball the doctor had thrown at them after Emily had been born, letting them know she would be their one and only. He supposed it made them appreciate her all the more, knowing she was it for them. As with the majority of couples, they'd ridden the roller coaster ride of ups and downs during their marriage, but it was mostly ups. They were happy, they balanced each other nicely, and they'd raised a remarkable daughter. He picked up the picture and smiled. "I always called you hardheaded. Guess your head wasn't as hard as I thought it was, huh? So, that being the case, I'd better find us a good neurologist."

CHAPTER 3

CLARK LEANED HIS FOREHEAD AGAINST the cool windowpane and looked down on the backyard. It was dawn, just a little overcast, but it was a sure thing the sun would burn that away in a short time; the weatherman on the news the night before had promised a scorching day. So what else was new? Clark took a deep breath and centered himself. Those moments between waking and getting ready for work when the house was quite were one of Clark's favorite times of the day. He gazed down on his wife's flowers and shrubs. She sure loved digging in the dirt. Then his mind flipped from her digging in the dirt to how she had been since the accident. They had gotten through the graduation and, as predicted, the ordeal had worn Faith out completely. But not only had it worn her out, she had been behaving uncharacteristically all weekend. He'd packed her camera bag, as he knew she'd want it, yet she hadn't touched it all weekend. When he mentioned to her that she might want to take some photos of their daughter, she had just looked at him with a little frown of confusion. So he took it upon himself to snap a few pictures with his phone as he knew in the long run they would want some.

When he'd talked to his daughter after the ceremony, Emily had agreed to move back home. But it wouldn't be until she and Chris got back from a trip they had planned. They had airline tickets and room reservations, all of which were nonrefundable. They'd be gone just shy of two weeks. That seemed to be the timeframe he'd been dealing with lately. When he had called to set up an appointment with the neurologist, the receptionist said the doctor's next opening was two weeks out. Well, it was one week down and one to go, and *what a week* it had been.

He looked back at his sleeping wife, then turned away again; he felt tears sheen his eyes, so to battle them back, he concentrated on focusing on the out-of-doors. He wasn't a praying man, but he sent a plea out into the early dawn, "Please help her."

During this past week, things had devolved from bad to worse; and it wasn't just the fact that she slept most of the time. He was noticing a lot of things going haywire and it really concerned him. It had been Faith's habit, when arising in the morning, to pour her first cup of coffee then sit down with the morning paper and get caught up on the news. The other morning, he hadn't headed out to the site before she'd gotten up as he usually did because he had some blue-prints to refine, so he was a firsthand witness to something short cir-cuiting in her head. When Faith sat down with the paper, he noticed she suddenly started getting agitated. She pushed her coffee cup away and spread the paper flat down on the table. She placed both hands on the paper, framing an article and looked closely at it. Then she started shaking her head and flipped a page; she looked at it for a few moments, pulled back, and flipped another page. Her frustration was apparent and her flipping of pages was becoming almost frantic. "What the heck are you doing?" Clark finally asked.

Faith was breathing funny. "Th-th-the w-words."

"Yes? The words?"

"Th-th-they don't m-make sense."

He walked over, put his arm about her shoulders, and looked down at the paper spread over the table. "What doesn't make sense?"

Tears started flowing down her cheeks, "I-I-I can read t-the wor-words, I-I-I know t-the words, b-but…"

"You can read the words but it doesn't make sense when you read them? You can't get the context of the sentence?"

She nodded while wiping the tears off her face. "I-I-I d-don't know th-things any…more." That had been their rocky start at the beginning of the week, but they managed to make it to Friday.

Clark always looked forward to getting home on Fridays. He'd have the whole weekend to recharge his batteries before starting all over again on Monday. Getting out of the truck, he spied Meghan watering her lawn. He waved, walked through his front door, made a beeline for the fridge, popped open his beer, and headed on upstairs to check on Faith. First and foremost on his mind was a shower to wash off his workday sweat. Dang, it had been a hot one today! He paused in the bedroom doorway, looking at the empty bed, taking a moment to process that she wasn't there. She'd spent most of the week in their bedroom sleeping, sleeping, and sleeping. In fact, he'd started calling her Sleeping Beauty. Then he had to explain to her who Sleeping Beauty was. But, surprise, surprise, she wasn't there. He went back downstairs and started looking around. No Faith, no Lola. So he made an educated guess that she had taken the dog for a walk. He pulled out his phone and punched in the speed dial for her phone. When he heard it ringing upstairs, he shook his head. "Rats!" He spoke aloud to himself. "She doesn't have her phone with her. And that's a first!" *Okay*, he wondered, *how long had she been gone?* Twenty minutes passed while he waited for her to get home, then he started to get worried.

Back outside, Clark looked up and down the block. The block was the usual suburban LA neighborhood. Originally, two- or three-bedroom one-story houses, but most of the homeowners had added on a family room here or another bedroom or bathroom there. Clark had done most of those additions over the years. Thanks to word-of-mouth advertising. It, of course, had all started when he had done the addition to his own house after he and Faith had married. When she was pregnant, he'd added the huge family room in back and their master bedroom and bathroom above that. He'd also added the second story over the original part of the house for a home office large enough for his drafting table along with a computer desk and his files. He'd basically more than doubled the square footage of his house and it looked good to boot. After that, one by one, the neighbors got on board with wanting additions to their small homes. It had been quite the lucrative time in their lives. Yes, life had been good, at least mostly, until the last few years. The economic collapse had people tightening their belts, and that meant not spending money on things like additions to houses. The trickle-down effect in reverse. When things dried up, they really dried up. Clark scanned the block both ways again and again. No sign of Faith.

Meghan was no longer out watering her lawn, so he knocked on her door, turned the handle, opened it, and hollered inside, "Meghan?"

"Yeah?" She came around the corner into her living room, drying her hands on a dishtowel. "What's up?"

"When you were outside, did you see which way Faith went?"

She walked to the doorway and pointed down the street. "She and Lola took off that-a-way."

"How long ago?"

Meghan shook her head. "I don't know. Maybe half an hour. It wasn't long after she took off that you got home."

"Great." Clark looked up and down the block again. "Look, I'm going to take the truck and drive around and see if I can find them. If she gets home, will you call me?'

Meghan was starting to look worried now. "Yes, certainly. Clark, I'm so sorry. I wasn't thinking. I should have kept an eye on her."

He waved his hand at her, stopping the flow of her apology. "Just call me if she shows up."

After fifteen minutes of driving around, Clark finally spied them in the distance. Faith was sitting on a bus stop bench, hunched over, crying into her hands. She still held the leash. Lola sat charmingly by her mistress's feet while looking at her with concern on her doggy face. It dawned on Clark that he had seen his wife shed more tears in this past week than she had in their entire marriage. It usually took a metaphorical brick in the face to make that woman cry. He guessed that the tears, like the stuttering, were going to be the new normal for a while.

As Clark pulled up to the bus stop, Lola jumped up with a happy yip. Faith looked in the direction of her husband's truck. Relief spread a wan smile on her tear-streaked face. She stood up as Clark got out of the truck, walked around to the passenger side, and opened that door. "I-I t-t-told Lola t-to t-t-take me h-h-home," she explained, "b-b-but she was l-l-lost t-too."

"It's okay, sweetie." Clark hugged her while snapping his fingers once and pointing. On command, Lola jumped up into the truck, taking the place in the middle between the two seats; she turned in a circle then bounded up onto the little bench seat in the back of the cab. Clark helped his wife into the truck, walked around the front, and climbed in. Putting the vehicle in gear, he said, "Let's go home."

"I-I was s-so con-confused. I-I know these st-streets, b-but..."

Clark patted her leg. "I know, honey. I know you know these streets. But I guess with this head injury, things are jumbled up in there." He ran one hand lovingly down the side of her head, smoothing her hair.

"B-but Lola sh-should have known th-the w-w-way. I-I didn't know sh-she was s-so-so dumb."

Clark looked at her quizzically. "Sure you did, sweetie. Don't you remember that your pet name for her is Du Mas—with the accent on the 'u', kind of classing it up—for dumb ass. Duuuu Maaas. She's as dumb as a post."

"D-d-du Mas?" Faith was shaking her head. "I-I d-don't-don't..."

"You don't remember dubbing her Du Mas?"

Faith shook her head.

Clark just sighed.

Sunday morning found them sitting out in the backyard at the patio table drinking coffee and just enjoying the morning. Clark watched Faith eye the newspaper on the table between them like it was a snake in the grass waiting to uncoil itself and sink its fangs into her. "You know what we should do?"

"W-wh-what?"

"I know you love doing the crossword puzzle. But because of your...you know, you are avoiding it, obviously so. I think we should do it together. Want to give it a try?"

"S-sure."

"Okay." Clark opened the paper to the correct page and read the first clue. "This one's easy, chocolate cookie, there are four spaces." He waited while she thought about it.

"C-ch-chip," she finally got out.

"Oh. Hmm? I was thinking Oreo. As it's four spaces, it could be either one. Let's fill in some other spots and see which one it is, chip or Oreo. An autumn color."

She thought then finally said, "R-red."

"Ah, no, there are five spaces, red is only three."

She thought some more, "Or-orange?"

"No that would be six spaces. We need five."

She thought some more, counting off on her fingers a couple of times, shaking her head, recounting, and then giving up. "I d-don't know. M-maybe b-brown?"

He could tell she was guessing. But as it turned out, it was a good guess. "I think that's probably right."

Faith began rubbing her forehead with her fingertips. "Th-th-this is a lot of w-w-work."

"One more. I think this is good mental exercise. So let's try one more."

She reluctantly nodded.

"The clue is in quotes, '…who sat down beside' and then a blank. So we need to fill in the blank for the word. And the word is three spaces long."

She just kept shaking her head.

"It's from a poem, a nursery rhyme actually. You used to tell Emmy nursery rhymes all the time when she was little. '…who sat down beside.'"

She shook her head again.

"I'll say the whole rhyme up to the blank part and see if you can fill in the blank, okay?"

Faith nodded.

"Little Miss Muffet sat on a tuffet, / Eating her curds and whey, / Along came a spider, / Who sat down beside and the blank."

She had been listening very intently, but after getting lost in the words, she started shaking her head. "I-I don't know th-that poem."

Clark put the paper aside. Of course she knew that rhyme or at least she used to know it. Faith had told all the nursery rhymes to Emmy so many times that their daughter had them all memorized by the time she was three years old. Shaken, but not willing to let Faith see that, he tried for nonchalance. "Okay, enough mental gymnastics for now. Why don't we figure out what we're going to want for dinner tonight? Then we can go do some grocery shopping."

"I-I-I'm tired, Cl-Clark." She stood and turned toward the sliding glass door. "I-I th-think I'll t-take a n-n-nap f-first. O-okay?"

While she was sleeping Clark's phone rang. "Hi, Hope."

"Hi, I figured I'd call your phone as she is usually sleeping when I call."

"Yeah, she just went up to take a nap. She'd only been up half an hour before she headed back to bed."

"That doesn't sound good."

"No, things aren't so rosy."

"Oh, dear. I was so hoping things were starting to turn around for the better. Do you think Cliff and I should head home to…I don't know…to do something? Help out?"

"Help out how, Hope? By watching her sleep? Really, there's no need to cut your trip short. Emmy will be home in a few days and before you know it, everything will be back to normal. I mean, things have to get back to normal."

"Are you sure you don't need us?"

"Meghan's right next door. We're good. Really. Enjoy your trip, and we'll see you when you get home. Okay?"

"Okay. Give her my love."

"Will do." Clark hung up and wondered if he had been trying to convince Hope or himself when he kept insisting that things would get back to normal. *Well, of course, things will be fine,* he chided himself as he swigged back the last of his coffee then grimaced as it was cold and yucky. It would just take some time for that brain swelling thing to go down, but after that, everything would be fine! He just knew it.

Well, they'd made it through the weekend and now it was Monday morning. Emmy would be back from her trip and moving home in a few days. And he'd talked to Meghan and asked her to drop in occasionally during his working hours. He pulled away from the window and started getting ready for the new workweek.

ANGER

There is nothing wrong with anger provided
you use it constructively.
—Wayne Dyer

CHAPTER 4

FAITH STOOD IN THE BEDROOM doorway while Emily unpacked a suitcase and hung clothes up in her childhood closet. There was no mystery whatsoever regarding Emily's parentage. She had her daddy's rich, dark luxurious hair and roundness of face, and she had her mother's height, quick wit, and organizational abilities. She had been an alert baby, a curious child, a straight-A student, and a young girl who had grown into an exceptional and beautiful woman. Her parents had raised her to treat others as she expected to be treated and that had served her well all her life thus far. Feeling a maternal tug, Faith smiled as she watched her daughter. "I th-th-thought you and Ch-Ch-Chris had signed a-a-a lease on a p-p-place for the t-t-two of you?"

Emily glanced at her mother. "Hmm? Dad says you are forgetting things, but you didn't forget that, did you?"

"Y-you m-moving in with a b-boy is something I-I don't f-for-get."

"Ha-ha. I talked to the woman and explained the situation to her. She let us out of the lease and told me to go do what I have to do. She was really very understanding."

"And Ch-Ch-Chris? Is he going t-t-to be very underst-st-standing t-too?"

"You know Chris. Goes with the flow." She noticed that Faith was picking up knickknacks she had on her dresser. She'd look at one, put it down, pick up another one and look at it. "You remember my souvenirs?"

"S-sou-souvenirs? F-from wh-where?"

"From the different trips we've taken over the years. We got that one on the cruise to Mexico. See where it's been broken and glued together? That happened in the store in that one little town. They had a 'You break it, you buy it' rule." Faith gave her daughter a look and Emily simply shrugged. "I bumped it and it fell off the display shelf and broke. So you bought it." They both chuckled. "That one we got when we were in Canada for the family reunion four years ago. Some street-corner artist had a little stand up and was selling those. And that little brass lobster was from when we were in Maine."

Faith made a sound that came out, "Humph?" Like this was all news to her. Then she sat down on the foot of Emily's bed and started staring at the painting she had hanging on the wall above her headboard.

"My self-portrait."

Faith looked from the painting to Emily, then back to the painting, appraising it. "Y-you p-p-painted it?"

"Yeah, when I was in high school taking that art class. I hadn't even wanted to take that class, but you talked me into it."

"W-why d-did I d-do th-that?"

Emily said down next to her mother and took her hand. "I guess because you took art in college."

"I-I p-paint?"

"No. No. You took art history classes, stuff like that. When I painted that—and I got an A on it, by the way—you really liked it. You called it Picassoesque."

"P-Pa wh-what? W-why d-did I s-say th-that?"

"I guess because it reminded you of a Picasso painting."

"H-he p-p-painted l-like th-that?"

"Yeah, it's called impressionistic or maybe it's called something else. Heck, I don't know. You're the expert on all that stuff."

"I-I am?"

"Yes, you are."

Faith stared at the painting shaking her head. "W-well, I d-do l-like t-the c-c-colors."

"I do too. Turns out, I have an aptitude for painting I'd never realized before that class. Maybe now that college is behind me, I'll find the time to dabble some more."

"Th-that w-would b-b-be n-nice."

"Come on." Emily pulled her mother into a standing position and then headed out of the room steering her mother with her. "Let's make pizza for dinner."

"D-d-dinner? A-al-ready?"

Emily focused on her mom, looking at her closely for the first time since she'd gotten home the hour before. She saw a haggard woman, and that gave her a little clutch in her stomach. Faith had always taken pride in her appearance and been such a fashion plate. "Look, Mom, it's kind of early for dinner, so why don't you go take a little nap and we'll deal with dinner later, okay?"

"K-k-kay." Faith almost stumbled as she headed up the stairs to her bedroom to take a nap.

When Faith entered her bedroom, she realized she had tears streaming down her face. She swiped at them and heaved a sigh. Why was she crying now, darn it? Then she felt it, that cloud descending over her like a damp woolen blanket, so very heavy and uncomfortable. She should be glad because her daughter was home. And she was, but, oh, damn it, life was so very hard now. So very hard. *Damn it, damn it, damn it, damn it, damn it,* she repeated over and over and over in her head. She didn't bother trying to swear out loud as she had so much trouble getting the words out, but she felt her rage rising and in her head she screamed, *Damn it damn it damn it!* She wanted to throw something but instead punched one fist into the palm of her other hand a few times. That made Crestline, her kitty, snap to attention. The cat had been on the cushion of the window seat. She jumped down and weaved herself in and out of Faith's legs. Faith picked the cat up and buried her face in its fur. She was so angry. She couldn't remember so many of the things Emily had been talking about. Trips, paintings, she just couldn't remember that stuff and it was so unfair. So wrong. And it just made her so mad! She put the cat down and sat on the edge of her bed. After heaving a couple of sighs, she sagged with tiredness. She was bone-weary and her head ached and her eyes burned. And the air conditioning was making her shiver.

Crawling under the sheet then wrapping the comforter around her, she rolled onto her side to settle in for a nap. Crestline bounded onto the bed and curled up next to her. She draped her arm over the purring cat and the two of them drifted off toward sleep. Faith found herself in that place between sleep and wakefulness. It was a place where she just kind of floated. And she found herself wondering about this journey called life. She wondered about the twists, the turns, the surprises. Was that all fate? Was it all preordained? Were certain things meant to happen? Was she supposed to have been in a car accident? And if things were fated, where did free will enter into the picture? Hmm? This seemed like a familiar quandary. Like it was something she had debated with herself before. These considerations floated around in her mind not really as thoughts but more as feelings. She felt she was missing something, she just didn't know what it was. It was some kind of answer she was looking for—that she knew. An answer she'd been trying to find for a long, long time. She tried mentally to reach for it. But couldn't. And then nothingness enveloped her as sleep finally captured her.

After making the pizza dough then setting it aside to rest and rise, Emily detoured to the family room. Clark was in his easy chair watching TV and drinking a beer.

"Hey, Emmy, what's up?"

"Mom."

"What about her?"

"Come on, Dad."

"Come on, yourself. What's on your mind?"

"I guess we have to figure out a plan of attack here. I mean schedules and such."

"What are you talking about? It's not like we can't leave her alone. She's not an invalid or an infant. With only two or three snafus these past couple of weeks we've done fine."

"It's not just the stuttering. You know she's forgetting stuff. But it's worse than I thought."

"What?"

"When I first got home, she asked me if Aunt Charity and I had gone shopping lately?"

"Whoa!"

"Yeah, whoa! Mom didn't remember she hasn't spoken to Aunt Charity since all that horrible angst and drama way back when."

"What did you say to her? I mean, did you tell her that she and Charity haven't spoken in, literally, years?"

"No. I just said, no, and left it at that. But it really threw me. So, my point is, it's more than just the stuttering or forgetting words and things."

"I know." Clark reached out and took his daughter's hand. "But back to Charity. I think we need to tell your mom something about that situation, or she might end up calling you-know-who and then getting slammed. I don't want her to have to deal with any rejection and not understand why."

"Yes, I know. It's just hard to talk about Charity sometimes. I mean, she used to spoil me so with gifts and spent time with me and now it's like we are all dead to her."

"Sad to say it's better this way. But I'll talk to mom about the Charity situation."

"Okay, good."

"By the way, sweetie, I'm glad you are here to help. And it's not just me." He glanced over toward the dog snoring by his chair. "Lola has missed curling up at night outside your bedroom door after you moved into the dorms. She'll be glad to post sentry like she used to do when you were in high school."

"Yeah, I missed her and Crestline too. And it does feel good to be home." The dog suddenly jumped up, ran out of the family room, and started barking at the front door. "Mail's here," they both said in unison, then laughed.

Then Emily got down to business. "I figured you are on the building site most mornings and during the day. So I asked my boss if I could be on a quasi-swing shift at the store. I'll have to go in around noon or one. That way I'll be here in the mornings when you are gone. And, as you told me every time I called the past two weeks, she's usually sleeping in the afternoons, so if neither of us are here at that time, no biggie. And then you'll be home when she's up after her nap. How does that sound to you?"

"It sounds like you are as efficient and as organized as you've always been."

"I noticed on the kitchen calendar that the neurologist's appointment is tomorrow afternoon at four, so that's on your watch."

"Got it," he saluted his daughter. "Now, what's this I under-stand about pizza for dinner?"

***

Chris, timing perfect, arrived just as the pizza came out of the oven. The four of them sat around the dining table and wolfed it down while it was still hot enough to take the skin off the tongue. Faith's eyes travelled back and forth between Chris and Emily. They were a lovely couple—almost bookends in coloring and temperament.

Chris winked at his girlfriend. "You make good pizza, Emmy. I'm glad you remembered to leave the cheese off my portion."

"After nearly five years together, I guess I can remember you're lactose intolerant."

Chris turned his attention toward Faith. "How are you doing? You look kind of tired."

"Th-th-th-thanks." Even with her stuttering Faith managed to insert irony and insult into that one word.

"Sorry, I didn't mean that as an insult. I'm just saying…you look kind of tired."

Clark good-naturedly reached over and knocked on Chris's head with his knuckles. "Try getting smashed on the noggin and see if you don't feel tired too."

Chris swallowed a bite of pizza then said, "I had a friend who was in an accident in high school. His car was really banged up, almost totaled. It was the other guy's fault, so his insurance company said not to worry. They'd go after the other guy's insurance and get the money to get him set up good as new. Then, turns out the other guy was insured by the same company my friend was. When that came to light, their tune completely changed. Instead of getting my friend the max for the damage that they'd pretty much promised him, they barely paid anything. Because it was coming out of their own pocket."

Clark was listening intently. "So your point is: we'd better hope this woman's insurance company and our company are not the same company."

"You got it."

"What about no-fault insurance?" Emily wanted to know.

Chris smirked. "Yeah, right. No-fault in theory."

"Terrific. One more thing to look in to." Clark shook his head in exasperation.

Faith pushed away from the table. "Th-tha-thanks, Emmy." She started to pick up her plate.

"Leave that for me, Mom. I'll clear and put everything in the dishwasher."

Nodding, Faith left the table and headed back upstairs to her bedroom. Chris watched Clark as his eyes followed his wife out of sight.

"So she has her appointment with the neurologist tomorrow?"

"Yeah, none too soon." Clark pushed his plate away too, no longer hungry.

CHAPTER 5

Faith awoke and lay as still as she could. Words whispered though her mind, *Where am I?* She turned her head first to the right toward a big bay window with a window seat. *Pretty.* She imagined a bed and breakfast might have a window seat and a bay window like that. Was she in a bed and breakfast? She looked to the left at a small jewelry armoire and an open doorway to a walk-in closet that was full of clothes. No, not a bed and breakfast; the guest closet wouldn't be full of clothes like that one was. The whispers continued, *Where is this place?* Ever so slowly pushing back the covers, she got out of bed and looked around trying to get her bearings. A cat strolled out of another doorway. Faith tiptoed over to it and peeked in; she saw that it was a bathroom with a kitty litter box butted up against one wall. The cat wound itself around her legs and opened its mouth in a silent meow. The whispers in her head said, *Cute kitty. I wonder what her name is?* Faith wandered over to the dresser and looked in the mirror. The woman staring back at her was a stranger. Faith touched her face. The woman in the mirror touched her startled face. Faith started grabbing at her cheeks. The woman in the mirror in horror was grabbing at her cheeks too. In her head, the whispers became a scream. *That isn't me! This isn't me! That isn't me! This isn't me!* She ran back to the bed and fell into it, pulling the covers over her head. The keening in her head said, *Who was she? Who am I? Who was she? Who am I?* Crying became sobbing, but it wasn't a release as it only made her head ache all the more. She pressed her face into her pillow and opened her mouth in a silent scream that went on and on and on. Then she wept some more. As she wept, she felt the kitty stretch out next to her. She didn't know where the cat came from, but it was comforting not to be alone in this scary place.

***

Emily entered the bedroom armed with a steaming mug of coffee and a plateful of scrambled eggs with little pieces of ham cut up in them. "Wake up, Mom. You've been a slug-a-bed all day and I have to go to work soon."

Faith struggled to wake up then sit up. Emily looked at her mom's face closely. She couldn't tell if that was just a sleepy face or if she'd been crying.

"Emm-Emily?"

"You slept through breakfast time, and so this is both lunch and breakfast. You need to eat, shower, and get dressed so you'll be ready to roll when Dad gets home."

"R-ready t-to r-r-roll?"

"Yes, you have an appointment with a neurologist this after-noon. Dad will take you. So eat, shower, and get dressed. Even if you fall back to sleep, you'll at least be ready when it's time to go." Faith simply sat on the edge of the bed acclimating herself to being awake. Come on, Mom. Chop-chop!" Emily set the mug of coffee on the nightstand and handed her mom the plate.

Faith obediently took the eggs from her daughter. She smiled after the first bite, nodded her approval, and said, "G-good."

When Emily smiled and left the room, she took only a couple more bites then set the plate aside. It wasn't really good. Nothing tasted good to her these days. She got up and paused, looking in the mirror over the dresser. She remembered her scare earlier that morn-ing. She hadn't known who or where she was. That was probably the most frightening experience she'd ever had. She pressed the palm of her hand over her stomach that had suddenly lurched under the combination of the few bites of unwanted food and the memory of the fear. At least she knew who she was now. She was a woman who was dealing with the trauma of having a head injury. She looked at her rumpled bed and at Crestline who was washing herself. The cat had become her little guardian angel, sticking by her side no matter what. She backtracked to the bed, bent down, and kissed the kitty between her eyes, then headed to the bathroom to shower.

***

Faith and Clark arrived at the doctor's appointment fifteen minutes early as requested. When the receptionist handed Faith a clipboard full of papers to be filled out, she didn't know what to do. She glanced at the jumble of words on the top page and felt like a little kid who was about to be scolded for breaking something. She knew she wasn't going to be able to fill out any forms. She saw what looked like a comfortable couch and sat down. Clark sat next to her, picked the clipboard up off her lap, and scanned it.

"Let's see what we have here." He flipped through the pages. "Ah, it's just medical history information. We can do this. First part, name, address, phone number, easy." He started filling in the form for his wife.

She watched him check something off. "Wh-what was t-th-that ch-check-mark for?"

"They want to know if you've ever suffered from a blow to the head. That was a yes."

"O-oh."

"Hmm? Honey, were you unconscious after you banged your head in the accident?"

She rubbed her hand over the side of her head. "I-I d-don't know."

"Well, it's asking if you were unconscious and, if so, for how long?"

"I-if I w-were un-unconscious, h-how would I-I know h-how long it w-was?"

"Good point. I'll leave that blank. Next question. Have you ever suffered from other head injuries before this one?"

"I th-think m-maybe, w-when I was l-l-little?"

"I kind of remember you telling me that once upon a time when you were a little kid you fell and bonked your head on the concrete apron of a swimming pool. So that's a yes."

"I-I, y-yes, t-th-that sounds right."

"Did you ever have mumps, measles, you know, the usual childhood diseases?"

She thought for a moment then shook her head as if she hadn't a clue. "P-probably."

"Well, we know you've had a baby." He checked that off. After scanning the papers and marking what he could recall about her medical history, he handed her the clipboard and the pen. "You need to sign it and date it."

"O-oh." She took the pen and signed her name. Clark took the clipboard back and filled in the date. Then he went up to the window and handed it to the receptionist. After that, they waited, but it wasn't that long of a wait.

"The receptionist came through the office door into the waiting room. "Faith? This way."

"C-come w-with m-m-me." She reached for her husband's hand.

"Wouldn't be anywhere else," Clark told her, giving her fingers a little squeeze.

Hand in hand, Faith and Clark followed the receptionist down a carpeted hallway. There were tasteful pictures on the walls here and there, and arrangements of silk flowers on a couple of credenzas. She opened a door and gestured into an office that boasted a couch, a desk, a couple of comfortable chairs, a coffee table with some magazines fanned out on it along with a box of Kleenex, a water cooler, and a bank of filing cabinets along one wall. On the opposite wall was another door that had the word "Restroom" on it in tasteful gold letters.

"Have a seat. Dr. Wellbrock will be right with you." They decided on the couch and sat side-by-side, waiting some more.

In moments, the doctor entered the room and took a seat in one of the chairs near where they were sitting on the couch. "Hello." He placed the clipboard of papers they'd just filled out on the coffee table, reached across it, and shook each of their hands in turn, then he held up a chart. "The emergency room just this minute faxed over your records, so give me a moment to look through this. Then we'll get started." The neurologist was a gorgeous, buff, fifty-something man with a goatee and a sexy German accent. He had a full head of grey hair and a chunky gold wedding ring with a black stone in its center. He didn't scan the chart, but actually read it. After a few moments, he looked up over the top of his reading glasses, put the chart aside, and reached over to his desk, picking up a tablet of paper and a pen. He smiled at Clark then turned his full attention to Faith. "My name is Dr. Wellbrock. What is your name?"

"F-F-Faith. F-Faith K-Kincade."

"A pleasure to meet you, Faith. I am going to ask you a few questions. But this isn't like a test. Okay?"

Faith nodded. Nodding was easier than talking, which she was starting to avoid if at all possible. Talking meant thinking, and sometimes, her brain just ached trying to find the words and get them out of her mouth.

"Are you married, Faith?"

She nodded and reached out patting Clark's knee. "Y-yes. M-m-my hus-hus-husband."

"What is your husband's name?"

"Cl-Clark."

"Do you have children?"

"Em-Em-Emily, our dau-daughter. And-and-and-and th-th-the st-strays."

"The strays?"

"Th-the r-r-rest..." She turned to Clark for help.

Clark explained, "Emily is an only child, but she has always had many friends. Our house was always full of kids when she was living at home, and my wife, who is a kind of clichéd Earth Mother, lovingly called the other kids her strays. It was like we had a very big family, always more than just the three of us at the dinner table."

"I see." The doctor focused on Faith again. "What are the names of one or two of your strays?"

Faith thought a moment. "C-C-Chloe and..." she looked over at Clark as if for verification, "w-was th-th-there a-a-nother Emily?"

"Yes, honey, yes, there was." Clark turned to the doctor to explain. "When our Emily was in high school, the school had an exchange program and the Japanese girl who stayed with us for one semester was also named Emily."

"Y-yes."

"Very good, Faith. You are doing very well. Where do you live?"

"On Aster St-Street."

"And where is that?"

"B-b-b-Burbank."

"And where is Burbank?"

"Cal-i-f-f-fornia."

"Do you have a job?"

"I-I ha-have a st-store. A clo-thing st-st-store."

"No, honey," Clark reached over and laid his hand on her knee. "You sold your store, remember?"

Faith shook her head indicating she didn't remember that.

Dr. Wellbrock drew her attention back to him, "You don't remember selling your store?"

She shook her head.

"Tell me about the store you had."

"I-I s-sell," she shook her head, "s-sold clo-clothing. A-and sh-shoes an-and…" She gestured with her hand for a word she couldn't find. "Sh-shoes," she ended lamely.

"Sounds like it was a lovely store. Do you have any pets?

"Y-yes. A-a c-cat and d-dog."

"Tell me your dog's name."

"L-La-Lola."

He smiled, then asked, "What Lola wants, Lola gets?" Checking to see if she recognized the line from the song.

She shook her head. "N-no. I-I'm the al-alpha."

That made the doctor laugh. "Very good, I like that. What about your cat, what is the cat's name?"

"Cr-Cr-Crestline."

"Like up in the mountains?"

Hope looked confused. "I d-don't know."

"Yes." Clark answered. "Don't you remember, honey? We were driving up Angeles Crest Highway years ago and there was that little baby kitty, stranded along the side of the road. You made me pull over and you picked her up. You adopted her on the spot and named her Crestline, as that's where we found her."

Faith just shook her head as all that was news to her.

"It's okay, Faith, if you don't remember things. Let's continue. Did you go to college?"

Her eyes flew to Clark's in questioning panic, "D-did I?"

"Yes, honey, you did."

"Oh y-y-yes. I did."

"What subject did you major in?"

She leaned back in the chair pressing the fingers of one hand to her mouth. "I don't kn-kn-know."

"You are doing fine, Faith. Remember, this isn't a test that you can pass or fail. I'm just looking for information for now."

"O-o-oh, p-p-painting. E-Emily s-said I t-took art c-cl-classes."

"What do you remember about these art classes?"

A tear spilled from one eye sliding down her cheek, "I don't kn-kn-know."

"No worries, Faith. Let's…"

"O-oh, 1066 wh-wh-what?" She looked at Clark.

He looked blank. "What, honey?"

The doctor said, "That date, 1066, is the Battle of Hastings. Does that have significance? Perhaps something to do with your schooling?"

"I-I-I ah…" she shook her head, "I th-th-think so. B-but I c-c-can't re-mem-b-ber. Cl-Clark?"

"Yeah, sweetie, I think it had something to do with what you were taking in school, but I was out building houses at the time, and we'd barely just met about the time you graduated, weren't even dating yet. So I wasn't all wrapped up in what you were taking in school. Sorry."

She kept shaking her head as if she was trying to shake a memory loose.

"That's okay, Faith. Let's continue, shall we?"

She nodded.

"Tell me about when you were a little girl."

She paused before speaking, "I-I tell you wh-wh-what?"

"Just anything that comes to mind. Did you ever go to Disneyland?"

"A-a-ah, yes."

Do you recall the first time you went to Disneyland?"

Faith thought for a moment, then just shook her head.

"Do you remember anything about Disneyland?"

After a long pause she said, "Sm-sm-small world."

On a laugh he said, "Yes. Very good. That catchy tune is probably stuck in everyone's brain forever. How old were you when you went on your first date?"

"I-I-I don't know."

"Were you in high school? When you went on your first date."

Faith shook her head uncertainly, "I-I m-must have been."

"Do you recall where you went on your first date?"

She shakes her head.

"How about your first date with Clark? Do you recall where you went?"

She thought for a moment. "D-dinner."

The doctor smiled at her; pretty sure she had just made an educated guess. "What kind of restaurant?"

She looked over at Clark. "M-M-Mexican?"

"Yes, it was," Clark confirmed. Although he, like the doctor thought she was guessing.

"How old were you when your daughter was born?"

Faith continued to shake her head, "I-I don't re-re-mem-b-ber."

"Who is the President of the United States?"

Faith gave her head another shake and her mouth turned down pulling a disgusted look onto her face. "Th.-that wh-wh-war monger!"

Clark reached over and rubbed her arm, "You're talking about Bush, sweetie, he's no longer the president."

Faith looked confused for a moment, thinking. "B-B-Bush isn't th-the president?"

"Not for a while, sweetie."

"Do you know who the president is, Faith?" The doctor was writing something down on the tablet of paper as he asked the question.

"I-I guess its n-n-not B-Bush."

"Correct. It's not Bush. Do you know who it is?"

Faith shook her head.

"What day of the week is it?"

Faith turned inward. It was clear she was thinking hard. Then an embarrassed little shake of the head, "D-d-darned if I-I-I-I know."

"Where are you right now?"

"In y-y-your off-office."

"And who am I?"

She tapped a forefinger on her forehead. "A h-h-head doctor."

"That's right. What floor is my office on?"

She thought again for a minute. Shaking her head, she said, "W-w-we got on th-th-the el-el-avator." Still shaking her head she added, "I-I don't know."

"That's okay, Faith. Let's take a little break from all the questions. When she sighed in relief, he said, "Go ahead and get up and walk up and down the hallway for a little breather. We'll reconvene and finish up with all this in say ten minutes? Will that work for you?"

"Y-y-yes. T-t-thank y-you."

CHAPTER 6

After the little break, Faith and Clark sat back down on the couch in the doctor's office. "How you doing, Faith?"

"O-o-okay."

"Good. We'll do some different evaluations now. Will you stand up and walk over toward the file cabinets and then walk back for me?"

She stood up and complied.

"Very good, now I want you to stand first on one foot, then the other."

She wobbled a little when standing on only one foot, but managed to do as the doctor asked.

"Go ahead and sit back down. Now I want you to look at me and smile. That's a girl. Now blink. Good, good. Now I want you to follow my finger with your eyes only, don't turn your head just follow it with your eyes. Very good." He picked up his pen again and wrote a few notes down on the tablet of paper.

"Tell me how you've been emotionally."

"W-wh-what d-do y-you m-m-mean?"

"Ups and downs? Crying spells. How have you been since the accident?"

She thought for a moment then said, "I-I'm up-up-upset. M-m-mad a-a-bout it. V-v-very m-mad!"

The doctor nodded. "It's not uncommon at all to experience angry feelings about this situation. Anything else?"

"I-I d-don't k-know." She looked over at her husband for help.

Clark blew out a breath and told the doctor, "She does shed more tears than she used to. I mean, she never was much of a crier and now she is."

Dr. Wellbrock finished writing down some observations, sat back, put the tablet of paper down, and looked first at Faith and then at Clark and finally back at Faith. "We are going to have our work cut out for us over the next year."

"A year?" Clark's voice expressed his surprise. "Getting her well is going to take a year?"

"Accidents happen in seconds, but it takes time for healing to occur." He turned his full attention to Faith. "Let me explain to you what has happened in your head. You are suffering from something called traumatic brain injury or TBI for short. TBI is distinguished from other types of brain injury in that it happens from external force. In your case, a car accident. They are other ways for TBI to occur. Shaking a baby is one. Sports injuries are common. Are you following me so far?" Faith nodded.

"Good. A closed head injury is different from say, getting shot by a bullet. If a bullet enters the head it enters at one point, that area is where the problems will manifest. With a closed head injury like you have, the brain damage..." He noticed Clark wince. "We have to call a spade a spade, Clark, it is kinder and more accurate to call it what it is." Faith was nodding in understanding. "Anyway," the doctor continued, "closed head injuries, where the brain has bounced around in the cranium, cause what is called diffused damage—it's not just one part of the brain but multiple parts of the brain that are affected. Still with me?"

Faith nodded again.

"Good. So with more than one part of the brain injured you might have varied symptoms. You might have problems with balance, standing on one foot. Something like that signals an injury to one part of the brain. You might have problems with vision. That signals the optical nerve, which is in a different section of the brain. Problems with words and cognition, all that's in, yet, a different part of the brain. And that seems to be the area of your brain that is most affected."

"S-so wh-what d-does th-that all m-mean?"

"See my file cabinet over there?" Faith followed the direction he pointed and nodded. "It has several drawers. And each drawer is full of file folders—lots of files—and in those file folders are lots of papers. Lots and lots of papers. Imagine what the floor of my office would look like if the cabinet was tipped over and all the files and papers were all over the floor all mixed up." He gave her a moment to visualize that. "The brain is like a filing cabinet. It takes information and files it away in a place where it can be retrieved when we want to retrieve it." Rubbing both his forefingers on his temples, he continued, "Your filing cabinet in here has been tipped over. All the drawers have opened up and all the file folders are scattered around on the ground. All the papers in the files are mixed up on the ground. This is why you have a hard time finding words or saying words. It is why you don't remember some things. You can't find the right file folder, and if you do find the right folder, it might be empty yet as the papers in it haven't been found and replaced. You are going to have a very hard task that will take you a very long time. You have to—and we are speaking metaphorically here as I am sure you are aware,— pick up each piece of paper and put it in the proper file folder. Then, you are going to have to take that file folder and put it in the proper drawer in the cabinet. All that takes time. My job is to help you get the filing cabinet upright again. But I can't do all the filing for you. That's your job and it will be hard work."

Faith looked like a deer in the headlights of an oncoming car. "H...how...how...how..."

"You won't be doing all this work alone, Faith. You are going to need to start seeing a speech therapist two or three times a week for quite some time. She isn't just a run-of-the-mill speech therapist. Her official title is speech pathologist. Her training is with people who have suffered brain injuries as you have. She is the best in the business. Between the three of us, you, me, and the therapist, we'll get your filing cabinet straightened out. Do you understand?"

Faith nodded.

"In addition, you should know that I have earned degrees in both neurology and psychiatry so I can serve you in both capacities. Often, a person with TBI needs to see both."

"I've got a question."

Dr. Wellbrock turned his attention to Clark. "Certainly."

"Can you give us an idea of what kind of…I guess symptoms is the word…that Faith will be displaying? I mean it's not just the stuttering. She's tired all the time. I expect that's a symptom of this… TBI."

"Yes, it is. Both extreme mental and physical fatigue are very common. Sleep disorders are another possibility."

"She's sleeping a lot. I mean *a lot*."

"That's called hypersomnia and it's not at all uncommon after a concussion. What else have you noticed?"

"She doesn't remember to keep her phone with her. That's never happened before."

The doctor nodded and turned to Faith. "It's not uncommon to become confused and misplace things and forget where you put things like keys or your phone. Here's something you can do to try to help you recall where you put things. After you set something down, immediately close your eyes and visualize it. Picture it in your mind's eye then open your eyes and look at it to reinforce the visual image. That might help." He turned back to Clark. "Anything else you've noticed?"

"She's not eating much these days."

"Again, not surprising. Loss of appetite and even nausea often occur after a concussion." He turned to Faith, "What about head-aches? When you filled out the form before our appointment, you didn't mark the line that asked if you had persistent headaches."

"N-no. Not per-per…" she brushed her hand through the air giving up on saying persistent. "J-just ac-achiness now a-a-and th-then."

"Okay." He picked up the tablet and wrote that down then con-tinued. "If the achy headaches persist, take some Advil or Tylenol. Other symptoms besides headaches would be sluggishness, reduced tolerance for stress, and then, of course, the cognitive symptoms we've been dealing with here today. The difficulty processing information or expressing thoughts. Problems with words. The memory loss. There may be difficulty in understanding others. Hence," he looked directly at Faith, "why I kept asking if you understood what I was saying. I realize this is a lot to digest at once. But we will address issues as they arise."

"O-o-okay."

"You will start to notice a pattern of good days and bad days. I want you to start noticing the patterns." He picked up the chart they had filled out when she arrived at the office. "Good, I see your signature, that means although you have trouble with words and speaking, you can still write. That's because writing is located in a different part of the brain than the speech centers are. So what I want you to do, Faith, is start to keep a log. Monitor yourself closely for things such as blurry vision, difficulty in concentrating, or for sudden tiredness. Write down days and times and see if a pattern emerges. In addition, use the log just to write down feelings and thoughts. For anything."

Faith looked so sad that the doctor gave her an encouraging smile. "Do you have a question for me?"

"I-I d-don't re-re-remember th-things. Wh-when will I s-start re-remembering?"

"Our brains contain both long-term and short-term memories. Your long-term memories should be returning to you slowly, in fits and starts. In fact, it's usually the memories you've had the longest that will return the easiest."

When Faith excused herself to use the restroom, Clark turned to the doctor and spoke in a low voice. "I can't believe it will take a year to get her back to normal. A couple of weeks ago she was fine. Surely, it won't take a year."

Dr. Wellbrock sighed deeply. "No, it won't take a year. I told her that for her well-being. I told her a year so she would have a light at the end of the tunnel, a goal. It will more likely take three years, maybe five or ten. Maybe it will never happen."

Clark was speechless, but only momentarily. "You mean this may very well be permanent?"

"No, not necessarily. But there is no overnight fix."

"So you essentially lied to her when you told her in a year she'd be better." He looked like he was ready to throttle someone. The doctor simply smiled at him compassionately.

"I didn't say she'd be well in a year. I said we'd have our work cut out for us over the course of this coming year. As I said, I gave her a goal. At the end of the year, even if she isn't better, and she very likely won't be, she will be able to look back and see accomplishment. She will be able to see that things have improved and will likely continue to improve with continued hard work. If I told her now just how long this process will be, she'd give up before she got started. Depression is so common with people who have suffered from brain injuries. And suicide is not uncommon at all. So I gave her a goal, a year to work hard. When she sees that in a year she has improved, then we'll work on more improvement that second year. It wasn't a lie. We will work hard this year. Not telling her she'll be working hard for *several years* is a kindness."

Clark thought about everything the doctor said. "I see." It didn't really look like he did. "And me? What do I do for her?"

"You need to be her rock. Stand by her and when she gets frustrated and she will, don't let that get *you* frustrated." He brushed a hand through the air as if erasing what he had just said. "Easier said than done as you will get frustrated too. Very frustrated. Here's some advice, hang a punching bag in your garage and take your frustrations out on that."

"Doctor's orders?"

"Doctor's orders."

After a penetrating look at Clark, Dr. Wellbrock asked, "Is there anything else you want to say? You seem to be holding something back."

"Yeah? Well, I guess these days I'm holding a lot back. I mean, she can't work, she can't socialize, she can't even replace the toilet paper when the roll runs out. It's like, I tell her something and she completely blows it off. I know it's not intentional. I know she can't remember what I told her. But it makes me feel like she doesn't care. And I know all that makes me sound like an unfeeling ninny."

"No, it doesn't. It makes you human. Try addressing her by name first before telling her whatever you need to tell her. Get her attention. It might help her to focus and realize what you are saying to her is important to you."

"It's like half the time she's impervious to things, the other half she's overwhelmed by normal stuff."

"You do understand she has trouble with the amount of information she can take in and process at a given moment? Most of what we talked about today went right over her head. That's why it's a good thing you are here, to remember for her at this point."

"I just can't get past that year or years thing. It seems that she should just be getting better and getting past all this."

"Denial isn't productive, Clark. Facing the facts and moving forward with that knowledge is what will help Faith improve."

Clark just blew out a breath then asked, "Are you going to be doing additional testing? I mean, I know she had a CAT scan at the hospital a couple of weeks ago. Are there other tests?"

The doctor gave a sigh. "Oh, Clark, there are so many tests. But, no, we aren't going to be doing too much right away. Later on, but not now. Faith is under a tremendous amount of stress. Just thinking is hard for her now, and so I need to weigh all of her stress issues against the value of the tests we should be taking. Now, at this time, she couldn't handle them. Later, we'll talk about additional tests."

Clark glanced at his watch. "She's been in there a long time."

"I can hear the water running. In fact, it has been for a few minutes. Want to go check on her?"

"No, she's probably just splashing water on her face. When she has hot flashes, she does that a lot. So this speech therapist you mentioned, is that the next step?"

"Yes, it is."

Clark blew out a breath. "I just keep seeing dollar signs flying out the window here. I know that should not be my primary concern right now, but well, it is."

"Don't spend too much time worrying about that at this juncture. I am sure the insurance company from the other car will be dragging its heels for as long as it can before it pays out one cent, but from what I see here, you're going to get the maximum from them. That will fray a lot of the medical costs that will be building up over the next months and years. It will probably be up to a year or even two years before the insurance company will be compelled to pay, so just let the bills pile up. Your lawyer will be able to get the max, I'm sure."

"*Lawyer*! Now we need a lawyer?"

"Always a smart move in a case like this."

Clark was still shaking his head in disbelief when Faith emerged from the bathroom.

Faith and Clark rode the elevator down to the lobby. In fact, it did look like Faith had shed some tears and washed her face before coming out of the restroom. But Clark kept his own counsel and didn't say anything about her red eyes. The lobby was cool and no one was around, so before stepping outside into the hot summer afternoon, Clark led his wife over to one of the marble benches and pulled her down next to him. He put his arm about her shoulders and kissed her check. She sighed.

"I know talking's hard for you, so you don't have to talk. Just listen. We are going to get through this together. We'll get you to the speech therapist that Dr. Wellbrock recommended, and we'll take it one day at a time."

"I-I-I...," and she proceeded to tell him, albeit haltingly, her tale of woe.

CHAPTER 7

WHEN THEY GOT HOME FROM the appointment with the neurologist, an exhausted Faith crawled into bed, pulled the covers up to her chin, rolled over onto her side, and slid into sleep with her faithful Crestline tucked under her arm. Clark sat in front of the television, not really watching the news. He was just going over and over all the doctor had said and attempting to process it. Rubbing his brow, he realized his head was aching and he felt a sudden sympathy for Faith.

Getting up, he went outside for some fresh air. He smelled the burgers before he actually heard them sizzling on the grill next door. "Hey, Brian," he hollered over the concrete wall that separated the two backyard properties, "you got one on there for me?"

"Sure, come on over."

Meghan was adding an extra plate to the picnic table when Clark arrived with a six-pack of beer. Handing one to Brian who was manning the grill, he said, "I see you've got an under contract sign hanging on the for sale sign. That all happened fast."

"That's the way it seems to go with real estate. Either a place sells right away, or it takes years. We were lucky."

"Not so lucky for us. We're going to miss you guys."

Meghan added her two cents worth. "Well, it might be one of those good news bad news things."

"What do you mean?"

"An Armenian family bought the house."

"Yeah?" Clark asked cautiously, "Was that the good news or the bad news?"

Both Meghan and Brain laughed. After flipping the burgers Brian said, "The good news is that they are going to do some remodeling, actually some complete restructuring. So play your cards right and you'll be able to work right next door for a while."

"The bad news is," Meghan added, "looks like they want to add not only the second story you've been trying to talk us into for over a decade, but they want to turn the place into one of those McMansions. On this little plot! Can't imagine how that will look in this neighborhood. Yuck!"

"I have to admit, potential work does sound like good news. Jobs have been few and far between the last few years. I'm almost done with the project I'm working on now. Next one I have lined up is out near Lancaster in the desert. And I have been dreading that ever since Faith got hurt."

"Why?"

"Because I'll have to be staying out there during the week. Not just me, the entire crew. Commuting back and forth would not be cost or time effective. So I'll have to head out on Monday mornings, and get a half day in then. Work like fury from dawn to dark on Tuesdays, Wednesdays, and Thursdays and after half a day on Friday, head home for the weekend. And that will go on for at least a couple of months, most likely longer. Thankfully, Emmy is home. But it will still be a hardship on all of us. But harder yet if I didn't have the income from that job."

"Yikes, bad timing on that job. You can't put it off for a while? Do something else first?"

Clark was shaking his head, "It's the only one lined up, and, as I said, we need the money. I can't let this fish off the line."

"When are you going to have to start out there?"

"Soon, maybe in the next three weeks."

When Meghan went back inside, Brian asked, "So how are things with Faith?"

Clark took a long drink of beer. "It seems like we are going one step forward, two steps backward. We used to curl up on the couch and watch a movie or some show. She can't concentrate enough anymore to follow the thread of the story. Or I'll tell her something in the morning and it seems to sink in, but when I mention it when I get home from work, she doesn't have a clue what I'm talking about."

Brian thought about that. "So it's short-term memory too on top of everything else. Well, patience is the key. It will just take time." He put the buns on the grill to brown, flipped the burgers for the last time, and added a slice of cheese to each. "Meghan," he gave a holler toward the backdoor, "time to bring out the potato salad. Let's eat."

"So? The neurologist?" Meghan plopped a spoonful of potato salad on her plate and passed the bowl to Clark.

Clark just heaved a sigh and put a scoop of the salad on his plate.

"That bad?" Brian held out his hand for the bowl.

"On the downside, it was not an encouraging experience at all. The doctor said it will probably be years before Faith is back to normal, if she even gets back to normal."

Meghan rested her hand on Clark's forearm. "Oh, Clark."

Brian was just nodding. "Head injuries are no walk in the park. That's for sure. So if that was the downside, is there an upside?"

"Well, Faith really liked the doctor. So I think she'll be okay working with him."

Meghan was upending a ketchup bottle next to her burger. "Well, that's a blessing," she said, "knowing how Faith feels about doctors—the whole medical profession for that matter."

"No kidding. When I told her we had an appointment today, I expected her to go off on her usual 'Medicine is a profit-driven business, yada, yada, yada.' But she didn't fight the appointment, so guess she's forgotten she doesn't trust doctors. Let's hope she gets better before she remembers that she considers medical doctors a bunch of drones brainwashed by the pharmaceutical companies who run the medical schools."

"Amen, to that." Meghan chuckled. "I can just hear her saying, 'Conventional medicine isn't interested in curing a person. Drugs treat symptoms. They don't address the real issue, blah, blah, blah.' Now eat up before that burger gets cold."

When Clark got home, he checked on Faith. She was sound asleep. Crestline looked up from her place beside her mistress and opened her mouth in a silent meow. "Good kitty," he whispered to her. The cat hadn't left Faith's side since this ordeal had started. In the early days after the accident, when Clark realized that the cat wasn't about to leave the bedroom if Faith was in it, he had brought Crestline's food and water bowls up and placed them on newspapers next to the dresser. Glancing at the cat's food bowl, he saw it was empty. "Are you hungry?" He upended the last of a box of Friskies into the food bowl, filled the water bowl at the bathroom sink, and detoured back into the bathroom to clean up the kitty litter box. Taking the used litter and the empty cat food box out to the trash, he rolled the trashcan and the recycle can out to the street so they'd be ready for pick up the next day.

That taken care of, he settled down in his easy chair in the family room and was reaching for the remote when Lola started barking. He heard the front door open.

"Shut up, Lola, it's only us. Anybody home?"

"Back here, Hope." Clark greeted Hope and Cliff. "Okay, Lola, stop. Go lay down." He pointed a finger toward the dog's cushion then shook hands with his brother-in-law and hugged Hope. "When did you guys get back?"

"Just now. Faith?"

"Upstairs sleeping. She does that a lot. Beers all around? Or do you want a white wine?"

"Wine, thanks. I'm just going to go upstairs and peek at her while you get us the drinks."

When she walked into the bedroom, Crestline, who had been licking a paw and washing her face after her meal, walked over to Hope and wound herself in and out of Hope's legs, greeting her with chirpy little purrs. Hope reached down and petted the cat, then walked closer to the bed and observed her sleeping sister. She looked more wan, more drawn, and more strained then the last time she had seen her a few weeks before. The fact that she had been through something was evident even as she slumbered. "Poor baby," she whispered and headed back downstairs.

Hope sat down next to her husband and reached for the glass of wine sitting on the coffee table that Clark had built for his wife: a wedding present a little over two decades ago.

"So fill us in."

And he did. "So then the neurologist drops all these bombs on us about how long it will take for her to regain a semblance of herself. I guess everything kind of hit Faith hard, I mean, it's not like she's going to be able to take a pill and get better. Not that she would."

"Yeah, she's like me in that she thinks all pharmaceuticals are poison."

"Yeah, yeah, I've heard all that before. So, anyway, she excused herself to go to the restroom, and, well, she was more shook up than even she knew. She probably won't mind me telling you what happened…"

"What?" Hope asked.

"She said that when she went in to the bathroom, she pulled up her skirt, sat down, and peed, only realizing that she hadn't pulled her panties down. She was sitting on the toilet with her panties still on and had peed right through them. She was mortified. She managed to get them off and washed them in the sink. Rinsed all the pee out of them then held them in front of that hand dryer blower thingy until they were only just slightly damp. Then she popped them in her purse so nobody would know."

"Oh, the poor thing."

"I tried to make light of it, teasing her. I said, 'So you're going commando, huh?' And she looked at me like she didn't know what I was talking about. In fact it wasn't *like* she didn't know, she literally didn't recall what it meant to be going commando."

Hope put her wine glass down and swiped a knuckle at a tear that had snuck out of one eye and was sliding down her cheek.

Cliff reached over and rested his hand on his wife's thigh. "We all know memory issues aren't uncommon with head injuries. So here's an idea, since you were raised together, sharing the same history, maybe you can be her memory while she gets better. You know, tell her stories of when you were little girls, all that. It might help her to restore at least part of her memory."

Clark nodded. "Good idea. I just hope your memory's better than mine. Half the time, I can't recall stuff she wants to know. On the way home from the doctor's office, she was asking me about classes she took in college. I guess because he had gotten her thinking about that. How the heck am I supposed to know what classes she took in college? We weren't even together then. And," he took a breath, "I can hear myself starting to rant. I guess all of this is getting to me."

"Understandable."

"So let's change the subject for a little bit and give me a break."

"Okay, so changing the subject here," Cliff pointed at the wall, "I see your neighbor's house is under contract."

"Yes, just one more disaster." Clark wasn't happy about that at all. "Meghan has been so great in all of this, and to have them move at this time is just really bad timing all the way around. They'll close and be moved about the time I have to start on that job out near Lancaster. No, not good timing at all."

"Looks like we got home in the nick of time then." Hope sipped her drink, considering. "Why don't I make it a habit of coming by and, as Cliff suggested, just start sharing memories with Faith. I can come after her speech therapy sessions."

Clark was shaking head. "That would be too much at a time for her. I can tell you right now, she will be heading straight up to bed after her therapy. Any and everything wears her out so quickly."

"Oh. Well, why don't I plan on coming on the days she doesn't have speech therapy? We'll figure it all out. Maybe have Emmy give me a call tomorrow before she heads off to work. She can let me know a good time to come over when Faith won't be sleeping."

"It's a promise."

***

When Emily got home from work that night, she could hear the television on in the family room, so headed in there. She squeezed into the roomy easy chair next to her father and curled up beside him resting her head on his shoulder. "How did it go at the neurologist?"

Clark muted the television then filled her in. He finished with, "So looks like speech therapy is on the agenda. Dr. Wellbrock's receptionist said she'd call the therapist and set up a schedule then she'd call us and let us know. She said it would likely be three mornings a week for…well for quite some time."

"That's good. Speech therapy is a positive step."

"Yes, it is."

They cuddled in cozy silence for a while then Emily asked, "Your knees? They really bothering you?"

"What makes you ask?"

"I can smell the Bengay, Dad, you smell just like Grandpa did when he rubbed it on his sore shoulder."

"Is that all you remember of Grandpa?"

"Of course not. I remember that he used to smuggle me gumdrops, the spicy ones, when you and Mom weren't looking."

Clark smiled at that memory. "Well, you thought we weren't looking. We chose to look the other way. After all, a girl and her granddad should have a secret or two, don't you think?"

"Yes, I do, but I also noticed how you managed to evade the question about your knees."

On a sigh, Clark confessed. "Yes, they bother me a lot, sometimes. But right now, we have more important things to deal with than my aching knees. Speaking of which, Hope's back. So she is going to be able to help out with Mom. She'll probably be touching base with you about coming over some mornings or afternoons, whatever. Oh, yeah, I guess she asked me to have you call her."

Emily nodded. "Okay, but I'm thinking afternoons will be better if Mom will be having therapy in the mornings. Plus, I have plans for the mornings that she doesn't have therapy."

"Oh?"

"I've been doing some online research."

"Of course you have." They both chuckled. "And?"

"One article was talking about the value of exercise when healing from traumatic brain injury. The article said something about walking is tied in to neuronal regeneration. Something like that. But, obviously, since Mom and Lola got lost not long ago, we can't let her do the walking alone for a while. So here's my idea. She and I will start walking on the days she doesn't have therapy. Pretty soon, she'll start getting the lay of the land again, and eventually, she won't get lost when she ventures out alone."

"We hope. So what else has this research you've been doing turned up?"

"One article said recent research shows that omega-3 fatty acids and vitamin E improve cognition in patients with traumatic brain injury. I think you should call Dr. Wellbrock and ask him if he thinks it's worth a try to give her some supplements."

"You know your mom hates taking pills."

"Yes, but these aren't prescription drugs, they're just supplements."

"Even so. She's recently started on how those companies aren't necessarily providing the best products to the consumer."

"Well, that was then, this is now. Maybe she's forgotten about all that."

Clark's laughter was tinged with sadness. "There is that."

"So let's give the supplements a try if the doctor okays it."

Clark kissed Emily's head, getting some hair in his mouth in the process. "You're right, it's worth a try. Good idea, princess."

***

Clark opened his eyes. It was dark, still the middle of the night. What had he heard? Lola hadn't barked, so it mustn't be anything to be concerned about. He shut his eyes then opened them again and rolled over. No Faith. He sat up in bed, rubbing the sleep out of his eyes when he heard a noise and noticed some ambient light spilling from the office. He got up, padded across the hall in his bare feet, and stood in the office doorway, watching his wife. She was sitting on the floor in front of the file cabinet. The bottom drawer was pulled out. She had the contents of one file folder spread out around her. She was looking first at one piece of paper then another. She'd put one down, pick up another one, study it, put it down, and go on to another one. She had tears streaming down her face that she didn't bother to wipe away.

"Honey, what are you doing?"

She looked up at Clark in despair. "T-tr-trying t-to f-f-figure out how t-to f-file."

He squatted down next to her. "Oh, baby, this isn't what the doctor was talking about."

But she wasn't listening to him. She focused on the piece of paper in her hand. "It-it s-says Em-Emily, b-but th-that's all I c-can get."

"It's Emily's birth certificate. Come on." Clark took the certificate from her, placed it in the pile of other papers and pulled Faith to her feet. "Let's get back to bed." As he led her out of the room, she turned and looked back at the pile of papers on the floor next to the open file cabinet drawer. Clark reached over and switched off the office light. "Come on. Bed."

Faith tossed and turned for a little while then dropped off to sleep like a stone off a cliff.

Clark, on the other hand, lay in the dark with his eyes wide open. He stared at the ceiling for what seemed like hours until the gentle wash of dawn lightened the room.

CHAPTER 8

THE ANGER WAS A RED burning haze not only blurring her vision but also scorching her throat. That smoldering coal where her heart had been had flamed into a furious living thing that was spreading through her bloodstream. The effort it took to hold herself back was making her pant through open lips. Her mind was racing around in circles. It was all wrong. Everything was wrong, so very wrong, so horribly, horribly wrong! Faith felt like a volcano ready to spew, but she had to wait, she had to wait, she had to wait. Emily was still home. Go, go, go, go she kept saying to herself in her head. Get out of here. Go to work. She wanted her daughter out of the house so she could be alone with her anger. So she could let the wrath fly out of her helping to ease the pain that raged behind her breastbone that coursed through her system and made her feel as if the top of her head was going to blast off like a rocket ship to Pluto. She crept to the head of the stairway and waited. It sounded like Emily was gathering her things together and getting ready to go. She heard her daughter say, "Be good, Lola. Don't wake Mom." Then the front door opening and shutting. Faith tiptoed down the stairs holding on to the railing for balance as the muscles in her arms and legs trembled with her pent up fury. She stood in the hallway until she heard her daughter's car start and finally, finally, finally pull away.

Faith's trembling increased as she called to the dog. "C-come on, L-Lola. C-come on." The dog followed her to the kitchen and Faith gave her a little shove out the doggie door. After sliding the board that blocked the opening to the doggie door into place, she finally allowed the volcano to gush forth.

The wordless sound that emerged from Faith's throat was pure anguish. "Ahhhherrrrrrashhhhhhhhhgggggggrerrrrrrr." It went on and on as she shook her head from side to side, her hands curled so tightly into fists that her fingernails bit into her palms. "Eeeeeeeehhhhhhhaaaarrrrrrrrrrgggggg." The sound emerging from the depths of her being was so primitive that Lola on the other side of the doggie door started howling too. Pressing her fists to her ears to close out the sound of the dog, she started panting, "S-s-stop it. S-s-stop it." But to say it was so hard, she shut up and started pounding her fist on a nearby cupboard. The pain along the side of her hand made her feel slightly better. The dog was no longer howling, but there was an occasional whimper and some scratching at the door. "Stop it, stop it, stop it!" But she was screaming it in her head so she could control the words.

Faith noticed that the cupboard door she had been pounding on had bounced open and the contents beckoned. She took out a glass goblet. Considered it for a nanosecond then let it drop onto the cold, hard tile floor. It shattered making the most satisfying tinkling sound. She grabbed another glass and threw it onto the floor, smashing it with an abandon she hadn't known existed inside of her. Then another one and another one after that, shattering each in its turn. The dog was whimpering now, but that didn't stop her. One more and one more and one more. She stopped to take a breath and something caught her attention, a knock on the front door, then she heard it opened.

"Faith?"

It was Meghan. Faith turned and stepped out of the kitchen into the dining room so she could see her neighbor. She winced as the ball of her foot inadvertently picked up a shad of slivered glass. Looking down at her foot instead of at Meghan, she thought to herself, *Drat.* She'd remembered to protect Lola from whatever her building wrath might have brought forth but hadn't thought to put on shoes.

By then a concerned Meghan had entered the house and wandered over toward Faith. Her eyes swept the kitchen. The floor was covered in broken glass. They could both hear the dog scratching at the back door making little yipping sounds, pleading with her mistress to let her in. When Meghan turned back to Faith, she raised one eyebrow and simply said, "Cathartic?"

Faith stared at Meghan blankly with no comprehension on her face.

Meghan tried a different approach. "Feel better?"

"K-k-kind of."

Meghan continued observing her friend. Faith was red in the face and panting a bit, but she no longer appeared to be totally out of control. She might have been so moments before, but not now. So Meghan just nodded. "Good." They both look back down at the foot that Faith was now favoring. She lifted her foot up and looked at the bottom of it. Yep, bleeding. "Sit," Meghan ordered. "I'll get something to fix that." She took the long way to the bathroom as the kitchen floor was impassable and returned with tweezers, ointment, gauze, and tape.

Meghan knelt in front of her friend and went to work. After Faith's foot was cleaned and bandaged, Meghan sat back on her heels and took a deep breath. "You planning on cleaning up that mess?"

"I-I w-was g-g-going to g-get t-to it. B-but…"

"But what?"

"I-I-I d-didn't th-think th-things th-through cl-clearly."

"What things?"

"T-the b-br-broom and d-dust p-pan are in t-the br-broom cl-closet on the o-other s-s-side of the k-kitchen."

"Humph! Lucky for you I'm a noisy neighbor. When I hear chaos, I come over to investigate. I'll go get my broom and dust pan and we'll clean this up before Clark gets home."

Faith just sighed then nodded. "Th-thanks."

"And, just out of curiosity, you have any more glasses? Clark or Emmy might want to, you know, have a glass of milk or water or lemonade."

Faith just scratched her head.

"Tell you what. I just boxed up some glassware I was going to take to Goodwill because I didn't want to haul it all the way to Sacramento. So I'll bring over the box. There's probably more in it than you need, but, hey, you might want extra in case you go on another spree." Meghan looked at her cautiously and sternly and with love all at the same time.

"O-o-okay, o-o-okay. E-enough with t-the s-s-sarcasm."

The red was slowly seeping out of Faith's face and neck and her breath was more normal. But she was now pressing one hand to her stomach.

"You feeling all right?"

"S-st-stomachache."

"It's probably all that adrenalin still floating around with no place to go settling in there." Meghan glanced at the kitchen then shook her head, stood up, and headed for the door. "I'll be right back with the broom and some soda crackers for your tummy."

"Th-th-thanks."

***

While Meghan swept, Faith nibbled on soda crackers to settle her stomach and hauled out the vacuum cleaner. Twenty minutes later, the kitchen floor had been swept, vacuumed, and gone over twice with damp paper towels to get up the little slivers of glass that had escaped both the broom and vacuum. When Faith unblocked the doggie door, Lola bolted through the opening, skittered across the floor, ran back to her mistress, and jumped up to see if she was okay.

"D-d-down y-you id-idiot." But she gave the dog a loving pat on the head.

Completely at home, Meghan filled the teakettle and dug some teabags out of the cupboard. While the water heated, she put her hands on her ample hips and stared at Faith. "Talk to me, girlfriend."

"S-s-sure. T-t-talk is s-so e-easy."

While the water heated, Meghan scurried back to her house, got the box of glassware she'd mentioned earlier, schlepped it into Faith's kitchen, and plunked it on the counter. Meanwhile, Faith poured boiling water over teabags and brought the two mugs to the dining room table. The women blew on the steaming brew and sipped in silence for a few moments. "Look," Meghan said. "I get it. You're ticked off. And believe me, I know the satisfaction of throwing some-thing and hearing it shatter, but…"

Faith simply crossed her arms over her chest, leveled a look at her friend, and said, "T-t-ticked off d-doesn't e-even t-touch it. I-I'm en-enraged! I-I-I *hate her* s-s-so *m-much*! L-look wh-wh-what she d-d-did to m-me! S-she t-took s-so m-much f-from me!"

"Yes, yes, she did." Meghan nodded in agreement. "But she didn't take everything. You still have so much more than so many people. Clark, Emmy, your house, your pets, your friends. You have a wealth of things so many people don't have. Don't let her have any more than she's already taken."

"W-what d-d-do you m-mean?"

"I mean that hatred is a very destructive emotion. It erodes, it subtracts, it destroys. You need to take the emotions she brings forth in you and try to harness them and deal with them in a way that isn't destructive."

"H-how?"

Meghan shook her head. "Darned if I know. But if we look to nature, we can see that wind can be stirred up into typhoons, and hurricanes, and tornados and wreck such havoc and damage. And yet that same wind can be harnessed in windmills and wind farms with all those turbines and some good can come out of all that power. When those emotions start swirling through you again…"

"I-I-I'll p-p-probably b-break s-something again."

"Sure." She reached over and laid her hand over Faith's. "Maybe on Saturday you and I can take in a couple of yard sales and stock you up on glassware." When Faith laughed, Meghan added, "You know they always have those ugly cheap wine glasses for a nickel or a dime. I bet they'd shatter nicely."

"S-smarty-p-pants." But Faith was still chuckling. "Y-you k-k-know you d-don't have t-to s-stay and b-babysit m-me. I-I'm o-okay n-now."

"Well," Meghan stood up, "let's get the new glasses in the cup-board and stash the rest in the garage, just in case."

***

LOST

Alone once again, Faith sagged in exhaustion. Weariness, her constant companion, wrapped itself around her. She made it as far as the couch in the family room and was asleep as soon as she pulled the throw comfortably up to her chin.

BARGAINING

You also bargain with yourself – I'll do this today so God will let me heal. You bargain every single day. You'll bargain with any entity, even the devil – you bargain let me not be so afraid of…everything!
—Susan Cade

CHAPTER 9

SITTING UP IN BED, FAITH tapped the pencil against her chin. She had just written a passage in her log and was feeling pretty smug. When Dr. Wellbrock had told her to start keeping a log of things, reactions, etc., she thought he was crazy. How was she going to be able to do that if she couldn't even speak clearly? If she couldn't read a simple article in a newspaper and make sense of it? Reading was simply too hard making her head ache and ache. But, amazingly enough, she had discovered as she moved the pencil across the page somehow words flowed from the tip and onto the paper. Her speech might be jumbled but her thoughts weren't. She might not be able to comprehend what others were writing about if passages were too long, but her own thoughts being written down wasn't a chore and wasn't that the most amazing thing! She didn't expect to write more than two sentences, but once she started writing, words bubbled out of her like a pot bubbling and boiling and she just went with it. For her first entry, she had written:

> I don't remember many things and that is
> a concern to me. Clark or Emmy will say some-
> thing to me with an expression on their faces
> like I'm supposed to know what they are talking
> about. I feel like a person in a strange land where
> everyone speaks a language different from mine.
> Some of the words are the same, but the mean-
> ings aren't. I feel like I have to learn their lan-
> guage because they won't be learning mine.

She could hear Emily bustling around downstairs getting ready to leave for work. Faith put her log away and looked around the bedroom. She took a sip of the coffee Emily had brought up to her a little while ago. She thought she remembered Emily saying that Hope was going to come over today. That must mean she was back from her trip. So she tossed back the covers, she should get up. After a quick shower, she dressed and was heading downstairs just as Emily sang out, "Heading to work, Mom. See you later."

"B-b-bye, h-hon-ey."

Faith heard the door shut just as she reached the bottom of the stairs. Her logbook was tucked under her arm. She put it on the coffee table in the family room and started to head toward the kitchen but instead stopped in the hallway. For the first time since the accident, she noticed that walls of the hallway were hung with pictures. She looked first at one and then another and then another.

***

Hope arrived just as Emily was leaving for work. They stood in the driveway chatting. "She just woke up, so she should be good for a little while. But she tires out so easily. Just be aware of that."

Hope gave her niece a hug. "I will, Emmy."

"I mean she *really* tires out easily, so don't…"

"I get it. Don't over do it. I'll keep it short."

"Okay, I've gotta go or I'll be late." Faith watched Emily drive off then turned toward the house.

The dog announced her before she had gotten one foot in the living room. "Shut up, Lola. Where's your mommy?"

"B-back h-here."

Hope headed toward the back of the house and saw Faith in the hallway, looking at the photographs that hung on the walls.

"H-hi, H-Hope."

"Hi, yourself." Hope gathered her sister into her arms and just held on for a while. "Ah, the Gold Dust Twins united again," Hope said, stepping back to get a good look at Faith.

Faith tilted her head, trying to catch an errant thought, "G-gold wh-what is th-that?"

"Did a ping of memory go off? Gold Dust Twins. Do you remember Daddy…"

"A-ah, of course I-I re-remem-b-ber D-Daddy!"

"No, no, you didn't let me finish." Hope patted her sister's arm. "I was going to say, do you remember that Daddy used to call us the Gold Dust Twins?"

"N-no. Wh-wh-why?"

"Well, I'll tell you all about that. But what are you doing here in the hallway? Looking at the photographs?"

Faith nodded. "T-t-trying t-to re-remem-b-ber."

Hope scanned the walls up and down the hallway. "Your Rogues' Gallery. So much fun stuff here."

"R-Rogues' G-Gallery?"

"Yeah, that's what you always called it."

"W-why?"

"Good question. Let me ponder that. Oh, okay, I've got it. In the old days, in police stations, they used to have drawings of all the most wanted criminals along the wall and they called that the rogues' gallery. So with your sense of humor, that's what you always called these family photos. These walls are your Rogues' Gallery."

Faith made a little humming sound in her throat.

"What was that little 'hmmm' about?"

"S-some-thing j-just m-made s-sense t-t-to m-me."

"What was that?"

"W-when you p-ponder-ed th-then an-swered my q-question, y-you w-were g-going th-through files," Faith was tapping the side of her head, "up h-here. L-like th-the d-doctor ex-explained t-to m-me."

"I guess I was. A couple nights ago when we dropped in, Clark told me how the doctor explained everything to you using a tipped-over file cabinet as an example. I guess I *was* going through mental files. Yeah. So you just had an epiphany. That's good."

The word epiphany made Faith frown. Then ignoring the fact that she had no idea what Hope had been talking about, she turned back to the pictures on the walls. "I re-re-recog-nize us. B-but I-I don't know wh-where…"

"You don't remember where the pictures were taken?"

Faith nodded. "Or w-w-when."

"Shall I tell you about them?"

"Y-yes, p-pl-please."

"This one, Emmy was all dolled up for the junior prom, I think it was. Yes, that one over there was senior prom."

Faith looked from one to the other and back again. "It-it's th-the s-same b-boy in b-both th-these p-pictures. B-but it's n-not Ch-Chris."

"That's right. She was dating this other guy in high school. Chris didn't show up on the scene until she was getting ready to head for college. She had just broken up with this guy," Hope tapped the glass-framed picture, "figuring as they were going to two different schools that it would be too hard to continue the relationship. They had really been more just friends than anything anyway."

"I-I d-don't re-remem-b-ber any of th-that."

"What about this picture?" It was of Faith and Clark. She had a flower in her hair. "Do you remember this one?"

"I-I d-don't k-know wh-where it was t-taken."

"Hawaii. Your tenth wedding anniversary. I was so jealous as I had never been. Still never have as a matter of fact. And there you are, you and Clark in this other picture, with that sunset behind you. Hawaii again on your twentieth anniversary."

"I-I d-don't re-re-rememb-er Ha-Hawaii."

"You will, someday. In fact, you'll probably also remember that after coming home the second time around, you said you guys were never going back. You said it had changed so much in ten years that it could no longer be called paradise."

"W-why?"

"Too many people was what you said. And it was so built up and commercial. You said you'd have had more fun staying home and playing in your own backyard."

Faith was staring at a picture of a mound of stones in a fallow field. There was a young pine tree rising up out of it with a little lilac bush cozily off to the side. "Th-th-this is p-p-pretty."

"That was taken one year when you guys came to visit Ross and me and the boys when we lived in North Dakota. We had been out picking chokecherries to make some syrup when we came across that pile of rocks. You were very taken by it, said it was a real Zen kind of expression and you snapped the picture.

"Y-yes. It's v-very p-p-peace-ful. Wh-what about th-this p-pic-ture w-with th-the d-don-key?"

Hope chuckled. "That was on our trip to the Black Hills."

"B-Bl-Black Hills?"

"Yes, in South Dakota. It was a great trip. Emmy was about three. Ross and the boys and I were along with you guys for the trip. The kids had been feeding the donkeys crackers. That guy was trying to stick his head in the car to find more crackers when you snapped his picture."

"B-b-by th-the way, h-how is R-Ross?"

That threw Hope for a loop. She and Ross had been divorced for years. After being alone for ages, she had remarried, and Faith had stood up with her as matron of honor. She cleared her throat and said, "As far as I know, Ross is fine. He and I are divorced, Faith. And I can see by your expression that's news to you. Come on, let's go sit down in the family room. That will be more comfortable than standing here in the hallway."

Hope, completely at home in her sister's house, detoured into the kitchen and found some lemonade in the fridge. She poured them both a glass and then sat on the couch with Faith and told her sister the whole dreary story of the divorce. "But, hey, it was a long time ago. And you really like Cliff."

"B-but I-I l-like R-Ross t-too."

"Sure, so do I. Who doesn't like Ross? We just weren't suited, and Cliff and I are very well suited. Don't tell me you don't remember Cliff."

"Y-yes, I re-re-remem-ber Cliff. *N-now*, d-don't t-tell him I for-forgot him."

"Of course, I won't. It will be our secret. One of many."

"W-we h-have s-secrets?"

"Yes, and now, considering the circumstances, I know you'll never tell them to anyone."

"H-h-ha-ha."

"You know the old saying: two can keep a secret if one of them is dead. Now I won't have to kill you."

"H-h-ha-ha once a-again."

"See, you still have your sense of humor, so all is not lost. Okay, serious time. Tell me how you've been. Really been. No sugarcoating."

So Faith did. "I-I j-just don't ha-have any en-en-energy any-more. A-and I-I get s-so co-confused. And m-my at-attention s-span is s-shot. I get l-lost in w-words and ex-explana-na-tions. I-I can't read any-anymore. I m-mean I-I c-can r-read w-words, like c-cat. Or a-a n-name on t-the phone. B-but p-put it in a-a sen-sentence. I g-get l-lost."

"But your doctor said that normal, right? For someone who has had a head injury? It will just take time?"

"Y-yes, t-time." Then she cocked her head as if an idea had flit-ted through it. "T-time. S-something a-about t-time?"

"What?"

"I-I d-don't know. I-l lost-it."

"So, what else? You haven't spilled all the beans yet."

"I-I've b-been so a-angry a-a-about e-every-th-thing. No, it's m-m-more than j-just anger. I-I j-just w-w-want t-t-to p-punch s-s-someone or s-something. I-I j-just k-keep a-asking w-why m-me?"

"Honey, I just feel so badly that this has happened to you. It's so unfair."

"T-tell m-me ab-about it." Faith looked off into the middle distance for a moment, then, her eyes focused on a little figurine sitting next to a cup and saucer on the mantel over the gas fireplace. Pointing, she asked, "Is-is th-that an an-angel?"

"Sure looks like it to me."

"W-why d-do I h-have an an-angel th-there?"

"Probably because you like it."

"N-no, I m-mean, d-do I b-believe in an-angels? It d-doesn't s-seem l-like I do? O-or m-maybe?"

"Well, you're not a traditionalist when it comes to religion. But with a name like Faith, you'd hardly be an agnostic or atheist."

"S-so I b-believe in G-God?" She had a little frown between her eyes as if to say she wasn't sure.

"You pretty much believe in energy, a universal energy. Some people might call it God, but you always felt that was way too limiting."

Faith listened very intently. "Th-that s-sounds r-right."

"You always said people were so stupid and shallow that they invented a God and then cast him in their own image. And then they claimed the reverse. If you had to try and explain your beliefs, you'd always come back to $E=MC^2$, the theory of relativity. It basically says that energy never dies. And to you that universal energy is immortal and can manifest in many forms. And people, you surmised, interpret those forms in different ways. So if somebody wanted to call a certain form of energy an angel, that would work for you."

"In-interesting. Th-this is f-funny. Y-you t-telling m-me my b-beliefs."

"I'm just repeating what you've said over the years. You kind of have your own Bible, *The Scriptures According to Faith,* as it were."

"I-I d-do? Wh-what d-do you-m-mean?"

After thinking for a moment, Hope nodded. "Here's an example. There's a line in the New Testament that says, 'In the beginning was the Word and the Word was God.' You always paraphrase that to, 'In the beginning was the Word and the Word was Ohmmm.' And then you'd go on to say that the vibrational energy that emanated out from that first Word caused the Big Bang that started all creation on its path."

"S-sounds l-like I had a l-lot of ideas."

"Yes, we have that in common. We both like to theorize about things."

Faith shook her head at the irony. "I s-s-said that a w-w-word 'ohmmm' started e-ev-every-th-thing and yet l-l-look what a hard t-t-time I have w-with w-w-words now."

"Life is full of little ironies."

"T-tell m-me m-more a-about *Th-The S-Scriptures A-According t-to F-Faith*."

Hope laughed. "Okay, let me think about that." She tapped a forefinger to her chin as she thought.

"Y-you d-don't r-r-remember?"

"Oh, I remember a lot. I'm just trying to think of the best way to begin. Okay, let's see if I can synthesize here. Maybe to understand *The Scriptures According to Faith*, we should start with the Vocabulary of Faith first."

"O-o-okay."

"So the first vocabulary word is *liberation*. It is a freedom from restrictions."

"I kn-know wh-what li-lib-liberation m-means."

"Sorry, I wasn't trying to be condescending. I was just trying to put it into a context for you. It's just that that freedom from restrictions, particularly restrictive thinking is key to *The Scriptures According to Faith*."

"D-do I h-have th-this s-stuff w-written d-down s-s-some-wh-where?"

"No, I don't think you do."

Faith picked up the notebook and pen lying on the end table that she was using for her log and begin to write the word *liberation*. "O-okay, I'm s-s-s-starting a v-v-vocabulary p-p-page."

Laughing Hope said, "Okay, here's goes with the second vocabulary word: *interconnectedness*."

Faith wrote the word in the notebook. "I-I kn-know w-what in-inter-c-connectedness m-m-means," she linked the fingers of both hands, "b-but wh-what is th-the c-c-context?"

"Well, you see the world—no, not just the world—the whole cosmos as interrelated and interconnected. You believe that all things are connected, that life, all of life, is, metaphorically speaking, one huge spider web and what jiggles the web over here," Faith spread her arms wide and wiggled the fingers of her left hand, "can affect a reaction way over here," she wiggled the fingers of her right hand. "So that the two things, this," she wiggled her left fingers, "and this," she wiggled her right fingers, "that don't seem connected at all are actually very much connected. *Interconnectedness.*"

Looking overwhelmed at all this information, Faith asked, "H-how d-did I c-come t-to all th-this?'"

"I'm not one hundred percent sure. I know you had some kind of a woo-woo experience at some point and you were trying to get a handle on it. Something happened that opened you up or lifted you above the mundane. It wasn't something you were able to put into words, hence one of your first maxims: *To talk about it is to lose it.* I think what you meant by that was that the experience counts, but to try to explain the experience lessens it. Like losing something in the translation."

"W-w-wow," was the only word she could think of to express the amazement at all she was learning about herself.

"You figured most people wouldn't get it, so you kept a lot of this to yourself."

Blinking as she processed everything, a sudden urge made itself known. Faith stood up. "W-w-wow a-again. A-and on th-that n-note, I-have t-to p-pee."

Hope almost sang out after her retreating figure, "Don't forget to pull down your panties," but thought better of it at the last minute. The old Faith would have laughed. But the new Faith, she didn't want to hurt her or make her cry. Clark had told her that Faith cried a lot more often since the accident. And speaking of crying, she felt tears welling in her own eyes. "No! Stop it!" Hope chided herself. "Don't let her see how this gets to you!" She rubbed her eyes a few times and brushed her hands over her cheeks to get rid of the moisture before Faith came back.

CHAPTER 10

As HOPE WAITED FOR FAITH to return to the family room, she wandered over to the bookcase on the other side of the room. On the bottom shelf were photograph albums. She pulled one out at random and sat back down on the couch. When Faith returned, the two of them looked at the pictures together. Most of them were pastoral pictures of nature in its glory.

Faith had a little concentration line between her eyebrows. "W-who t-took th-these?"

"Why, you did! You don't recall that?"

Faith simply shook her head.

"You're an amateur photographer. Actually more than just an amateur."

They flipped through a few more pages. There was a particular grouping of photographs that caught Faith's attention. It was a series of pictures of a very small island full of pine trees spearing into the sky and fronted by a large boulder that abutted it like a sentry. The island sat in the middle of a small lake, and Faith had taken pictures of it from different perspectives: close, far away; from the north, south, east, west; during a clear sunny day, a morning with mist rising off the water. One picture was of the lake with a pair of ducks floating peacefully on the surface; one with the reflection of trees and clouds in the water; one with a bullfrog on a lily pad that was so clichéd that it was actually the antithesis of a cliché; and one of raindrops falling on the water. And in all the pictures, the island resided either centered or off to the side, but always part of the picture.

"W-wow. Th-these are a-amazing. I-I d-did all of th-these?"

"You guys took a trip to Maine a few years back. Rented a cabin on a lake for about a week. Or, as you told me when you got home, a camp, they call a cabin a camp there. Who knows why? Anyway, you told me you liked to get up early and kayak around the lake and around your island. It was a kind of Zen time for you. You are big on Zen time, and during your mornings on the lake, I guess the island became a focal point for you."

"T-tell m-me wh-what Z-Zen t-time is?"

Hope sat back and thought about it. "It's just a peaceful, natural time when you don't worry about things, don't even think about things. You just exist in the moment."

"Th-that s-sounds n-nice."

"Yes, it is. And most people don't take the time for Zen time, but you are pretty big on that."

Faith wrote *Zen time* down in her log before turning back to the album. They turned pages looking at a few more pictures.

"Th-there a-aren't any of p-p-people. J-j-just na-nature."

"You take some of people. They are in other albums. But mostly you stick with nature. You are a bit of a Druid."

"Wh-what is th-that?"

Hope laughed. "I guess I don't really mean that. Druids were a mysterious group of people in ancient times and some say they even participated in sacrifice: animal and human! So scratch that Druid comment. What I was trying to say is that you're a bone-deep tree hugger. You always related to nature. Your gardening, your kayaking on the lake, your Zen time, all that is kind of what I was referring to." Hope looked closely at her sister. "And you, sis, look exhausted. Emily's going to skin me alive! I promised her I wouldn't overstay my visit so I best skedaddle."

Faith put a hand to her head, which had started to ache with all the concentration it took to keep up with Hope let alone look at the pictures. "I-I am k-k-kind of t-t-tired."

"So I'm out of here." Faith stood up to walk Hope to the door. "I can find my way out, you go up to bed." Hope kissed her sister on the cheek and picked up the empty glasses of lemonade. She rinsed them in the kitchen sink and put them in the dishwasher. She heard her sister making her way slowly up the stairs to the bedroom. When she got to the front door, Lola who had been sleeping on the living room couch popped her head up and looked around. Hope put her finger to her lips. "Mommy's going to take a nap, so no barking." Then she slipped out the door.

When Faith entered the bedroom, she had tears streaming down her face. She didn't remember any of the things Hope had been talking about. Taking pictures, trips to Maine. Nothing! A big fat blank! She picked up a tennis shoe that was on the bedroom floor and threw it against the wall. And the red haze fell over her eyes again.

***

When Faith finally came back to herself, every shoe in her closet had been thrown around the room as if they had been caught up in a whirlwind and her cat was cowering under the bed peeking out with trepidation. And her stomach was starting to hurt too. She went back downstairs and got some soda crackers. She munched as she gathered up her shoes and started putting them back in the closet. When she picked up one shoe with the nice spiked heel off the window seat, she saw a little pit in the window. *"Oh, oh,"* she said to herself in her head. Touching the pit with her finger, she realized the heel must have hit the glass. She looked around and understood she'd been extremely lucky that she hadn't broken any of the mirrors or the television. Thank goodness. She reached over and pulled the drapes a little to the left and, voila, the pit was hidden.

Shoes finally all put away, Faith sagged. The skin over her forehead felt like it was drawn so tautly over her skull that the slightest movement would tear it. And the pounding inside her head was increasing, like someone was beating a tom-tom drum. She popped an Advil then wet a washcloth in the bathroom sink, getting it as cold as she could stand. Folding it up, she held it to her head and just sat on the edge of the bed for a moment. Laying down flat on her back, she pressed the wet cloth over her eyes, letting the cold dampness penetrate.

That didn't stop the tears that slid out of her eyes only to be absorbed by the wet cloth. In her head, she just kept repeating to herself: *why me?* and, *it's not fair!* over and over again. The visit with her sister had drained her beyond belief. And the subsequent tirade had taken her to the edge of complete exhaustion. She felt limp and worn out and the unfairness of everything that had brought her to this point was getting her ire up again. She took a deep, shuddering breath, for all the good it did to get upset. Her thoughts turned to that higher power that Hope said she believed in. That energy that was all encompassing and everlasting. Could it help her? "Please," she said to it in her head, "please make me better. I want to be the old me. The one who is never confused, who is never forever exhausted. The one who was never angry. Well, hardly ever angry. The one who takes charge of everything. Please, make me better so Emmy can get back to living her own life. Please make me better so I can start helping Clark again with the business. Please, please, please." Her tears continued to fall and to be absorbed by the cloth while the word *please* echoed in her mind.

Crestline jump up on the bed, stepping delicately onto Faith's stomach, making herself comfortable by turning around a few times, before curling up into a little ball of purring fur. Faith fell asleep petting her kitty with one hand while holding the cloth to her eyes with the other.

That's how Clark found them a little while later. He stood in the bedroom with the box in his hands. He turned around and was tiptoeing out of the room when Faith sensed him. She pulled the washcloth off and opened her eyes. "C-Clark?"

He came back into the room. "Hey, Sleeping Beauty. Did I wake you?"

"N-no. I wa-was j-just resting m-my eyes."

"You're not a very good liar. Here." He held out the box to her as she pushed the cat off her stomach and sat up in bed."

"Wh-what's th-this?"

"If you want to find out what a present is, you have to open it up."

She picked up the box that Clark had placed beside her, opened it, and pulled out a laptop computer. Confused, she asked, "W-wh-why? W-we al-already have a-a co-computer."

"But we don't have a laptop. Well, Emmy does, but you don't. And the desktop is both of ours. This is yours."

She still looked confused. "B-but wh-why?"

"I've been thinking about what Dr. Wellbrock said, about inside your head was a filing cabinet that was tipped over with all the files mixed up. And I thought, computers have files too. A person does something on a computer and puts that document in a file to keep things organized. So I figured if you started doing, I don't know, stuff on this, and putting stuff in files, it might," he moved a finger back and forth between the computer and her head, "you know, cross pollinate or something and help you with organizing your internal files. And, as it's a laptop, you could do it in bed or wherever, not just in the office. What?" Her face had crumpled up like she was about to cry. "Did I mess up?"

Faith was shaking her head. "N-no. Bu-but I-I…"

"You what?"

She was still shaking her head. "C-c-computers use w-words. I-I d-dis-covered I c-can-can w-write, but I s-still c-can't r-read wh-what other p-p-p-people w-write if th-there are t-t-too m-many w-words."

"We don't have to deal with words, honey. Not just words. I was actually thinking we could start with pictures. I have a ton of photographs I've taken over the years on the desktop. I'll email a few to you each day. You could then open them up and organize them in appropriate files. This one when we were dating. This one from our wedding. That one after Emmy was born. Files could be set up by years or events. See, just organizing them and putting them in appropriate files on the computer might help put things in the right file in your head. We'd start with just three pictures a day and see how it goes. It can be like a daily game we play. Okay?"

The tears were falling in earnest now. "Oh-oh, C-Clark. Wh-what a-a good i-idea."

"And even though you have trouble speaking words, I know you can read some words and write them. So you can maybe start a little log like the doctor suggested, only on the computer, not just in a notebook, things like that."

She started crying harder but was nodding too. "I-I-I d-did s-start a-a l-log." She looked around. "I-it m-m-must b-be d-downs-stairs." Her tears kept falling and falling.

Getting on the bed next to her and taking her into his arms he asked, "Why are you crying?"

"Be-because." And for the first time since the accident, in Clark's presence she didn't just cry, she let the dam burst and she *wept* in her husband's arms. She wept for many reasons: for the unfairness of life; for the multitude of frustrations she had been enduring since the accident; for the knowledge that the world she had known had ended and a new one had begun in an instant of time; and she wept for happiness that her husband would be so thoughtful as to bring her a gift to try and help her through her nightmare. In time, she finally sobbed herself into an exhausted sleep.

Clark carefully extricated himself, and, after heading to the kitchen for a beer, went into this office. He booted up the computer and got to work. He knew how hard it was going to be on Faith when he had to start the job in the desert. So he organized several emails with photographs attached to them and stored them in the draft file. That way when he was out of town, he could access his email, and choose one with the pictures already attached and send it to Faith. It would give her something to look forward to on a daily basis. For good measure, he decided right then and there to shoot one of them off to her before he closed his email. He didn't write much as he knew that would be futile. He just wrote: *First Batch of Pictures. Love You.* And if she woke up and turned on her new laptop and opened her email tonight, he'd be there to help her get started on their new game.

CHAPTER 11

CLARK KNOCKED ON MEGHAN'S DOOR then opened it and walked in. They had never stood on ceremony. Packing boxes lined one wall. "Hey, Meghan, where are you?"

"In the kitchen." Her voice sounded like she had a bag over her head.

Clark made his way to the kitchen and stood in the archway, looking at what must have been a recent earthquake. All the cupboards were open and mostly bare. Dishes, glasses, cereal boxes, canned goods, and who-knew-what-else were piled up on the counters. And the kitchen table looked like it was all but sagging under the weight of a multitude of things. All he could see of Meghan were her ample hindquarters. She stood on a stepstool and was reaching back into the farthest reaches of the top shelf of a cupboard, head and shoulders deep. "Good grief, what's this?" she was mumbling to herself.

"Need any help?"

"Just give me a minute, Clark, I've got this one nearly empty, but something's stuck up here." She gave a yank while making a disgusted sound in the back of her throat. She handed a half-empty glass jar of something toward Clark. "How this honey got way back there on the top shelf," she was shaking her head. "What a mess! Would you be a lamb and put it in the sink for me?" While he complied, she started ripping the shelf paper off that shelf. "Lucky it was up high. The ants never found it. Yuck, yuck, yuck." She backed down off the stepstool, tossed the crumpled up shelf paper into an overflowing trash bag, and washed the stickiness off her hands before drying them on the seat of her pants. "Anyway, what's up?"

"A snafu. I was going to ask you to do me a favor, but," he gestured all around him, "I can see you have your boots full with all this packing. So never mind."

"Ignore the mess. What's the snafu?"

"Faith has her first appointment with the speech therapist tomorrow morning. Emmy was going to take her, but she just called me from work. There is going to be a staff meeting tomorrow morning and she is expected to attend. And I've got inspectors lined up to sign off on some stuff tomorrow. That can't be put off or it will be the domino effect of biblical proportions. I simply can't do it. I've really got to finish up this job that ended up running longer than expected. Anyway, never mind, I'll just call Hope. I'm sure she can help out."

"Don't bother Hope. I'll take Faith to her appointment."

"You sure?" Clark looked around at the chaos.

"Look. Once I'm gone, you'll be relying on Hope a lot more. No need to start now. I've got this one covered."

"Thanks, Meghan."

"No problem. Now, as long as you're here, I could use some muscle in the other room."

Clark helped her turn the dining room table over on the rug so it looked like a turtle on its back. Then she handed him the tools. As he removed the legs he said, "Brian sure was smart to take that job in Sacramento so he'd have to be there instead of here during the packing phase."

"No kidding!"

"There," he laid the final table leg next to the other three, "all ready for the moving van. Anything else?"

"Not at the moment."

"Okay," he moved toward the front door then nearly jumped out of his skin when he heard a bunch of firecrackers go off down the street.

Meghan chuckled. "It's just those Randall boys starting the celebrations early." Noticing his frown, she added. "Didn't you ever light off firecrackers on the 4th of July as a kid?"

"Sure. But it wasn't against the law then. Nor was there fire danger as we have now. It hasn't rained in months and they're doing that?"

"Aw, pshaw. They're not going to start a fire and they're not hurting anybody. Stop being such an old curmudgeon."

"Plus the fourth isn't for another week."

"As I just said, curmudgeon. Stop."

"Yes, ma'am." He saluted her. "By the way, the appointment is at ten, but chances are she won't be up and ready to go unless she's prodded."

"Don't worry. I'll go over and prod her in plenty of time."

"I knew I could count on you."

***

The therapist greeted them at the door to her office with a sunny "Hello."

"Hi, this is Faith. I'm Meghan, the driver." Meghan looked around the office. "How about I just sit over there and read a magazine while you do your thing?"

"Pleased to meet you, Meghan. Yes, that would be great. Hi, Faith, I'm Cheryl." Cheryl was a petite brunette with a winning smile. The splash of faded freckles across the bridge of the classic button nose added a winsome little-girlishness to her otherwise no-nonsense can-do attitude. She was a woman who exuded confidence and competence, making both Faith and Meghan feel completely at ease. The therapist had Faith sit at a table. Cheryl sat opposite her and smiled. "How are you doing, Faith?"

"O-okay."

"Good. Glad to hear it. Before we get started, I'd like to ask you if it's all right with you if we record the sessions we'll be having here?"

"R-r-record th-them?"

"Yes, it's good to have a record of where you were when you began your treatment later on so we can look back and do accurate assessments."

Faith shrugged. "I-I-I g-g-guess it's o-okay."

Taking a piece of paper out of a drawer, Cheryl explained, "This is a release form saying we have your permission to record the sessions." She looked over at Meghan who had been listening to the whole exchange. "Meghan, would you please witness Faith's signature and then sign indicating I explained this to her and she agreed?"

Meghan walked over to the table and rested her hand on Faith's shoulder. "You don't mind them recording you?"

"No-no…h-harm in…it." Faith picked up the pen and signed her name and handed it to Meghan who signed in turn.

"Thank you." Cheryl put the paper in her drawer and turned aside to flick on a switch for a recording device that was bracketed to an upper corner of the wall focusing down on the chair where Faith sat. Turning back to Faith, she began the session. "We'll just talk for a little while so I can do some assessing. When you first got here, I asked how you were doing and you replied, 'Okay.' Tell me," this said with a friendly and inviting smile, "how are you *really* doing?"

Faith gave a little laugh at being caught. "W-well, n-not o-okay."

"Tell me."

Faith thought for a moment. "M-m-my m-mind s-seems t-t-to w-w-wander a lot. Or-or n-not w-wander s-s-so m-much as I j-just g-g-get l-lost." She swirled her fingers in the air next to the side of her head. "Y-yes, th-that's it. L-lost. I-I am s-s-so l-lost."

"And?"

She glanced over her shoulder at Meghan and turned back to the therapist. "A-and I h-have t-temper t-tantrums and b-break th-things."

"And?"

S-some-t-times, I-I-I g-get s-so ov-overwh-whelmed at s-sounds or-or l-lights and th-things."

"That's called sensory overload. And there are some things I can teach you to do that will help with that."

"G-g-good."

"We'll do that in a few minutes. Why don't you tell me about something you did yesterday."

Faith made a little self-deprecating moue. "I-I s-slept m-m-most of t-the d-d-day a-a-way."

"Because you're exhausted or because you're bored?"

"Ex-exhausted. B-but," she rubbed her head, "I-I'm j-just s-so bl-blank up h-here m-most of th-the t-time."

"Tell me about it. Tell me what you are feeling."

"I-I d-don't k-know if I'm f-f-feeling any-th-th-thing. M-most of th-the t-time I'm j-just ex-existing. H-hour t-to h-hour, m-minute t-to m-minute."

"That sounds normal considering your brain injury. That fatigue that you are experiencing, the fatigue that accompanies a concussion is a very different type of fatigue than you have probably ever been used to. The reason I asked you before if you were exhausted or bored is that I wanted to know if *you* understood that this is a whole new can of worms that's been opened here. It is not only bodily exhaustion that turns your limbs into dead weight, but it fogs the mind as well. So you fall into sleep as the body desperately tries to regain some semblance of equilibrium. But sadly, the naps don't make the confusion or the weariness go away."

"Ex-exact-ly." She looked so relieved that someone recognized what she'd been struggling with.

"Yes. I do get it. So when you are up and about, tell me what you do."

She gave a little laugh and her cheeks flushed slightly with embarrassment. "I t-tied m-m-my sh-shoes."

"You tied your shoes? That's what you did yesterday?"

"I w-was g-getting ready t-t-to go f-for a w-walk w-with m-my d-daughter. And I h-had f-for-gotten h-how t-to tie m-my sh-shoe l-laces. E-Emily sh-showed m-me."

So your daughter taught you how to tie your shoes." Cheryl glanced down and saw that Faith was wearing sandals, but that her friend who was sitting over in the waiting area had tennis shoes on. Getting Meghan's attention she asked, "Would you mind if Faith unties your shoes then reties them for me?"

Faith untied them, then after a false start or two, she managed to get them tied again.

"Good. You remembered what your daughter showed you yesterday. So that's all positive."

Back at the table, Cheryl continued, "Are you able to prepare meals?"

Faith thought about that for a minute. "M-my d-daughter d-does th-th-that f-for our l-lunch b-before s-she g-goes t-t-to w-work. A-and C-Clark g-gets t-takeout f-for our d-dinner."

"And you. What did you do yesterday while your daughter fixed your lunch?"

"W-well, l-last w-w-week m-my hus-hus-husband g-gave m-me a co-computer. A l-l-lap-t-top. S-s-so I w-was tr-trying t-to use it yes-yester-day."

"What do you do on the laptop?"

"T-try-trying t-to p-put p-pictures in f-files. B-but, it's h-hard."

"Tell me what's hard about it?"

"A-after a wh-while, it b-b-bothers m-my eyes. A-and," she pressed her fingers to her forehead, "and m-my head. S-so I-I h-have t-t-to t-turn it off."

"I see. I can tell you this, Faith. The computer bothering your eyes is just one more symptom of this brain injury you suffered. So let's talk about your brain injury, okay?"

Faith nodded.

"Just a little physiology lesson here: the brain is divided into sections. The two biggest sections are called hemispheres. Are you with me so far?"

"Y-yes. I k-know, th-the l-left and th-the right h-hem-hemispheres. A-and the l-left one c-controls th-the r-right s-side and v-vice v-versa."

"That's correct." Cheryl seemed only mildly surprised. "Have you been doing your homework?"

"M-my n-n-neighbor is a s-s-psychologist. He h-has b-been ex-explaining s-some th-things t-to m-me and m-my hus-husband."

"Very good. The part of your brain that has been injured, at least primarily so, has to do with the cognition and speech centers. Hence your trouble with words."

"A-and y-you c-c-can h-help m-me?"

"I can. Let me explain a bit of what's happening. When you want to say something, you have to find the words to use. That has become hard for you. When you finally do find the right word, you are so afraid it will disappear again before you can say it that you get in too much of a hurry. And in your rush to say the word, you start tripping over the word. Your hurry contributes to your dysfunctional speech. For you, words have become the enemy. Does that sound right?"

Faith nodded. "I r-really h-h-have a n-new em-empathy f-for P-Porky P-P-Pig."

"I need you to recognize one thing up front. Your verbal deficits are a transient symptom of your injury. They are not a permanent disability. Do you realize that?"

"W-well, I h-hoped t-they w-weren't p-p-permanent."

"Well, they're not. Just keep reminding yourself of that. One of the things I am going to do is teach you how to slow down when you talk. We will be doing exercises that will help you to do this. And one of the things we will be doing is using the breath to help you get the words out. So instead of hurrying to get a word out and going t-t-t-t you'll learn how to stretch the word syllables out. First from t-t-t to ta-ta-ta then to taaaaaaa and finally then blend it into the rest of the word. Taaaaaalk or taaaaable. So instead of being in a hurry and say-ing b-b-b, we'll, again, stretch the word out letting the breath work with us and say baaaaath or booook. Do you see?"

"Y-y-yes." Faith shook her head at the way she had said, yes. "I-I g-get it in th-theory."

"Don't worry. It's not going to be an overnight fix. Just because you know what we will be doing now doesn't mean you can do it immediately. It will be days or weeks before you even start to get the hang of it. It will be weeks or months before the dysfunctional speech is corrected. But if you work hard, it will happen."

"G-guess th-that's w-why I-I'm h-here."

"Just as a concert pianist didn't start out playing Beethoven's fifth symphony, you won't start out reciting the Gettysburg Address. The key is practice. And just like our concert pianist who probably as a little kid had to practice the scales over and over and over again," she mimed playing the scales on a piano, "you will be practicing certain exercises," she pointed to her throat, "over and over. But before you can practice, you need to learn the basics."

"Wh-hat are th-the b-basics?"

"Well, let's stick with our piano analogy. Before a little kid learns the scales, what does he or she learn?"

Faith thought a moment, "Th-the n-n-notes?"

"Yes, to play the piano, you need to learn the notes before you can play the scales and then progress from there. So we will begin at the very beginning and, like our piano player, progress from there. Are you ready to begin?"

Faith nodded. "I-I'll t-try."

"Good. Now, the exercises I will show you today, you will need to practice when you get home. Even when you get tired or frustrated, you will need to set aside a block of time each day, even twice a day, and do the work. And keep doing the work every day even if it doesn't seem like you are making progress. You need to continue with the practice. What we are beginning here today is a process, and what you need to do, above all things, is to trust the process. In fact, I want that phrase to become your mantra. When you get frustrated, stop what you are doing for a moment and repeat in your head: trust the process, trust the process, trust the process. Then go back to what you were doing and practice some more. And before you know it, you will be making progress."

"O-o-okay."

"In a few minutes, we are going to work on repeating a list of words, but first, let's talk about your sensory overload. Anything can trigger it—repetitive sounds like a barking dog or a jack hammer. As far as eyes, flickering lights like a florescent light sometimes triggers overload. Even certain colors. So I want you to start keeping your sunglasses and a set of those little foam earplugs with you at all times. If you are outside and the traffic sounds suddenly start stressing you, put in the earplugs. If bright sunlight is suddenly causing the sensory overload, put on your sunglasses." Cheryl looked over toward Meghan and saw that she was listening to this. "Will you pass that message on to her family?"

"Absolutely."

"Also, let them know that sometimes, unnecessary clutter can trigger these sensory overload symptoms, so have them clear off countertops in the bathroom and the kitchen. Neat, tidy, sparse surroundings really help counteracting or even preventing these episodes."

"Got it." Meghan took out a little notebook and wrote a note to herself to share all this with Clark.

Cheryl turned her focus back to Faith. "It may take weeks or even months to pinpoint the triggers, but when you do notice what is suddenly stressing you, try to take note of it. Write it down in a log. In fact, maybe start carrying a little notebook with you to write observations down in."

Faith nodded. "Y-yes. D-Dr. W-W-Well-b-brock t-told m-me t-to k-keep a log."

"Have you been doing that?"

"Y-yes."

"Next time you come here, bring your log with you and we'll look at it together and discuss it."

"O-okay.

"Good." Cheryl reached into a drawer on her side of the table and extracted a stack of photographs on sturdy card stock. "Let's get started on some evaluative exercises. I'm going to show you some pictures one at a time and you tell me what you see." She held up the first card. It was a picture of a Boy Scout troop saluting the flag.

"Th-they are s-s-saluting th-the f-f-flag."

"And why are they doing that?"

Faith had to think about that for a moment. "B-be-cause th-th-they are p-patriotic."

Putting that card face down, she showed Faith the next one. "What do you see here?"

Faith smiled. "It-it is a-m-m-mother f-feeding her b-baby."

"How is she feeding her?"

Faith wasn't able to pull the word she wanted out of her head, so she held an imaginary baby to her breast. "L-like th-this."

"Correct, she's nursing the baby."

"Y-yes. N-n-nursing."

"I noticed you were having a hard time trying to find that word. This is not uncommon. You did a good job of showing me what you couldn't say. Try not to get too frustrated when you can't find a word for something. It will happen. It will be like the word is on the tip of your tongue, but you can't get it out. In time, this will improve."

"I-I h-hope s-so. B-but a lot of t-the t-time, I know the w-word I w-want to s-say. B-but I c-can't g-get it out."

"When that happens, close your eyes. Picture the word in your brain. Look at it with your mind's eye, then try to say the word."

"O-okay, I'll t-try."

"What about this picture?" Cheryl held up another one.

Faith blinked like she wasn't sure what she was seeing at first. Then she looked shocked and tears filmed her eyes. "It-it's a-a l-little g-girl."

"What about her?"

"S-she's a-afraid and r-running."

"What is she running from?"

"I-I th-think w-war?"

"That's right. Have you ever seen this picture before, Faith?"

Shaking her head, she said, "I-I d-don't know."

"It's a very famous photograph taken during the Vietnam War. I think it won a Pulitzer Prize."

"O-oh. It-s-sort of s-seems f-familiar, I th-think."

"You are doing great. A few more of these, then we are going to start doing the word exercises that I'll want you to be doing for homework as well."

***

ON THE WAY HOME, MEGHAN looked over at Faith. "You look pretty optimistic."

Faith nodded. "I th-think th-this is g-g-going t-to h-help. If I j-just w-work h-hard, I'll g-get b-better. A-and t-the h-harder I w-work, t-the s-s-sooner it w-will h-happen."

Having been married to a psychologist who worked with patients dealing with all levels of life's crud, Meghan realized that

Faith was in a bargaining stage. If I do this and work really hard at it the bad stuff will go away. The reality was it probably wouldn't. It was just a vain hope that the bad stuff that the person had been dealing with was reversible. Brian often preached to her that pointing his patients toward the inevitable, even if it catapulted them into depression wasn't a bad thing because they needed to move through a depression stage on the road to recovery, anyway. But Meghan wasn't Brian. She wasn't about to burst Faith's bubble and tell her that while all the hard work would clearly be helpful to some degree, it wouldn't make her turn into her old self again overnight. Instead, she just made agreeable mouth noises and kept driving.

***

Meghan filled Clark in when he got home from the site. "It was actually quite the interesting experience. At one point, she showed Faith some pictures and had her explain what she saw. What I surmised was happening was that the therapist was reading Hope's reactions as well as seeing if she knew what the actual picture was because each picture was more than just a picture, it was also a concept, such as patriotism or nurturing or war. I think she was testing to see if Faith got those concepts. It was really fascinating to be a fly on the wall observing the process. As far as the word exercises, as often as she is supposed to practice each day, I think you are going to get sick of hearing the word 'ball, ball, ball, ball, ball' repeated about a zillion times in a row."

"Maybe it is a good thing I'll be starting that project in the desert in a few days."

"Hardy har-har. Oh yeah, Faith told her about the laptop you got for her. So just as we were leaving, the pathologist gave Faith some additional homework. She told Faith that playing computer games can help with concentration. So maybe when she's up and you have some time, you can show her the ropes for a couple of computer games so she can work on that exercise when you're not around."

"Okay, will do."

"And," Meghan flipped open the little notebook she'd written her reminder in, "you need to clear clutter off the kitchen and bathroom counters."

"Because?"

"Too much clutter can contribute to sensory overload."

"Sounds like a chore for Emmy."

Meghan just shook her head. "You men are all alike. Anyway, she also said sunglasses and earplugs help diffuse sensory overload, so get her some of those little foam earplugs to put in when noises get to be too much for her."

"I've got lots of those. We use them on the worksite all the time." He turned to go then turned back to Meghan. "By the way, thanks again for taking her today."

"You know it really isn't that far away. Once she gets into that walking habit that Emily is pushing, she may very well be able to get herself to the therapist and back."

Clark was shaking his head. "I don't know about that."

"I don't mean now, or even this week, but she's going to be in therapy for a long time. Like months. So let's be optimistic here. Surely, if Emily walks her there and back some of the time, it will sink in."

"Maybe, but I expect the therapy will wear her out so much that she wouldn't have the energy to walk home afterwards."

"Yeah, I hadn't thought of that. Oh, by the way, the therapist suggested you get her playing some children's card games too like Go Fish or Old Maid."

"You're kidding? Why?"

"I guess it's something that helps the cognitive process do something. I don't know. She just said to do it."

"Oh yeah, I can hardly wait. And on that happy note," he, once again, turned toward his house giving her a little wave, "I've got a beer calling my name and I need to go get it."

CHAPTER 12

SHARPENED PENCIL IN HAND, FAITH flipped open her log and then just stared at what she saw. "Wh-what?" She shook her head and looked hard at the page, trying to understand what she was seeing. She must have done that. No one else would have. But she had no recollection of doing it. The words "I HATE HER! I HATE HER!" were written over and over and over again on the page. At first written neatly and then more sloppy and the words got larger and sloppier as the writing continued. When she turned the page, the phrase had changed to "I HATE YOU I HATE YOU I HATE YOU" and the pencil had dug into the page so deeply the paper was torn in one long deep gash. She flipped a couple of pages. Yes, the words on the previous page had penetrated through the next few pages as she had been pressing down so hard with the pencil. *"Oh, Lord, please help me,"* she said to herself in her head.

Standing up, she walked away from the log for a moment then came back to it and stood over the log lying on the coffee table. She just stared at the notebook still trying to remember writing all that. She couldn't. She was drawing a big, fat blank. Sitting back down, she flipped open the log again with the intention of ripping out the pages and tearing them up into little pieces and throwing them away. But something stopped her. She looked at the pages again, placed the palm of her hand flat down on the words. No, she wouldn't tear them out and throw them away. She needed to keep this as a reminder of her anger, of the place where she'd been emotionally that made her write those words. She needed to be reminded, because only then could she try to do something about all this, to try and move from that out-of-control angry emotional place to a new calmer and more rational emotional place.

Faith scanned a couple of entries. One simply read:

> I look forward to the day when I wake up and talk & think freely.

She sighed, picked up her pencil again, and began writing.

> Every day is a battle. It's a struggle to wake up and get up. It's a struggle to talk. It's a struggle to think. And sometimes I just want to give up. But then I'll hear Emily humming a little tune and my heart feels lighter and I know I can get through one more day.

***

Faith answered her phone after first looking at the readout. "H-Hope. Hi."

"Hi, yourself. Thought I'd check if it's a good time to come over for a visit."

"Y-yes. P-please d-do."

"Okay, I'm about ten minutes away. See you soon."

Faith was pouring two glass of sun tea when Hope knocked on the door, sending Lola into paroxysms of barking. Hope entered the house greeting Lola in the usual way, "Shut up, Lola. Where's your mommy?"

Faith sang out, "I-I'm in th-the k-kitchen."

"Is that sun tea?" She gave her sister a hug and a kiss on the cheek. "I think you're the only person left alive that still makes sun tea."

"G-guess I-I haven't for-forgotten how t-to d-do th-that."

"How about we have the sun tea on the patio?" Hope picked up both glasses and headed outside. "It's not too hot today and there is a breeze."

The sisters sat on the patio being refreshed by the tea, the breeze, and just being together. A bird trilled in a nearby tree, making both sisters smile.

"So yesterday was the first day with the speech therapist. No miracles yet?"

"S-she g-gave m-me ex-exercises."

"Ah! The dreaded homework. Have you done your homework for today?"

"Th-this m-m-morning. C-can't t-tell, r-right?

"Hey, it's only day one. If on day twenty I can't tell a difference, I'll let you know."

"D-d-deal."

"Emmy tells me you guys are getting up and walking in the morning."

"Y-yes. S-she k-keeps m-me on a s-schedule. W-we will w-walk on th-the d-days I d-don't have sp-speech th-therapy. S-so w-we went t-today."

"Good for you guys. You must remember that I am a firm proponent of walking. I've been doing my three miles every morning before breakfast for years."

"R-really?"

"Diet and exercise, the two most important things to keep you healthy. But I won't get going on all that." Hope looked around the backyard. "I love it out here. You worked so hard getting it to look like this."

"I k-know, b-but I-I h-hardly h-have en-energy t-to d-do any w-weeding anymore."

"Then why don't I help with that."

So for the next few minutes, the sisters knelt, side by side, pulling weeds from the garden bed next to the garage."

Hope sat back on her heels and looked at what they accomplished then pulled a few more weeds. "Do you remember that Emmy used to have a tortoise?"

Faith thought deeply for a moment. "N-no."

"At one point in school, she did a report on tortoises. You and Clark had gone somewhere so she was staying with me at the time, so

I was helping her with her research. We discovered that the markings on some turtles are thirteen which is the same number of moons in the lunar calendar each year, and that is one explanation why turtles symbolize the feminine. You know, moon, lunar, female. So we counted up the little squares on her tortoise, but it was like sixteen or eighteen, or something like that. She was disappointed it wasn't what the article on the website she was researching had said, 'but, oh well.' Anyway, back to Emmy's pet. You used to let the tortoise roam around out here when you worked in the garden. And one day it was gone. Just wandered off. You guys looked everywhere. It moved slowly, but I guess it also moved with determination and focus. Like I said, it was just gone." Both women paused from their weeding and looked around the yard, perhaps hoping to spy the little bugger even though it had been years. "I bet it's still out there somewhere."

"I-if it w-wasn't r-run over b-b-by a c-car."

"True. But there was never any evidence of that after it took off. At least around here. They are very long-lived animals, you know. In fact, in some cultures, they represent immortality. At least that's what I remember from the report Emmy wrote for her class."

"I-I r-really d-don't re-member a-any t-t-tortoise."

"No matter."

"B-but w-wait." Faith looked excited and she was making a circling gesture with one finger. "W-wasn't th-there a s-silly p-poem a-about a t-turtle?"

"Yes." Hope laughed. "Mom paid us allowance if we memorized a poem a week and one summer she was all about Ogden Nash poems. Let me think, 'A turtle lives twixt plated decks / Which something-something conceal its sex. / I think it clever of the turtle—something like that / In such a fix to be so...'"

"F-fer-fertile!"

Hope clapped her hands. "Yes! You remembered."

"W-we were wh-what? In j-j-junior h-high s-school?"

"Actually about fourth or fifth grade. We cracked up about the sex part and the fertile part. That silliness must have stuck in your brain."

"S-so w-we m-memorized p-poems? T-tell m-me another one."

Hope cast her mind back, thinking. Then her smile crinkled the corners of her eyes. "Here's a favorite: 'The Moon's the North Wind's cooky / He bites it day by day / Until there's but a rim of scraps / That crumble all away. / The South Wind is a baker. / He kneads clouds in his den, / And bakes a crisp new moon that…greedy / North…Wind…eats…again!' Do you remember that one?"

Faith shook her head, "N-not r-really. Is th-that O-Ogden N-Nash t-too?"

"No, I don't remember the poet." Hope brushed that away. "But that you remembered the turtle poem. I call that a victory. And," she sat back on her heels, shaking two fingers for emphasis, "I just remembered Emily's tortoise's name: Ogden Nash. Ha! You had a tortoise not a turtle, but the name was inspired, don't you think?"

Faith shook her head. "I s-still d-don't re-re-remember the t-tortoise."

Hope looked closely at her sister and saw she was flagging. "How you doing? Shall we call it a day as far as the weeding?"

"Y-yes, l-let's s-sit and h-have our t-tea and y-you c-can t-tell m-me…tell m-me-"

It looked like Faith was having a hard time filling in the blank, so Hope guessed, "Tell you about The Gold Dust Twins?"

"Y-yes."

"Okay." They settled down at the patio table after refreshing their glasses of tea. "When I was born," Hope began, "I was a tiny, skinny little baby. Then, eighteen months later, when I was still as skinny as you can imagine, you were born. A nice, healthy, robust baby."

Faith laughed. "N-nice way of s-saying I-I had b-ba-baby fat."

Hope laughed too. "Well, not fat so much as chubby. So time goes by, and by the time you were eighteen months and I was three years old, we were the very same size. Or I guess height is a better term than size. I was little for my age, you see, and you were big for yours, so we were the same height. That's when Daddy dubbed us The Gold Dust Twins. Cause we looked like twins. Eventually, no one could tell that I was older and you were younger. I was the brunette and you were blonde, but other than that…twins. In fact, wherever we went, people who didn't know us thought we actually were twins. Not only did we wear the same size clothes, Mom often even dressed us alike, just like twins. So that's the story of The Gold Dust Twins. That went on until, well, I guess, until junior high school when you shot up taller than me."

Faith nodded and sat up straighter. "I-I-I do re-remember being t-ta-taller than an-anyone."

"Yeah you were a tall one. And when you shot up so tall, your baby fat disappeared so you were as skinny as I was, just way taller. You were so tall and skinny they used to call you the frozen string bean."

Faith looked shocked. "W-who did?"

"Oh! Sorry, honey," Hope rubbed her sister's arm. "The kids at school. You didn't remember that, but the residual emotions from that time in your life are probably why even now you remember being taller than the other kids."

"Fa-fa-frozen st-string bean. H-how m-mean!"

"Yeah, they were mean. Junior high kids can be the worst. But it didn't last long. You were the ugly duckling that turned into the pro-verbial swan—and by your expression, I can see that's another story I'll have to tell you, so what I just said will make sense—but, as I was saying, soon, you were the most popular cheerleader in school. No lie! And with those long legs that could kick so high, well, by high school, there wasn't a football player on the team who wasn't besotted with you. That's for sure."

Faith had gotten lost in a lot of what Hope had said, but she did catch the cheerleader part. "I-I was a-a ch-cheerleader?"

"Yep. You and Sharon."

"Sh-Sharon?"

"Your best friend in high school." Noticing her sister's blank expression, she added, "Surely you remember Sharon?" Faith just shook her head. Hope sat back and took a long sip of tea. "Well! I guess I can say I feel kind of vindicated then, after all these years."

"Wh-why? Y-you didn't l-like th-this Sh-Sharon?"

Hope groaned. "Oh, honey, to explain the whole story would kind of be too much for you right now. You'd need a lot of back story to understand the Sharon stuff."

"I-I'm n-not g-go-ing any-wh-where." Faith had already learned she had a hard time keeping up with Hope's tempo of talking. Sometimes, the give and take of conversation just hovered around her like smoke. Maybe this was what they called sensory overload. But she like the cadence of her sister's voice and promised herself that she'd really pay attention and do her best to understand what Hope was saying.

Hope debated the wisdom of relating this bit of history then shrugged. "Okay, here goes. Suffice to say, I'll just hit some high-lights. We can flesh it out later if you want to." Hope fortified herself with some more tea then began. "After Charity got pregnant at six-teen and Mom married her off to that boy, well, poor Mom was so distraught over that disaster that she kind of emotionally abandoned us. She'd come home from work and go into her bedroom and we never saw her until morning when she was getting ready to go to work again. You and I were literally left alone to pretty much raise each other. Oh, Mom was around, but in body, not in spirit. And she left us to fend for ourselves."

"Th-that's t-terrible." Faith looked shocked. "Th-thank g-good-ness E-Emily is an a-adult, or th-that's wh-what I'd be d-d-doing to her n-now."

"Not exactly the same thing, Faith, not the same thing at all. But it was terrible for us. No mom, no big sister, nobody. Daddy was working, and, as I said, we were left to fend for ourselves. Mom didn't even buy us our first bras. I was a year ahead of you and so embarrassed in junior high school when it was P.E. time and I was the only one in the class with no bra. So, just mortified, I went to J. C. Penney's and bought my own first bra, size 28AA. All by myself. I'll never forget the feelings that were inside me, almost shame. Shame that I had a mother who didn't care enough to do this. Anyway, a year later, when you were going into the junior high school, I knew you'd need a bra too. So I took you shopping so you wouldn't end up feeling that same shame of having to do that all by yourself."

"Y-you b-bought m-me my f-first b-bra? H-how s-sweet y-you w-were t-t-to m-me."

"See, it was you and me against the world. Just the two of us. But then something happened. With Mom's emotional abandonment of us, I kind of turned inward and became so very shy and timid. You did just the opposite. You turned outward and became very gregarious. Sharon lived down the street from us, and she was a loud, out-there, gregarious type person too and you guys just bonded. By high school, you two were inseparable. You were both cheerleaders, etc. So I got left in the dust. Suddenly, we were no longer just the two of us against the world. You had Sharon and I was left out in the cold."

Faith had tears running down her cheeks. "Oh-oh, H-Hope. I-I'm s-so sorry!"

Hope patted Faith's hand that rested on the patio table. "Water under the bridge and over the dam."

"B-but if sh-she is s-such a good f-fr-friend, wh-where is she n-now?

"Ha! I'm getting to that part. You guys did everything together. Started dating at the same time and double dated with your boy-friends. You swore to each other when you got married you'd be each other's maids of honor—all that jazz. So Sharon gets engaged right out of high school. And you two are thick as thieves planning this perfect wedding. Then, about two weeks before the big day, Sharon tells you that she doesn't want you to attend her wedding. Her excuse: she didn't want anybody prettier than her in the wedding party. So she tossed her best friend out because you were prettier than she was. And the fact is you were! She was as plain as a post and she knew it and she didn't want to be upstaged by a gorgeous blonde."

Faith was shaking her head. "W-wh-what a h-horrible th-thing t-to do t-to a fr-friend. And I d-don't even re-remember her. I truly d-don't."

"Well, then."

"Sh-she sounds v-very cr-cr-cruel t-to t-treat a-a fr-friend like th-that."

"Just insecure, I guess, but it was a nasty thing to do to someone you'd been joined to the hip to for half a decade."

They sat in silence for a while, sipping their tea. "F-f-funny th-th-that I d-d-don't re-remember her."

"I've got an idea." Hope jumped up and entered the house through the sliding glass door. In a moment, she came out again holding a book. "Your high school yearbook. I noticed last time I was here you kept them on that bookshelf in the family room." She flipped through the book and found a picture of Faith and Sharon in their cheerleading outfits each kicking a leg up in the air in almost a vertical split.

Faith laughed. "C-c-can't d-do th-th-that anymore."

"Here." Hope pointed to a picture of a blonde girl with a winning smile. "Do you remember her?"

Faith looked at the picture for a long time. "O-oh y-yes, th-th-that's S-Susie B!"

"Another good friend of yours. Do you remember why you call her Susie B? Even now after she's married and her last name no longer starts with B?"

Shaking her head, Faith asked, "N-No. W-Why?"

"Because there were three girls named Susie in your class and two of them refused to be called Sue or Susan and both had last names that started with B. So one of them was just Susie and Susie B became Susie B."

"I-I d-do re-remember th-that n-now."

"Do you remember that she moved to Nevada not long after high school? In fact, I just remembered, she was in a car accident too, a few years ago. She barely survived. I remember you telling me that almost every bone in her body was broken."

"H-h-how aw-awful. I don't re-remem-ber th-that."

"You should probably give her a call. I'll bet you two would have a lot to talk about."

They flipped through the book some more. "What about her?" Hope pointed to another picture.

"O-oh! Th-that's B-Bar-bara!"

"She lives up north now. You flew up a few months ago and spent a few days with her. She'd probably like to know what's going on with you too."

"O-oh y-yes. O-oh, th-thank y-you s-s-so m-much for th-this." She patted the yearbook.

"How you doing here, sis? Is it time for me to head on out or are you up for some more tea and talk?"

"D-don't g-go."

"Then, tea it is." Hope picked up the empty glasses and headed into the kitchen to refill them.

When Hope returned, she could see that Faith was deep in thought. She tuned in to her sister and could almost hear wheels turning inside Faith's head. "What?"

Faith held a finger up while she thought about something, then she finally voiced her thoughts. "T-twins? N-not t-tr-triplets?"

"Oh, oh." Hope cleared her throat. "No, Charity was several years older than you and me. She'd never be a triplet to us. Do you really want to go there?"

"C-Clark ex-explained that Ch-Charity isn't sp-sp-speaking to us. Wh-why?"

"Oh, honey, it's such a long, sad story. Let's save all that angst for another day, okay? Suffice to say Sister Dearest is the one who severed the ties and it's for the best."

"S-s-sister d-dearest?"

"Yeah, that's what we call her. You know, from *Mommie Dearest*. Oh, I can see that doesn't ring a bell either. Well, better to talk about Joan Crawford than Charity at this juncture."

"J-Joan w-who?"

"Joan Crawford was a famous movie star in the thirties and forties, decades before we were born. She had adopted some kids and when one of them grew up, she wrote a book called *Mommie Dearest*. It was a tell-all book about the worst mother in the history of the world. Well that's an exaggeration, but you get the idea. They even made a movie of the book staring Faye Dunaway. Anyway, long story short, our sister became Sister Dearest to us. God! I just thought of something. There was this scene in *Mommie Dearest* with the mother going ballistic on the daughter for hanging her clothes on wire clothes hangers. Anyway, you were always such a great mimic. You would do that scene, walking down your staircase shaking a wire

115

coat hanger and screaming just like in the movie. Now, we are going to have to rent that movie and watch it again. Just for fun."

Faith started shaking both hands at Hope as if to say, enough. "S-stop. I-I don't re-remember any of th-that. B-but n-no m-movie."

"You don't want to see the movie?"

"It's n-not th-that I don't *w-want* to. I j-just ca-can't."

"Oh, I get it. I'm sorry. It's the concentration it takes to watch a movie. It's too much?"

Faith nodded. "I d-don't even w-watch TV n-now."

"Well, that will change once these doctors and therapists get on the ball." Faith didn't look convinced, but she did suddenly look beyond tired. "And on that note," Hope, gulped down her glass of tea and stood up, "I've got to get going so you can get some rest or Emily will read me the riot act. She warned me to keep our visits short so I don't wear you out. And it looks like you just hit the wall."

"O-o-kay." Faith tried not to look relieved, but she suddenly so desperately wanted to crawl into bed and sleep.

Picking up the tea glasses, Hope brought them into the kitchen, rinsed them, and put them in the dishwasher. Then she hugged her sister and skedaddled so Faith could rest.

Faith sagged against the door in relief. She loved having Hope drop by, but she was glad it didn't happen every day. The last time, it had taken her forever to bounce back from the visit. Today, her brain just ached trying to keep up with everything. Her bedroom seemed too far away; she made it as far as the family room couch, laid down and fell instantly to sleep.

Faith woke up to the sound of a barking dog. She guessed the mail had arrived and Lola was just greeting the mailman through the door as was her usual habit. Instead of going out to bring the mail in, Faith picked up her log and flipped it open. She continued to be amazed that writing was so much easier than talking. She wondered why and realized she should have asked Cheryl about that yesterday. Then she had a thought. As Cheryl had asked her to bring her log to therapy, she should write her a note in there so she would see it tomorrow. That way if she forgot to ask her the question, she'd see it written down. Faith wrote:

LOST

Hi Cheryl, In case I forget to ask you during our session, I just want to know why it is so much easier for me to write than to speak. That's all.

Thanks, Faith.

DESPAIR

Life begins on the other side of despair.
—Jean-Paul Sartre

CHAPTER 13

Log Entries

July 7

Therapy. Therapy. Therapy. Fri will be my 5th session. I need to be ready. Homework time.

July 11

Universe! I am tired of crying!

July 14

Things that have changed: I am more ma… thought…a…cul (don't have dictionary). I am not open to change. I no longer trust.

July 19

Issues:
Triggers – travel in all forms
Money- we are broke
Noise – certain sounds hurt
Not understanding how something works – can opener
Feeling like slow special ed student

Speech – not being able to get words out
Forgetting what I wanted to say

July 22

Tired of fighting for words – thoughts.
Speech improvement if calm. Hate feelings of lost,
fear. I wonder how I'd feel if all of a sudden it's
gone? NO, not gone, but, you have to claw it out!
Tired
Need a mini me to do my old job. As I can't.
THAT'S WHAT TICKS ME OFF!

Aug 1

My life has no purpose. I know, I know,
patience. You'll hele heal, oh drat, I can't even
spell anymore. May the people that caused this
learn their patience! I'm so tired of all this!

Aug 4

I feel trapped! I want out! I need to heal!
Old self lost. Victim of destruction. Surviving
PTSD means re-invent self. Like Phoenix rising.
Learning new info is <u>very</u> difficult. And now she
wants me to do math! Ah! I hate math.
Timelines don't exist. There is no parallel –
it just goes on.
No past
No future
Just now
Everything
Every emotion
Just now –
Write

Tell your feelings

You live a different parallel then the rest of the world. A side step. You are not in sink with the universe.

But you're not out of step

You observe – from a distance

You are removed yet you feel you hear (too much)

Aug 9

This morning I am calm as I have no events that demand I be there. I am able to putter at home.

One of the triggers I have focused on surprises me – being alone...

Aug 12

Worst day of life – and you keep reliving it.

Let go of day

Let go of day

Let go of day

It's over – it's gone – past – finished

Free to redefine new life

Now is scary – unknown – frustration - fear

Aug 17

Had therapy today. Clark must have had day off? As he drove me. I feel frazzled – tearful. I am tired of this ride. I want OFF. I look tired and pale pail? Bags – unhealthy. Headaches. I live on advil & am tired of being told Patience------------

You, yes, I'm talking to you! YOU live this one nightmere mare day & night. The kaleidoscope of sites, sounds, smells and YOU find YOUR patience, then YOU have the right to tell me "patience." Until then,…this is living hell! Childbirth is easier.

But still I get homework. Told to get out of comfort zone. Think about doing something completely new to you. Get a few instructions – and go do it. Remember that feeling, the pit of your stomach, the confussion, then step out, now do that daily, day after day after day. Hey, guess what? It wears you down!!!

Aug 20

PTSD I realize it's all consuming – it goes from brain to body take over – it's horrible. So, Cheryl, here is my question: Does PTSD ever go away, or is it once you've got it, you've got it forever, and you just have to learn to live with it? Here I am afraid of your answer. I think it is here to stay – like a cold sore – always in your nervous system waiting for too much sun, wind, rundown etc. And once I learned to feel the triggers for the cold sore, they wouldn't be so big or last so long. So is this the same? As I slightly tear up. Damn the woman who altered my life! That's how I feel this a.m.

It is easy to pretend nothing happened & all is ok. Cause to look at me you can't tell. I walk into therapy and I see so many broken bodies and they look back at me – you can't tell that I am as broken as can be. Everyone says: "You're so lucky – you're fine." Little do they know. I wonder if I will ever be Faith again. It's like having your bff taken away.

I don't want to accept I have been broken – I'm crying – I want to be me again. I don't want my brain broken. I want my life back.

Aug 22

Did good 2day – didn't work on the list or the math Cheryl gave me – but did errands around town. Went out 2 get items for house instead of doing homework. Had 2 fight some feelings of justifying in staying home vs. getting what we needed. Didn't plan any dinner. Oh well, baby steps.

Aug 24

Struggle to recover from less visible emotional scars – because no one can see my scar – a mark – you are preceeved (?) as ok. It wears you down. I get so tired of…saying, I'm ok.

Today I am going to go slowly, breathe, and follow my daily list. And may be I won't "feel" the tingly anxiety coursing thru my body.

Slow – oh, wait! Like the special ed student I have become.

Aug 25

Over Exhaustion
Over Tired
Can't Sleep
Get Mean
Watched a neighbor's baby for an hour
Took 2 days to recoup.
Was too long, too much.

CHAPTER 14

EMILY GENTLY SHOOK FAITH'S SHOULDER, "Wake up, Mom. Come on, time to wake up and get out of bed. Chop-chop. Rise and shine."

Faith forced her eyes open. "Wh-wh-what time?"

"What time is it? It's time to make the donuts." At Faith's blank look she said, "Just…never mind. It's ten o'clock. Time for our walk." She gave her mom a friendly little swat on the butt. "There, that's for all the times you did that to me trying to get me up for school. Come on, get a move on."

"M-m-man you a-are ch-ch-chipper in th-the mor-mornings."

"Slow down, Mom, stretch the words out."

"Is-is-is thhaaat c-cooofffee I ssmmeeell?"

Emily pointed to the nightstand. "Ready and waiting for you. Drink up. We're going to put on some miles today."

They had gotten into the habit of going to the grocery store during their morning walks. They'd pick up what items they'd need for lunch and dinner and then walk home. Usually, they'd walk straight to the store and back. But other times, Emily would lead them toward the park that was a few blocks in the other direction or up to Magnolia Boulevard to do some window shopping. Then they'd head toward the grocery store. At those times, Emily would say, "Okay, let's get the marketing done." She would then walk next to her mother, but not turn first at any of the appropriate corners. She'd hang back and make sure Faith made the correct turns. Soon, she felt confident that her mom was learning her way around the neighborhood again, so if she ever was out on her own, Emily wouldn't have to worry that she couldn't find her way back home.

It was during one of their walks that Emily discovered an interesting phenomenon. Faith had laughed at a dog riding in a car with his head sticking out of the sunroof. The dog was literally grinning as the wind blew his ears back from his head. "What's so funny?" Emily had asked.

"Th-th-there, on th-the-left," Faith pointed.

Emily saw the dog and chuckled along with her mom. It wasn't until a couple of blocks later that the phenomenon dawned on her. She decided to test her hypothesis. "Mom, look to the right, see that squirrel running up the trunk of that tree?"

Faith turned her head, saw the squirrel, and nodded.

"Okay, this is weird," Emily said.

"Wh-what's w-w-weird?"

"You don't know your left from your right. You never have. And yet today, twice, you didn't mix them up. You told me a dog was on your left and it was, and when I told you to look to the right you immediately did. You didn't do that L thing with your thumb and forefinger that you usually do to remind you which is left and which is right. That clonk on your head might have mixed you up about a lot of things, but it looks like it straightened out your left and right."

When they got to the store that day, Emily kept up the little test. As they walked down the aisle looking for produce, she asked, "See the tomatoes, Mom? Are the on the left or right?

"R-right."

"And the cucumbers?"

"R-right."

"Yes, again! And the potatoes?"

"L-l-left."

"Bingo! This is so great."

Faith smiled at her daughter's excitement. She didn't feel as if anything momentous had happened; she still felt confused, angry, tired, and drained most all the time. But if playing the left and right game made Emmy happy, she'd surely comply.

On another occasion, Emily had to step between her mother and another woman to prevent what for all intents and purposes might have devolved into a cat fight. They had been walking on the oval walking path not far from their house. It was a path that got a lot of foot traffic. And, as it turned out, the time they took their walks was also the time a woman who practiced singing first scales then an aria walked the walk. They walked in opposite directions around the oval so ended up passing each other a few times during their walk. That first morning they came across her, Faith was just alongside the singing woman when the woman hit a high note that threw Faith straight into sensory overload. She threw her hands up over her ears, stopping dead in her tracks. When the shuddering started, Emily led her mom to a nearby bench and had her sit. "Put your earplugs in, Mom. That will help."

"O-okay, b-but let's g-g-go h-home."

A few days later, they tried that oval path again, and the same woman was there walking along and singing, hitting high note after high note. This happened several days in a row no matter what time they walked.

One day, when they came abreast the woman, Faith held out her hand in the universal stop signal. The woman complied and looked at Faith questioningly. "Yes?"

Haltingly, Faith tried to explain to the woman that she had been injured and she couldn't handle high-pitched sounds, so would the woman please refrain from singing. Well, that went over like a ton of wet cement. The woman, who had taken a step back once Faith started speaking, her body language clearly saying, *keep this crazy person away from me*, immediately got her back up. "I have every right to practice my instrument," she rested one hand with long manicured fingernails on her throat, "while I exercise here. If you don't like it, walk somewhere else."

"Th-this is a p-p-public p-place."

"You got that right!" And the woman opened her mouth, hit a high note, and started walking away."

With both hands, Emily literally grabbed her mother who was in midstride heading after the woman.

"I-I-I-I…" Faith was starting to see red and her face, following suit, was almost scarlet.

"Let it go, Mom. She doesn't care one whit about you, and she did give us good advice. We'll walk elsewhere or come here at a different time. Come on."

"I-I w-want to b-b-bash her."

"We got that, Mom. However, you always told me I have to learn to choose my battles. So right back at you. This is one of those battles we're not going to fight. Come on."

So from that point on, they avoided the walking path and found other places to stroll and get their morning exercise.

Today, Emily decided to walk to the bakery first before they headed to the store. She and her mom both had a sweet tooth and she was in the mood for a chocolate croissant.

They sat at the little table outside the bakery and watched the cars go by while they munched on their croissants. After a few moments of constant pedestrian traffic heading into the bakery and out again, Faith began to fidget.

"Mom, put your sunglasses on. It will help you." Emily had discovered that the sunglasses helped not only with visual sensory overload, but also with activity going on around Faith. She wasn't sure why it worked, she just knew it did.

Sunglasses on, Faith relaxed a little. "I-I wweeent ttooooo thheee baaaaank yes-yesterday."

"Yeah?" Emily knew her dad had worked late on the site yesterday and wouldn't have gotten home before the banks closed. "Who took you to the bank?"

"Nnoooobody. I waaaaalked theere by mys-ssself."

"Mom! Really!" Emily could barely contain her excitement. "Tell me, why did you go to the bank?"

"I ssaaaw on thheee ccaaalender in thheee k-kitchen that thheee hoooouse p-paaaayment was due. Ssoooo I went in and tooooold them t-to taaaake the moooonEy out of ch-checking and paaay it."

Emily pressed her hands together and brought them to her smiling lips. "Mom, I am so proud of you. See, you really are starting to get better."

Faith just looked off into the distance and kind of shook her head. "S-soooometimes it s-seeeems l-like I am geettting beeeeetter, b-but other tiiiiimes, it d-dooooesn't."

"Well, good days and bad days, isn't that what the doctor said to expect. Seems to me like the good outweigh the bad."

"M-My little op-op-oppptiiiimist." She reached out and gently squeezed her daughter's hand.

"Come on, let's finish up our treats and get to the market. Dad wanted us to remember to get some ice cream. So let's not forget that."

After the marketing, they were a block away from the store and heading home when Faith started pawing around in the bag she was carrying.

"What are you looking for, Mom?"

"Cr-craaaaackers. We forgot m-m-mmyyyy craaaackers."

Emily looked in the bag she was carrying although she already knew there were no crackers in there either. "No crackers here, Mom."

"I ate up aalllll m-mmyyy faaaaavorite cr-craaackers l-last night. Daaaarn, I waaaaanted t-to get mooore."

A light bulb went on in Emily's head. If her mom could get to the bank and back all by herself, she could go to the store too. "Look," Emily took the second bag from her mom. "Why don't you go back to the store and get your crackers. I'll just keep walking home and get this ice cream in the freezer before it starts to melt."

Faith looked behind her. She could still see the store a block away. "O-okay."

"But here. You didn't bring your purse so you'll need money to buy the crackers." Emily handed her mom a five. Then she stood there watching as her mom crossed the street with the light and head back to the store.

Whistling as she walked the rest of the way home, Emily was confident it wouldn't be long before Faith completed her little chore and arrived home too. After about fifteen minutes, Emily started getting worried.

When another five minutes elapsed, Emily jumped in her car and zoomed back to the store looking for Faith along the way. She parked and ran across the lot into the store skittering to a stop when she saw a knot of people at the head of one of the aisles looking at something. Then she heard the crying. Pushing through the crowd of people, she saw her mother sitting on the floor surrounded by boxes and boxes of crackers.

"Mommy?" Emily knelt down beside her mother. "It's okay, Mommy. Come on, let's go home."

"I-I…" Faith sniffed and wiped her nose on the back of her hand. "I c-can't re-remember wh-what m-my fav-favorite cr-cracker is." And she continued sobbing as if her heart was broken. "I d-don't re-remember. Is-is it th-this one?" She had picked up a box of graham crackers.

"This one, Mommy." Emily held up a box of the soda crackers that Faith devoured almost daily. "This one is your favorite. Come on, let's get it and go home."

"O-okay." Faith let her daughter help her up. As they walked away from the boxes of crackers scattered all over the floor, Emily's expression caused the knot of gawkers to melt away. She led her mom out of the aisle and to the checkout.

When they got home, Faith went up to bed for a nap. Emily put the crackers away in the cupboard and felt tears sliding down her cheeks as she did so. "Oh, Mom," she whispered to herself. Then shaking her head and swiping the moisture off her cheeks, she finished her chore and started getting ready for work. Tomorrow and the next day were her days off. She was still getting used to having days off midweek; she would have preferred to have her weekends free. But she really liked her job and the paychecks were fabulous. If it wasn't for her mom, life would be pretty much perfect.

***

When Faith awoke from her nap, she decided to write about the cracker incident in her log. After she finished that entry, she looked back at some recent entries. That was a habit she'd gotten into. She liked to see where she'd been hoping it would give a clue as to the direction she should be heading. One entry read:

Discovered that when I have a busy day (hold attention for a long time) I get cranky – impatient and don't sleep well that night. When I putter – body/brain calm & I can think. Hate crowds – tooooo much energy. And yet, I saw a commercial on TV for Knotts. Wonder when I will be ready for that. I love enjoyment parks. But know I can't handle crowds. This a.m. very tired.

Another entry made her smile at life's crazy twists and turns.

New challenge: singing lady. NO matter what time I do my walk, she's there 7:30 or 9:00 or 10:30. I just can't keep my stride. She hits a certain note & my anger trigger is immediate. I wear ear plugs but her high note goes thru. So since I keep running into her, she is either stalking (jk) me or the universal big picture is testing me to see if I can learn yet another lesson. I hope she is not there today, tho – Yea! She wasn't!

And as she and Emily had altered where they walked, that *challenge* had become a nonissue. Ah, challenges. Faith knew without a doubt there would be more. That's just the way it was.

CHAPTER 15

THE NEXT DAY, EMILY TOOK Faith to her therapy appointment and brought her home. Then, as it was her day off, she and a girlfriend took off to do some shopping. She didn't get home until after suppertime. But that was no biggie as her parents were accustomed to having dinner without her there. She was going to be switching hours at work once her dad started the job in the desert, which was imminent. She'd gotten Hope on board to do the therapy run in the mornings and she'd be home to be in charge of dinner. She was trying to be optimistic that all would be well. Her plan was to switch the walking routine to the evenings after supper. Getting out of the car, she saw her dad in the driveway putting a bag of trash in the barrel.

"Hey, Dad, s'up?"

"You wouldn't believe it!" And he began to fill her in.

Faith stood at the kitchen sink loading the dishwasher and looking out the window. Emily and Clark were standing in the driveway with their heads together deep in intense conversation. Faith didn't have to be clairvoyant to know she was the topic of that conversation. Good grief, what had she done now? She could see Clark gesturing and pointing north. What was north? Her shop. It had been a while since she'd been in the shop. She sure hoped her employees were, wait, no, she no longer had the shop. She brought her damp fingers to her eyes and gently pressed on them for a moment. That's right, she no longer had the shop, but she couldn't remember why. What had happened that she no longer had the shop? All she knew was that she had really loved her shop and now she no longer had it. That seemed so wrong! She'd go out and ask Clark why, but not yet. He was still talking up a storm and Emily was nodding. She'd let them have their powwow. Then she'd ask. Ask? What was she going to ask? Oh, she was so tired. Faith dried her hands and decided it was time for bed.

Faith stood in the bathroom and stared at herself in the mirror. Then she closed her eyes and looked inward, sighing from the depths of her soul. She was just so tired of everything. She was tired of being tired. She felt tears leaking out of her closed eyes. *Lord,* she said in her head, *I just want this to be over. It's too much. It's too hard. I just want to go to sleep and not wake up.* And more tears fell. Wiping off her cheeks with the palms of her hands, she walked into the bedroom and stood there looking at her bed. Usually, seeing Crestline curled up on one of the pillows waiting for her made her smile, today it just made her want to cry harder. She sat on the edge of the bed and scooped her kitty into her arms. If she had been her old self and in so much despair, she would have whispered into her kitty's fur, "I just want it to be over." But these days, she didn't talk unless she had to so she said the words in her head. And what she said in her head was true. She did just want it all to be over. Despair, she had come to realize was darker than anyone could ever imagine.

***

"So did you get everything straightened out at the bank?" Emily asked her father.

"Yes. Thank God, the teller was on the ball. It had suddenly dawned on her that this was the third day in a row your mother had been in making the house payment. Sheesh! Three house payments in a row. We barely had enough in the account to cover two let alone three. What was she thinking?"

"That's just it, Dad, she isn't thinking clearly. That's all. She's working on her own internal logic. She knew the house payment had to be made and she made it."

"Yeah, over and over again." He blew out some breath. "Anyway, I got everything straightened out at the bank, as I said. The teller didn't put the third payment through. That's when she called me.

134

And they now know to call me first before doing anything if she goes in there again."

Brian had wandered over and gotten the tail end of their conversation. "I had a patient once who'd had a head injury. He started giving money away. Just indiscriminately writing checks to people. His wife was beside herself doing everything in her power trying to keep him from giving away their house and everything in it."

"Gee, that makes me feel better, Brian."

"It never hurts to know these things."

"I guess you're right." His tongue wasn't completely in his cheek when he added, "When I go in, I'll lock up the checkbooks."

"Say?" Emily wanted to know, "Did you guys finally get that mix-up with the house closing dealt with?"

"Yeah. It put us a couple of weeks behind with the move, but all systems are go now."

"Well, we're going to miss you guys." She gave him a friendly punch on the arm. With that, Emily excused herself and headed into the house, leaving the two men alone to talk about manly things.

"So other than the usual, how's life treating you."

"It could be treating me a whole lot better." Clark crossed his arms and leaned back against the concrete wall. "The bills are starting to roll in. Ambulance, emergency room stuff, it's not pretty."

"Isn't insurance covering all that?"

"Yeah, right."

"I thought you guys had a really great insurance with your business."

"Oh, Brian, the nineties are long over. Haven't you been aware of the economic turndown when Bush screwed everything up? And on top of that, a few years back, the great state of California pretty much screwed all small businesses. We had to completely restructure the business in order to get out from under the requirements by the state to insure all the employees. We had to incorporate and the employees had to actually become part owners so the business didn't have to pay the outrageously backbreaking premiums for insurance for them. Sheesh, I lost half my crew back then, the good ones, because they knew the ship was starting to sink. And the one's that stuck it out? Ha! We barely broke even most months and didn't even do that some of the time. That's why I've had such a tremendous turnover of employees. Can't keep the good ones when you have nothing to offer them. So, no, we haven't had any insurance for a long, long time."

"Sorry, buddy. I had no idea. But what about Obamacare? No help there?"

"Oh, we've looked into it, but it's not all it's cracked up to be. You heard about the Rasmussens down the street? They got a policy for their daughter under Obamacare as she was no longer eligible to be on their policy. Well, she passed out at work, an ambulance was called and she was taken to the hospital for tests. The upshot was she hadn't bothered to eat breakfast. That's all it was, and the bills for the ambulance and the hospital and the tests weren't even covered under the policy they had. So there they are making a monthly payment for insurance and they still get all the other bills on top of that. Not good! Good grief. In the old days, if a female fainted, she'd be laid out on the couch until she came to. End of story. Now it costs *someone* thousands of dollars to deal with some dolt who passes out because she's not smart enough to eat right. So, no, we haven't jumped on the Obamacare bandwagon. But not having insurance is the least of it."

"Tell me."

"Well, it gets better. Jobs were fewer and farther between. With my shoestring crew and barely breaking even most of the time, in order to help float the business, first we had to cash out our IRAs, taking that hefty penalty at tax time. When that was all gone, we refinanced the house not too long ago. I mean, Emmy was in college and, well, it paid those bills—the ones her loans didn't cover—and it kept the business going for a few months, but the upshot is we are so financially screwed right about now. And now these bills from the accident, and they are only a harbinger of what's to come. It's going to turn into a financial maelstrom that will suck us under. I'm afraid I'm anticipating bankruptcy in our future."

"It can't be as bad as all that? What about the woman who caused the accident? Her insurance company should be ponying up a bucketful of cash."

"They're dragging their heels on that. The insurance company is saying because it was a construction zone where the accident happened, it was the city of Burbank's fault or, beyond that, the state of California's fault. So they aren't paying a penny until all the wrinkles get ironed out."

"Ouch!"

"No kidding, ouch."

"Have you found a good lawyer?"

"Working on it."

"Well, here," Brian took a business card out of his wallet. "This guy is really good. And if he's not the right fit for you, he'll be up front with you about that and point you in the direction of someone who is. Give him a call."

Clark pocketed the card. "Thanks, Brian. Is he one of those lawyers who will wait for a percentage of a settlement in lieu of payment? Cause that's the kind of boat we are in."

"Ask him. But, hey, the light bulb just went on in my head. If that woman's insurance company is pointing the finger at Burbank and/or California for being at fault for the accident…are you starting to follow my drift?"

"What?"

"If they are responsible, you can sue them! Might be the answer to a prayer for you. Oh yeah, might as well include the construction company in that mix." Clark winced at that. "Yeah, I know that one hits close to home, but it's a dog-eat-dog world. You know that."

"Oh, man, this whole thing just keeps getting more and more complex. I can barely keep up with it all."

Brian pointed to the pocket the business card had disappeared into. "Hence why you need to call that lawyer pronto. Get a professional sorting out all this stuff."

"Yeah, sure. Guess that's my next step."

"Anyway, what I was dropping by to tell you is that the moving van will be here at first light day after tomorrow. When they are done loading all the stuff, we're out of here."

All Clark could do was shake his head.

"So looks like this is it. Meghan said she'd pop over in the morning on Friday to say bye to you and Faith."

"It'll just be Faith as I head for the desert tomorrow. I'll be spending the night out there and home later on Friday."

Brian just blew out his breath. Then said, "You picked a heck of a time of year to work in the desert. What will it be out there, a hundred and ten in the shade?"

"Probably."

"Well, good luck with all that."

"Yep." The two men shook hands.

"Chin up, buddy. It's always darkest before the dawn."

"Yeah, clichés help," Clark mumbled to himself as he watched Brian make his way back home. The man had a jaunty little step. All was well in his world: a new job, a new house, a new life. For a moment, envy swamped Clark. What wouldn't he give to be taking off into something new and positive right about now. He turned toward his own house and all that awaited within. Not ready to deal with that reality, he opened the back door, reached in, took the dog's leash off the hook, and hollered, "I'm talking Lola for a walk." The minute Lola heard the "w" word, she skittered around the corner and slid up to Clark, panting with a happy grin on her doggie face. "Come on, let's get out of here," he told her. And they took off into the dark.

***

The television was on but Clark wasn't really watching it when Emily came into the room, budged his feet over, and plopped down on the hassock in front of him. "Did the walk help?"

"Kind of-not really." He picked up the remote and muted the television.

"How are you doing, Dad?"

"I'm...doing."

"That's not an answer."

"Well, it's the best I can do." And with that, he took a long swallow of his beer.

"You heading out to Lancaster tomorrow to prep the jobsite?"

"Yes. At least this first week in the desert will be a short one as it's already Wednesday. Did you get your boss to approve your moving to days?"

"Yes. Tomorrow's my second day off then I start on days Friday."

"And speech therapy?"

"Hope's on board for that on Mondays and Fridays. I'll still be able to take Mom on Wednesdays as I'll still be off Wednesdays and Thursdays. So really, Tuesdays will be the only day Mom's alone most of the time, and she'll be swamped with homework from the therapist. So that should be okay. Or, if need be, Hope can drop by that day too to check up on her."

Clark was shaking his head. "I just don't know how this is going to work. Hope can't be here all the time."

"Dad, she's more than willing to pitch in. In fact, I think she'd be insulted if we didn't depend on her. She's family."

"Still, it's asking a lot. And your mother, being alone most of the time, with her confusion, I don't even want to go there."

"Don't worry, Dad. Remember that she is still sleeping most of the day away. And beyond that, I've been thinking about the logistics of all our different schedules and I have a plan."

That made him smile. "I can always count on you for a plan. So what is it?"

"I'm going to hang a white board on the kitchen wall and we will write down schedules and things."

"Are you forgetting your mom has a hard time with words?"

"Just talking. She can read small bits of this and that. If we write, 'Monday, Speech Therapy 10:00 a.m.,' she'll get it. Anyway, it will be for you and me too. If you are home and I'm not around, there will be information on the board that you might need to know. And vice versa."

He picked up his phone from the nearby table and wiggled it under her nose. "So you're not going to be calling me or texting me anymore? Just leaving notes on a white board?"

"Don't be silly. The board is mostly for Mom. I just think it's a really good idea. That's all. It will give her a place to look and get anchored in what's going on each day."

Nodding his agreement, he said, "It is a very good idea. And, thanks, Emmy, for all your ideas and your help. I don't know how I'd be able to cope without you."

"Like I said, Dad, family. I'll try and get the board up soon."

***

Clark sat at his office desk and pulled open the drawer. He tossed in two more bills that had arrived in the mail that day. This was the drawer he had designated for accident-related bills. He didn't even bother to ponder how long it might be before they got paid or before the drawer would be full to overflowing. He just shut the drawer on them and did his best to put them out of his mind. Booting up the computer, he needed to work on scheduling for the job in Lancaster. This was where he missed Faith's—the old Faith's—help. She had been a full contributing partner in the business. She had done all the accounting, payroll, and the secretarial stuff. She arranged appointments, scheduled the inspections, and did numerous other things. He was only just discovering how much he had counted on her now that she could no longer do the work. Her ability to organize and prioritize had flown out the window with so many of her other abilities. She couldn't even take care of the household business anymore, which she had done singlehandedly for most of their married life. Sometimes, he just marveled at how she had done it all. He sighed and pulled on his beer. So not only had his workload doubled just to keep the business on track, add to that all the household stuff too. And add to all that the additional time and energy for Faith. It seemed like everything was all on him now. And the worst was, he couldn't even use Faith as a sounding board as she didn't recall any of the nuances of the job or the household stuff either. Thank goodness, he was heading for the desert tomorrow. Getting away from all this might stem the feeling that he was heading toward a serious burnout. And boy, did all that make him feel guilty! But realistically, he rationalized, if he burned out, where would they be? Getting away was going to save his sanity. And he knew he could count on Emily.

Sitting back in his chair, he considered Emily. He could put her in charge of keeping track of the electric bill and stuff like that. On one hand, he hated burdening her with yet more stuff to deal with, but on the other hand, he was enough of an admitted male chauvinist that he felt she'd probably better handle the household stuff anyway. But as Chris, Hope, and Cliff were all pitching in too, it wasn't all on his daughter. With a sigh, he settled into the chair and started hunting and pecking his way across the keyboard.

***

Faith lay in bed starting at the ceiling. Sometimes, she'd wake up in the middle of the night and be unable to fall asleep. Probably because she slept a large part of each day away. Getting up, putting her laptop under her arm and picking up her log, she crept out of the bedroom as quietly as she could so she didn't awaken her husband.

An hour later, she was still sitting in her comfortable chair by the gas fireplace with a throw over her legs and a cup of hot tea that had gone cold next to her on a little table. The laptop was still on but abandoned on the floor by the chair, and she was writing in her logbook. She had tried keeping a log on the computer but discovered typing on the keyboard was too challenging. Yet writing—holding a pen or pencil—wasn't. That was still a mystery to her and because it was on her mind, she chose to write about that:

> I discovered writing by hand is easier for me than typing on a keyboard. One more mystery. And, I still don't know why writing is easier for me than reading. Cheryl tried to explain it to me but I got lost in her words. Lost again. Lost. Lost in so many ways. Be that as it may, back to what I was saying. I am trying to challenge myself each day with written words – not my written words but written words from other sources. I woke up

tonight and for some reason kept thinking about fate. What is fate? So I looked it up on my computer. There was too much to try to read, but when I looked up fate, the words free will kept popping up too. There was a sentence by Isaac B. Singer that caught my attention. It said: *We must believe in free will; we have no choice!* I had to reread it several times to get it, but, WOW, it really speaks to me. I don't know why it does but it does. Probably because I feel so much has happened to me that I have no choice about. I didn't choose to be in an accident. I didn't choose to have a brain injury. I don't know if I am even choosing to write this passage tonight. Is there no choice in anything? So here I am in the middle of the night writing. And wondering. Wondering what's next? I can't see around the next bend of time. All I can see is more of the same. More therapy, more therapy and more therapy. Endless therapy. Now that does make me tired, so sad, and so tired. I guess I'll go back to bed.

Faith slipped between the sheets and rolled over to snuggle against Clark. He rolled his shoulder pulling slightly away from her. For some reason that small movement cut her to the quick. She felt tears well in her eyes and fill her throat. Clark seemed to be pulling further away from her each day and tomorrow he was going away to work in the desert. She tried swallowing the blockage in her throat and couldn't. Unable to take a breath, she sat back up in bed. There was a glass of water on the nightstand. She took a sip of the tepid water and while it didn't slide smoothly down her throat, she managed to get it past the tightness in there. Lying back down, she closed her eyes. For a long time, sleep didn't come.

PART II

Ascending

***

Depression
Grieving
Acceptance
Resolution

DEPRESSION

Depression is the inability to construct a future.
—Rollo May

CHAPTER 16

Hᴏᴘᴇ sᴛᴏᴏᴅ ɪɴ ᴛʜᴇ ᴅᴏᴏʀᴡᴀʏ of the family room watching Faith who was tummy down on the couch sobbing into a pillow.

"Hey, there!" Hope entered the room and hurried over to her sister. "What's wrong?"

Faith sat up and brushed the tears away. "Oh, H-Hope. I-I didn't knooow you w-w-were here."

"Just arrived. Now tell me what's gotten you down? Or is that a stupid question? Is it because Clark was gone overnight? He'll be home later today."

"N-n-oooo. M-M-Meghan's o-off-officially g-gooone. T-the m-moooving van t-took off a l-little while a-go."

Hope started to tell her to slow down her words and breathe like the therapist was coaching her to do but decided now wasn't the time. "So sorry she had to move. We're all going to miss her."

"Itttt's juuuust nooot faaiiir!" Faith sniffed. "I juuuust caaan't taaake anymooore. I juuuust caaan't."

"Shush," Hope rubbed her sister's back. "It's all going to be fine in time. It will be. You just have to have…faith." Such a play on words usually made her sister roll her eyes. It had been their habit all through childhood to make word games with their respective names. But today Faith wasn't in the mood. The only thing that comment elicited from her was a heartfelt sigh. "Chin up, sis. It's all good."

Glancing at the clock, Faith said, "Y-you're h-here earlier th-than u-usual."

"I'm taking you to the therapist, remember?"

"Oh? G-guess I d-didn't re-re-member that." Then, through her tears, she gave a small depreciating laugh. "N-nooo suuuurrprise thh-heeere, huh?" Then, "I-I d-doooon't feeeel like gooooing."

"No playing hooky. I heard that Meghan let you get away with that one day last week, but can't make a habit of that."

Faith just nodded her understanding.

Something had snagged Hope's attention. Their grandmother's china teacup and saucer that had always sat on the mantel was gone. So was the little angel. Looking around, she glanced at the bookcase, the coffee table, and the end tables. They weren't anywhere.

"Wh-whaaaaat arrrre yooooou looookkkking foooor?"

"Grandma's china teacup and saucer."

Faith's eyes slid to the side.

"Faith?"

Unable to meet her sister's questioning eyes, Faith mumbled, "Itttt brrrroooke."

"And the angel?"

"Ittt brrroooke tooo."

"What happened?"

Faith sat up fully on the couch and gave a little half shrug. "Theeeyy juuuussst brrrooooke."

Hope could tell there was more to it than just that but decided now wasn't the time to pursue it. They had to get rolling.

***

On the way to the therapist's office, Hope mentally cast around for a topic of conversation to get Faith's mind off Meghan's departure. Finally thinking of something, she said, "I had my acupuncture appointment this morning. So, just conversationally, I was telling Dr. Lee about your accident and your exhaustion and all that. She said that people suffering from chronic exhaustion often respond well to acupuncture. I think maybe you should give it a try and see if it helps."

"I-I ssuuuuppose it coooouldn't h-hurt." Remembering to breathe through the words, she continued, "I'll aaassssk Drrr. Weeelllbrock n-nneext ttttiiime I s-seeee hhimmm."

Hope knew the old Faith would not have deferred any decision to a medical doctor. She'd have made up her own mind about whether to do this or that. But she kept her own counsel. That Faith had, well, faith in the neurologist was actually a positive thing.

"You are going to get better. I can already hear your speech improving. And you are going to start remembering things too. I know it."

"Yyooou s-ssooound ssuurrre of yyooour-s-s-ssseeelf."

Hope reached over and patted Faith's hand. "What I'm going to tell you may sound crazy, but it's been something I've been reading up on. Research suggests that memory exists in places other than just the brain."

"Wh-whhheere ellllse wwooould it beeee?

"Would you believe your heart or your liver or your kidney?"

Pulling back a little, Faith looked at her askance. "Wh-wwhhhat are you taaaalking abooout?"

"Well, listen to this. I read that people who have organ transplants sometimes end up with memories that aren't theirs. They have memories and likes and dislikes that belonged to the person whose organ they received. Someone who never liked hot chili peppers suddenly has a craving for hot chili peppers. Or someone who only loved classical music suddenly listens to country. Or someone else remembers the pangs of childbirth except that person is a man who just had a heart transplant. So the theory goes that memories are in those transplanted organs. And the person receiving the organ starts having that other person's memories. So, by extension, I have a theory of my own. I say your memories must be in your organs too, organs other than your brain. So it's just going to be a matter of time before they get funneled back into your healing brain and you will have your memories back."

Faith smiled at her sister and shook her head. "Sssooounds w-weeeird-ttooo m-mmmeee. B-but, hey, I-I'm open t-ttooo anythiiiiiing."

"Me too." Hope parked the car. "I mean, that idea can't be such a far stretch from muscle memory. Our muscles remember things like typing. Or you are knitting those scarves now. Mom taught us to knit eons ago. And you didn't forget how to do that because the memory is in your muscles." Faith was listening intently to her sister. "But enough of all this. Come on, let's get you to therapy then if you're not too tired, we'll have lunch before we head home."

***

"A new driver?" Cheryl smiled at Hope and extended a hand to shake.

Hope took the hand and gave it a friendly little squeeze. "Hi, I'm Hope. I'm on the Monday and Friday shift."

"Please to meet you, Hope. Do you want to stick around or come back?"

Hope looked around the pleasant office that was really as much a workstation and playroom as it was an office. I'll just sit over there and read a magazine and wait."

Cheryl nodded then turned her attention to Faith. Gesturing Faith toward the table she asked, "How are the exercises coming?"

"W-w-well…"

"Slowly, breathe, try again."

"Wweeeelll. I'mm d-ddooooing theemm."

"Good, I can hear that you have been. And you, how are you doing?"

"Oookkkkaaay."

"We've been this route before. I can see you must have been crying today. So let's try again. How are you *really* doing?"

Faith rubbed her hands over her face self-consciously. Cheryl noticed a little chin wobble, but Faith managed to get a hold of her emotions and answered, "I crrrry a lot."

"Tell me about that. What makes you cry? Why do you cry? When do you cry?"

Faith took her time to digest what she wanted to say. "Tooday beeeecause Meeeghan is moooving aaaway. Buuuut otttthher times toooo."

"Tell me."

"Wh-wheeen Emmmily is drrrrriving tooooo or frrrooom wor-rrk. I wooorrry th-thhhhaaat shhhee wiiilll beeee in annnn accident. I wooooorrrry soooo muuuch, I st-stttaaaart crrrrying. I crrry unnn-til she geeets hooome and I knnnnooooow sheeee is okkkkkay."

Hope was pressing the fingers of one hand to her mouth. She had known that Faith got distraught at times, but she hadn't realized how bad it was.

Cheryl, clearly a professional listener, nodded as Faith explained her travails. "What you are experiencing is anxiety. No secret there. Tell me what you are experiencing when this anxiety arises in you."

"I-I-I haaaave emmmpathy for cutttters. I geeet it. I haaaave sympathy for turrrrrrets – they screeeam s-swear wwords, and the braaain reeeleases indorrrrphins and theeeeey go ahhhhhh, and there issss reeeeelease. I ggget it. If I haaaave a tempeeeerrr tanttttrum and hiiittt my haaaand against thhhhe walll, it hurts. I feeelll bettter. If I brrreak something, I feeeellll better. And when Emmmmily is drrr-riving, I wooorrry and I cry. I know alllll thhhaaat is anxiety."

"What's happening is that the anxiety is controlling you. We can't let that happen. You need to control the anxiety. You can't let it control you."

"Hooowwww doooo I doooo thhhhat?"

Before Cheryl answered, she dropped down to the floor, removed Faith's shoes, and looked at her feet, separating each toe and looking between them. Giving a deep breath of relief, she slipped Faith's shoes back on and sat back down.

"Anxiety is energy that needs to be expended and you are expending it through your crying. You need to find other avenues through which to expend the energy that is manifested because of the anxiety. Think about little kids. They are little balls of energy. And what do they do? Run and skip and play hop scotch and jump rope and do all kinds of active things to expend their energy. So you need to do something active to expend the energy that wells up when you are feeling anxious. Scrub the floor, clean out the refrigerator, *do* something. *Do* being the operative word. Okay? You understand?"

Faith was nodding. "Yeeeesss, I unnnnderstand. But, whhhhat were yoooou doooing with myyyy feeeeet?"

"You said you understand cutters. Cutters usually begin with cutting between their toes as no one can see that area of the body. I wanted to check to see if you were cutting. You aren't, so that is good." Cheryl kept things matter of fact. "You understand why I was looking?"

Faith nodded.

"Now back to the anxiety issue. We were talking about your need to be doing something to relieve anxiety."

"Yeeeees, I understtttand."

"Good, but realize you don't need to be a hero, Faith. There are medications that Dr. Wellbrock can prescribe that will help with the anxiety you are experiencing. Do talk to him about this, okay?"

"Ooookkkkaaay."

"Now, what else is going on with you these days?"

"I g…guuuueess I geeeet frrruustrated. Annnd I'm allllways tiiirred. Ittt's s…soooo muuuch wooork juuuust toooo get upppp sooome days. Annnd fooor soooo litttttle p…paaayoffff."

"You are making great strides, Faith. Great strides. It's normal to get frustrated. There is no overnight fix. Just remember to *trust the process*," she made little finger quotes around the words. "Okay?"

Faith gave a frustrated little nod. "Oookkkkkaaay."

"All right. You'll get there, I promise. What you'll notice one day is that a window in your brain will open and you'll make a quantum leap through it and be on the other side, and all this work will have paid off. That being said, we need to get to work. Now, these past few weeks we've gotten into a little bit of a rut doing the same things over and over, so today we're going to be doing something a little different." Cheryl handed Faith a tablet of lined notebook paper and a pen then she picked up a stack of flash cards that were on the table. "We're going to start with these flash cards but don't let that word *flash* stress you out. We're not in a hurry here. There is one word on each card. I want you to look at the word. Just look at it at first. Read it to yourself. Then, say it in your head a couple of times. And finally, say it out loud using your breath and stretching it out as we have been practicing. After you've said the word, I want you to write it down on the piece of paper." She held up the first card.

Faith read it silently at first and then said, "R…rruuunn." Then she wrote it down on the paper.

"And this one?"

"Gggrrreenn."

"Yes. And next."

"S…sssaaiidd."

"Good, let's keep going."

When they had finished the stack, Cheryl sat back and took the tablet Faith had written the words on. "Good. Your writing's really good. Everything's readable, but I think your penmanship needs a little boost. Here's a little homework exercise I want you to do. It will help with your hand-eye coordination and translate to your writing. On your way home, buy some crayons and coloring books, the kind for really little kids with big pictures. Each day, or maybe twice a day, color a page in the book, staying in the lines. Go slow. It will help with the mind connecting to and moving the hand to do the task."

"Oooookkaaay."

"And that will translate to your writing make it a little neater."

"She always did have sloppy handwriting. Or wait, no. That was me. Hers was always pretty neat," Hope volunteered.

All three women chuckled.

"Be that as it may, this is a good exercise for a number of reasons. It's an eye-brain-hand connection. Now," Cheryl tapped the stack of flash cards, "there is a reason I've started you with individual words rather than just repeating certain words. In a couple of weeks, Dr. Wellbrock will be giving you a test." Cheryl noted the flash of panic in Faith's eyes as they shot to hers.

"Wh-whhhhaaattt kkkkiiinndd of ttteeest?"

"One that has sentences in it."

"I-I-I…"

"Slow down, breathe."

"IIII ccaaan't rrreead sseeentences."

"Yes, you can. I know it's a chore to read them, but you can read them. What we are going to be doing are some exercises that will get you ready for the test. You did just great with individual words." She tapped the cards again, "We'll be starting on short phrases next. By the time you take the test, you'll be able to handle the simple sentences in it without a problem. Trust me on that."

"Caaann yooou exppllaaaine thhe teeest toooo meeee?"

"It's one that's been around for decades. It's actually a psychological test called the MMPI2, but Dr. Wellbrock is not using it as a diagnostic tool, at least not yet. So don't you worry about that. What his rational is with this test is to establish a baseline so when you take the test again a few months down the road, we'll be able to determine your progress."

"Ooookaaaay."

"One thing they will be testing this time as compared to when you take it again is simply how long it takes you to complete the test. If you do it the second time around in say half the amount of time, it will show remarkable progress in comprehension."

"Oookkkkaaayy. Wwhhhat…?"

"I'll explain it. It is a true-false test. You will read statements, fairly short sentences as I already said, and just put a T for true or an F for false next to each one. It will be as easy as that. I know, however, that reading is hard for you, so I'm going to work on that with you so it will become easier by the time you take the test."

"Ooooookaaay."

Hope had been listening to Cheryl's spiel. It sounded like she'd embedded some disclaimers into that little explanation and that made her a bit curious, even cautious. So she unobtrusively pulled her iPhone out of her purse and started doing some sleuthing online about this MMPI2 test.

As they were getting ready to leave, Cheryl gave Faith an additional homework assignment. "I want you to start going to the library. You're to check out a bunch of children's books. Little, little kids' books with just a few words on each page. Then I want you to read a book every so often throughout the day. Pick one at random. Something short that you can read in one sitting. After you have finished the book, in your logbook, I want you to write down the date, the name of the book, and then write one sentence telling what the book was about. Try to get through three books a day. Two is fine, but three will be better. Then, we'll go over the logbook each time you come to therapy and see what you've read."

"Ooookaaay. Hooommewoork, liiibraary boooks."

"And coloring books."

"Aannd ccooloring boookks."

"And your regular exercises of repeating that list of words I gave you last time."

"L-liike prraaacticing ppiiiiano sccaaales."

"And the math sheet."

"Ugh."

Cheryl laughed. "Oh, and one other thing for homework. I want you to try singing along when you listen to the radio. Singing is good therapy to help you with your speech. Plus, singing sometimes helps chase away the blues. Give it a try."

CHAPTER 17

SITTING AT A LITTLE SIDEWALK table, Faith pushed her empty plate away and looked in the bag that held three coloring books. She smiled at Hope. It was the first genuine smile Hope had seen all day. "I ffffeeeel jjuust llliiiike a kiiid."

"It does sound like fun doesn't it." Hope took the bag from her and extracted one book and flipped through it. "You always were good at coloring, more patient than I was. I was constantly in such a rush to get on to the next one that I scribbled more than colored. You had much more attention to detail." Next, she extracted the box of crayons and opened it. "Don't you just love nice pointy brand new crayons and that smell." She sniffed. "I love that new-crayon smell."

Taking the box from her sister, Faith took a whiff. She looked puzzled at first then another smile spread across her features. "I dddooo reemmmember thhhiiis." The sudden sound of a siren racing down the street startled Faith and had her dropping the crayons in her lap as she covered her ears with both hands. When the screeching had faded away, Hope asked, "Do you need to put your earplugs in."

"N-noooo a lliiittle laaate fooor thhaat. I'mmm oookkkay."

"You sure? You've suddenly gone deathly pale."

Faith shook her head then blinked a couple of times. "I'mmmmm oookkkay. Reeeaaallly."

After an intent look at her sister, Hope gave a nod. "Okay. Good. Do you remember what Aunt Laura used to say whenever she heard a siren?" Faith shook her head. "She'd always say, 'Help is on the way.' I've never forgotten that. Whenever I hear a siren, her words just automatically pop into my mind."

"I hoooppe s-sooommeday m-mmeeemories liiike thaaat pooop innntoo myyy mmiiind."

Hope reached across the table and caressed her sister's hand. "They will. Now, before that interruption, we were talking about the smell of new crayons and it reminded me of something."

Faith picked the box of crayons up out of her lap and put them back in the shopping bag. "Whhhaat?"

"I recall reading that the sense of smell often evokes memories. I think we need to look into that. Like, bake some chocolate chip cookies and when the aroma of baking cookies fills the house, see if any memories are triggered. Or, no, better yet, brownies. You love brownies."

"Aannd on thhat n-nnoootte, I thhhiiink weee n-nneeed tooo orddeeer ddeessseert!"

They decided to indulge in a sweet, gooey treat, but in the interest of their waistlines, they ordered one desert with two spoons.

The waitress placed the piece of Death-By-Chocolate Cake ala mode with vanilla ice cream and drizzled all over with chocolate sauce in front of them and handed each her spoon. "Ladies, en guard! Last woman still conscious after all that sugar is the winner." All three laughed.

When they had practically licked the plate clean, Faith said, "Thhiisss waass a rreeeaallyy g-grrreeat iddeeea.'"

Hope rubbed her tummy and groaned. "Yes, it was, and now I'll have to do something aerobic to burn off all these calories. Now, not to change the subject, but I looked up that test online that your speech therapist was talking about. There are mixed feelings among professionals as to the validity of that particular test. But since it's been around forever, they keep on with it."

"Itttt's trrruue f-faaalse. S-ssooo thhaaat's easy."

"There were some sample sentences." Hope scrolled through her phone. "Ah, here they are. It will ask you things about yourself such as 'My father was a good man' or 'I seldom worry about my health' or 'My sleep is fitful and disturbed.' Then you simply assess them as true or false. I think the trick with a test like this is not to overthink any of your responses. Just mark what first pops into your head. That will be the best answer."

"R-rreeeading isss s-soooo hhhard."

"Hence why you have homework to start practicing reading."

Faith had been listening to her sister with her elbow resting on the table and her chin propped in her hand. When she realized her fingers were caressing the scar on her upper lip that she had noticed—barely noticed—in the mirror that morning, it reminded her to ask, "Hhhooow did I g-geet this s-scccaaar here?" Faith fingered the faint, almost imperceptible scar on her upper lip.

Hope took a sip of water then said, "I guess you were about three years old. You had a temper fit about something and slammed the basement door. The window in the door fell out and smashed over your head. Voila, your lip got sliced on a piece of jagged glass. Luckily, it didn't slit your throat. Come to think, that is just another example of you getting banged on the head!"

"S-sooo whhhaaat ggoot mmeee s-ssooo mmaaad th-that I s-sll-lammed th-that dddoooor?

"Not what but who."

"S-ssister ddeeeear…est?"

"Shall we start picking at that scab again?'

"I gggguuuuesss I d-dddooo waaant t-toooo knnnoooow."

"Okay," Hope cleared her throat then began, "Charity. She was always a bit of a bad seed. When it comes to the unhappiness in our family, I often think of the first line in Leo Tolstoy's *Anna Karenina*. He wrote, '*Happy families are all alike; every unhappy family is unhappy in its own way.*' I don't know if that's completely true, but it seems that Charity was always at the root of our family's unhappiness. She was like a cancer in the heart of our family, and you and I finally chose to cut it out before it poisoned us. So it's done and over with, but it did leave its scars." She ran her finger over her own upper lip. "They're just not all visible like the scar on your lip."

"I d-doooo rrreeemember s-sssoome thhhings from the p-ppaaast. At leeast I'mmm s-sstarting toooo. S-ssadly, a lot of the m-mmmemories I rrrecallll aren't fffun s-sttttuff. Mmmost of it's p-ppaaainful, hurtful."

Hope pointed to her lip again. "More scars, just of the emotional kind. You are probably remembering the sad things because they left a powerful emotional punch on your psyche. What you're discovering or rediscovering is that the past is always with us. Sometimes, the burden is light, so we don't notice it. But other times, it's like a sackful of scalded, angry cats we carry around on our backs—all of them scratching and biting to get out."

"Wwwwhhhat an immmage. Yooou s-ssoooound liiike a wrriiiter."

"So now I'm going to change the subject. What happened to grandma's cup?"

So Faith fessed up. She revealed that on occasion, she just couldn't control her anger; she'd let her temper get the best of her and she'd throw something. Sometimes, several somethings. The sound of shattering glass helped her when she was so angry. She didn't know why. Then she'd clean up the mess before Clark or Emily came home so they wouldn't be the wiser. She had thrown the cup and saucer and the angel too and, again, cleaned up after herself and didn't realize anyone would really notice that they were gone. "I rrreeeeaaally feeelt baaadd abbbout it. I meeeaaan, thhhis morning whheeen yooou noooticed, I knew I'ddd reeeealllly goooofffffed. But beeefffore that, I didn't knnnnoooww it was a sppppeeecial cuuup."

In her mind's eye, Hope saw the cup and saucer sitting on her grandmother's sideboard. It was a very rare set made of bone china, very thin and fragile. It was for show only. No one ever drank their tea from it. The pattern was old, obsolete. It was a one of a kind that could never be replaced. After their grandmother had died, all three sisters wanted the cup and saucer, but their mother chose among them and gave it to Faith. She had said Faith was the only one who was artistic enough to appreciate a rare piece of fine china.

Hope sighed deeply over losing that precious piece of their family history. Then sighed again and reluctantly let it go. "Well, what's done is done. But these temper tantrums? You're not going to go too far? I mean, we don't want you hurting yourself."

"I'mm trrryying toooo sttooopp."

"As long as it doesn't get too far out of hand. I saw Cheryl looking between your toes to see if you were cutting yourself."

A long sigh. "I saaaaid I'mmmm trying toooo stttop my temper taaaaantrums."

"Maybe you should talk to Dr. Wellbrock about the anger."

"Maaaayyybe."

And Hope knew when it was time to drop a subject. "So are you up for a trip to the library or is it nap time?"

Faith shook her head and started gathering up the bag with the coloring books and crayons. "Noo liibbbrary. Itttt's n-nnaaap tttime."

"Okay, I'll text Emily and let her know you guys have to go to the library this evening when she gets home from work and get some books. Maybe at bedtime, you can read her a story. Déjà vu all over again, huh?"

Faith didn't respond as she was in the middle of a huge yawn.

**

Faith woke up from her nap and heard some banging around in the kitchen. She looked at the clock and figured Emmy must be home from work and fixing something for dinner. She went downstairs and stopped stock-still in the kitchen doorway.

Emily stood on the stepladder with the power drill in hand. She was screwing a new white board to the kitchen wall. "There!" Glancing over her shoulder, she spied her mom. "Here." She held out the drill to Faith then stepped off the ladder. "Guess I learned a thing or two from Dad, didn't I?"

"I g-guueesss yooou did. Whhaat's alllll thhhiss?"

"This is a whiteboard for notes and things. So here's the plan. Every evening before bed, you and I will put the next day's schedule on the whiteboard, so all you have to do is look at the board and it will tell you what's up. For example, if Hope is coming over to take you to speech therapy, it will be written right down here. Okay? Or if you and I are going to the library for some books—which is actually too late to do today as they close early on Fridays—that will be written down here too."

"I s-sseeee." Faith noticed a pot on the stove that was simmering away. She lifted the lid and took a deep whiff. "Mmmmm. S-smmeeels goooood."

"I started some spaghetti sauce when I got home and I tossed a salad. So dinner's all figured out. But back to the whiteboard. Tomorrow is Saturday, and while I have to work, Dad will be home. So whatever you guys will be doing tomorrow, we'll get it down on the whiteboard tonight before bed."

"Oookkaaay. Buuut I waaasss s-suuuppposed tooo get liiibrr-raary booooks."

"No biggie, Mom, come here." Faith followed Emily to the Rogues' Gallery hallway and watched as Emily opened a cupboard that was built into the wall. Inside were shelves lined with dozens of children's books. "My books from when I was little. You saved them all. So we can get you started with these. Then move on to library books when these have been read." She knelt down and pulled out *Hop on Pop*. "Here." She handed it to her mother. "Dr. Seuss is a good place to start."

"Dr. S-Ssseeeuss?"

"You remember, Mom? Surely, you remember Dr. Seuss. *One Fish, Two Fish, Red Fish, Blue Fish*?"

Faith simply shook her head.

"Okay." Emily put her finger to her temple to help her dredge up a memory. "What about this? 'Today you are you! / That is truer than true! / There is no one alive / Who is you-er than you!' Do you remember that?"

Again a head shake, but she was smiling at the sing-song way Emily had recited the passage.

"Okay, this one's from the *Cat in the Hat* which you read to me only about ump-teen million times. 'Look at me! / Look at me! / Look at me NOW! / It's fun to have fun / But you have / To know how.' Remember?"

"Heeee s-sssooounds innnteeeeresting." *Hop on Pop* in hand, Faith headed into the family room, and sat on the couch.

Emily sat next to her. "Okay, Mom, just like when I was little. Tell me a story. And!" Emily admonished shaking a finger at her mom, "*No* skipping pages."

"Diiiidd III s-skiiiippp p-paaaggges?"

Laughing, Emily explained. "Yeah! *Cat in the Hat*. I just loved it and I made you read it every night for months and months. And you got so tired of it. You'd try to turn two pages at a time to get through it faster. But I had it pretty much memorized so I knew when you were skipping pages. I called you on it every time!"

"Hmmmmm. Bbuussstted, huh?"

"Yep. Now, start reading."

***

Lola lay curled up sleeping in her bed by Clark's empty easy chair while Faith and Emily colored in a coloring book. "Thiiiiss is eaaasier thaaan reaaading."

"And fun too. It's reminding me how much I grew to like that art class in high school. I think I'm being inspired to try my hand at some more painting."

Faith had just finished coloring the last bit of her page when Lola awoke, leaped into the air, and started up a ruckus as she bolted toward the living room. "I'll bet Dad's home. Perfect timing, as you just finished your coloring homework."

"Calm down, Lola." Clark's voice carried. "Anybody home?"

"Family room," Emily hollered in response.

Clark grabbed a beer out of the fridge then joined them. "Oh, man!" He stretched, arching his back. "What a heck of a commute on a Friday afternoon! I now remember why I decided to stay out there during the week when we are on this job. Doing that drive everyday would be a killer." He leaned down and kissed Faith. "How you been, sweetie?"

"Oookkkaaaay. Eemmily and Hoooope taaakke g-goooood caarre ooff m-meeee."

"Glad to hear it." He gave his daughter a kiss on the head. "So what's for dinner?"

"You didn't notice my spaghetti sauce simmering on the stove?"

"Guess I did, but," he held up his beer, "I was more intent on getting this."

"You were going to call that attorney today before you headed for home." Emily was curious. "Did you get an appointment?"

"I got his receptionist and set up an appointment with her. He's on vacation right now. He and his wife are taking some kind of six-week long second honeymoon traipsing around Europe. Guess he must be pretty successful if he can afford something like that."

"Well, at least it's on the books." Emily stood. "And on that note, I have garlic bread to get ready to go with the spaghetti."

***

That night, Faith couldn't sleep. As she tossed and turned, she kept thinking about what Hope had mentioned about organ transplant patients having memories that weren't their own. Giving up on sleep, she slipped out of bed, scooped up her laptop and her log, and headed downstairs. Sitting in her comfy chair, she booted up the computer and looked up memory in transplant patients to see what came up. She tried reading one of the articles and while most of it challenged her, she did get something out of it. She discovered that there are things called neuropeptides that exist in the brain, but not exclusively the brain. They are found in all tissues throughout the body. Some scientists think that these neuropeptides store memories in various organs in the body. And the heart, it seems, has more of them than other organs. That may be why heart transplant patients have memories that aren't theirs. Of course, the article pointed out, not all transplant patients experience such memories. But then, Faith reasoned, not everyone is really and truly tuned in to his or her body. The article gave Faith hope. She placed her hands over her heart and sent a little message to it. *If you hold my memories, please release them in such a way that I will have them back.* Turning off the laptop, she picked up her log and wrote about this idea that, while kind of far out there, did seem possible. Yes, indeed, it was something that gave her hope. She smiled at that because it was Hope that had told her about this. Hope giving her hope. She liked the eloquence of that.

Back upstairs, she slipped between the sheets next to her husband who was sputtering softly in sleep. She rested her hands on her heart; they were still there when she nodded off to sleep.

CHAPTER 18

AFTER LAZING AROUND MOST OF Saturday morning, Clark figured he should be getting some paperwork done and most of what he needed was on a clipboard in the truck. When he stepped outside to go get the papers and blueprints, he saw the new neighbor pulling into the driveway next door. Lacing his fingers, stretching out his arms, and cracking his knuckles he said to himself, "No time like the present. Go get him." Walking next door, he introduced himself. "Hi. I'm Clark Kincade, your neighbor," he jerked his thumb in the direction of the house behind him. "I understand from Brian, the previous owner, that you might be doing some renovating?"

"Gregory Saroyan," he shook Clark's hand. "Yes, Brian told me you are the one to talk to about all this." Gregory, a distinguished-looking man with a barrel chest and dark piercing eyes, spread both hands encompassing the entire house with his gesture.

"Do you have a few minutes now? We could talk about what you are envisioning."

"Well, my vision is something very different from what we have in front of us here."

"You looking to add a second story?"

"Yes, that and more. Brian said you remodeled your house years ago. Maybe I could see what you did and get an idea of your craftsmanship?"

"Just what I had in mind. It has been a while since I did my place, so keep that in mind. But it has surely held up well, even though those little quakes that roll in every now and then."

Gregory nodded. "That's good to hear. In these parts, we do want houses to be able to withstand earthquakes."

Clark brought the prospective client into his family room and explained how he went about designing and then building the addition. He had used his addition to make numerous sales over the years to this neighbor and that neighbor. They could see with their own eyes how he magically took a one-story two-bedroom smaller home and turned it into a nice-sized family dwelling. "If we were doing this with today's styles, we'd have French doors here instead of this sliding glass door. But the gas fireplace still holds up, both functionally and decoratively, over time."

Gregory took his time examining closely every nuance of the addition from the fireplace to the stairs that ascended to the master bedroom. Every now and then, he would nod to himself like he approved what he saw. Clark felt more confident with every nod. "I'd like to be able to take you upstairs to see the master bedroom and bath as well as the walk in closet, even the window seat, but my wife is napping. We can do that some other time."

"Of course. But speaking of time, if you have a block of free time now, why don't we drive over to my brother's house and you can see what he had done. I am in the market for something similar. It would save explanations. You know that saying about a picture being worth a thousand words. Well, the actual house would probably be worth two thousand words."

Picking up a notepad and a pencil, Clark asked, "Your car or my truck?"

They took Gregory's car and drove up to the base of the foothills. When Gregory parked in front of his brother's McMansion, Clark's first impression was, *Ugh, what a monstrosity!* But he was savvy enough to keep his expression interested and his words to himself.

Gregory held open the impressively massive and carved front door and gestured Clark in. "My brother is away on business for the next few days. So you are free to roam without intruding."

Clark entered and cast his eyes around, noticing the amazing use of space. He admired the spacious entryway and the high ceiling adorned with a chandelier dripping crystals. So far, the inside of the house was much more appealing than the outside. From the outside, the house took up the entire lot dwarfing the houses on either side of it. It was a giant among pygmies. And while the inside was inviting and roomy and very nice, the outside was still an out-of-place eyesore in this adorable little neighborhood nestled in the foothills.

Upstairs, Clark looked out a bedroom window and saw a very clear view of the neighbor's backyard boasting a swimming pool with blue tiles, making the water look invitingly blue as well. His thoughts ran toward the neighbor with the pool who he hoped hadn't been fond of skinny dipping as a halt would have been put to that practice as soon as the second story on this house was built. It also gave him pause as he realized that his own backyard would no longer be a private space once Gregory's house was reconstructed. But it was hard times and he needed the job. They'd just have to deal with the loss of privacy as a small secondary price to pay. Keeping the wolf from the door was primary. That's all there was to it. So he continued on with his grand tour and got a real good idea of what Gregory had in mind for turning the little house on Aster Street in to a trendy McMansion.

Dropping Clark back at his house, Gregory took off to a previously arranged business meeting. Clark watched his retreating car as it sped down the road and rounded a corner. They had agreed that Clark would draw up some blueprints according to what Gregory had in mind and they would move forward from there. Then they shook on the deal. Clark pumped his fist in the air. Things were looking really good. He headed up to his office to dig out a contract and get it sent over next door to be signed when Gregory got home.

Glancing into the bedroom, it dawned on Clark that Faith hadn't been out of bed all day. As an idea bloomed, he detoured back into the office and decided to get something in stone before waking his wife. He called Cliff. "Hey, there buddy. You and Hope have anything on the agenda this evening?"

"Not a thing."

"Good, because I'm getting Faith out of the house one way of the other. So we're coming over."

"How's she doing? Hope said Faith's been a little depressed ever since Meghan's exodus."

"She's been more than a little depressed. She's slept a lot anyway after the accident, but today, she's sleeping even more. Her doctor said that would be one sign of the depression kicking in. So I don't want it to get too bad."

"Hence why the phone call to come over tonight."

"Exactly. We'll be over for dinner. Just toss something on the grill, okay?"

"Sure, we were planning on marinated chicken breasts anyway. We've got plenty. And Hope just took a freshly baked peach pie out of the oven. So bring over some beer to go with dinner and vanilla ice cream to top off the desert and we're all set."

"Great! See you in a few hours."

"Hey, anything we can do. You know that."

Back in the bedroom, Clark looked down on his sleeping wife. "Hey, come on, Sleeping Beauty," he tugged the covers down a little bit. "Rise and shine it's already afternoon and the day is escaping."

Faith rolled over and looked at her husband with bleary, tired eyes. "Whhhaaat?"

"Come on, get up. I think we need to go out and do some celebrating. Looks like I'll be doing a renovation next door once I'm finished in the desert."

Faith rubbed her hands over her face. "Ohhhh? Thhhaat's goooood. Bbuuutt, I'mmm toooo tiiirrred tooooo goooo ouuuutt." She started to roll over and pull the covers back up.

"We're just going to be heading over to Hope's for dinner this evening. She baked a peach pie. Your favorite."

"Hoooonnney, reeeaaally, I'mmmm toooo tiirrred."

"You'll be fine once you get up and move around a little bit. We'll take Lola for a walk. After that, you have to read a book and do some coloring. Emmy put that on the whiteboard. Then, you can rest a little bit before we head on over to your sister's. Come on." He tugged the covers back again, and this time, on a sigh, Faith sat up in bed and rubbed the sleep out of her eyes.

***

Cliff dipped a chip into the guacamole and came up with a mouth-ful. "This is really good, Faith. Glad you brought it for an appetizer."

"Well, I know yooooou liiiike it."

"I do." He helped himself to another scoop of the dip. "Not to change the subject here, but Clark tells me you've been down in the dumps lately, well, not just lately. I want you to know that I am not a stranger to depression or grief. So if you ever need to talk to some-one, I'm here for you."

"Yes, t-taaaalking. That's s-soooo easy fooor meeee."

Rubbing a hand over her back, Clark said, "No need for sar-casm, honey. Cliff's just trying to be helpful."

Cliff cleared his throat, a sure sign, Hope knew, that he was about to go into lecture mode. "You know, Faith, when Eileen died, it took me years, literally years, to come out of that dark place I'd descended into. So I really do know what I am talking about. And I am here to tell you, you can get through all this and come out on top."

Faith knew her brother-in-law had been married before to a woman who had died unexpectedly. But she had never known much more than just that. So now that he had opened the subject up, curi-osity got the best of her and she jumped in. "Tell m-meee about it. What diiid you d-dooo? How did yoooou feel after sheee died?"

As he looked back in time, his eyes became slightly unfocused. "She and I were so very well suited. We were just plain and simple lucky in love. And when she died so suddenly with no warning, it knocked me flat. I did fall into a deep depression and that, of course, affected my work. And yet, ironically, it was work that helped pull me out of it again. I gave up my desk job that I'd worked so hard to get and went back to riding in a squad car, getting out there and dealing with people. To help me through the grief, I focused on the job, on those people I was helping. And for a long time, that was all there was for me. I was like one of those little hamsters running on a wheel. That's all I did. I had no hope for anything else. It was just work, work, work. Then, one day, there was Hope. And when fate tossed us together for a second time, well, the rest is history."

"Yeah, and it wouldn't have been history," Hope interjected, "if I hadn't asked you out."

Cliff smiled over at his wife who had just dug another beer out of the cooler and was handing it to him. He accepted the beer and said, "Oh, I was working up to asking you out. You just beat me to it."

"Really? I never knew that."

"See you're still finding things out about me. Keeps it all interesting, doesn't it?" He winked at her.

As Faith watched the domestic teasing between Hope and Cliff, she felt her throat thicken with tears. Tears she refused to shed. How long had it been since she and Clark had teased each other in just that way, a comfortable bantering way? They'd become not so much strangers as just roommates. She cleared her throat and raised her wine glass in a toast. "T-tooo finding new thhhiiiings out abbbout each other." And they all drank.

***

Sunset found the sisters sitting out on Hope's balcony overlooking the foothills while the guys took Cliff's new Corvette out for a spin. "Just like old times, huh?" Hope asked, gesturing toward the hills with her glass of wine.

Faith took a sip of her wine and set the glass on the table between them. "Yeees. This is s-soooo beautiful. Yooooou are s-sooo lucky. I am slooowly remembering things. Annnd I remember your condo annnnd yooour old balcony. This is almost liiiike your old baaaalcony."

"When my condo went up in flames and my balcony with it, and Cliff told me he would remodel his house and build a balcony just for me, well if I hadn't already fallen in love with him, I would have then."

"I remember hoooow much yooooou loooooved your old b-baaaal-cony. Do yooou stillll m-miss it?"

"Not anymore. Things change, times change, and this is home now. More of a home to me than the condo was and that's saying a lot as you know how much I loved my condo."

"I d-doooo."

"It's so great to hear your memories are coming back."

"Thhhere's still a lot oooof blanks."

"Tell me what you do remember. Is it like refilling the files the doctor talked about?"

Faith tipped her head slightly, thinking. "Everrrry fiiiilllle you puuulll up, you reeelive it."

Hope found it interesting that her sister was putting things in the second person. It was like Faith was removing herself slightly from the experience.

Faith continued. "Yooouu'lll have soooo mmmany upheavals. Youuu'lll have toooo reeeelive it and deal with it aaaaagain. You are dealing with Dadddddddy's death again. Mooooom's death again. Charity's reeeejection again. Ittt's soooo hard."

"I can imagine it is."

They sipped their wine in comfortable silence for a few minutes, drinking in the evening and enjoying the little nip in the air that was such a break from the heat they'd been subjected to for months. Faith broke the silence asking, "Hooow did it g-goooo with the t-teeeenants in Cliff's reeental hooouse in the valley?"

Hope blew out her breath with a little puffing sound. "Not good. They've gone MIA after two months of no rent and even with the eviction notice and all, we still aren't legally allowed in the house until after the eighteenth and only then with a police presence. The fact that Cliff is an ex-cop and knows the rules doesn't make it any easier. We looked in the windows and the bags overflowing with trash, well, it is just sickening."

"It s-sooounds hooorrible. Does it maaake him not want t-tooo beee a l-landlord anymooooore?"

"Actually, no. He takes it in stride. Points out the silver lining when he talks about the tax write off and stuff like that. The fact is he made some pretty wise investments in rental properties before the boom and the bust with land all those years ago. The houses are all paid off, and it's pure income to supplement his retirement. So it's all good."

"Until yooou have deadbeat t-teeenants whooo won't pay the rent and leeeave the place full ooof smelly trash."

"Yeah, I know. But last night, we got home from that white trash mess, parked my Accord which we'd been in, put the top down on the Vette, jumped in it, and zoomed off into the hills for a ride. Before you knew it, we didn't have a care in the world, and after a nice little cruise, we ended up at Joselito's for dinner. While we were eating, we realized how great it was to be us and how it really sucked to be them. I mean it must really, really suck to be them! So that made us feel better about the mess we'll have to clean up when they're finally out of our hair for good."

Faith put her hand up by her ear. "And sp-speeeaking ooof the Veeette, I think I heeear the roar ooof the engine coming b-baaack down the road."

***

Once Emily had started dabbling in painting again, she had moved some of the junk out of the garage and turned it into a quasi-studio. After all, no one ever parked in the garage—hadn't for years—so she'd felt fully justified in cleaning up the space and putting it to better use than just storage of stuff that needed to be hauled to the dump anyway. She didn't mind sharing her new space with the second refrigerator they had in the garage for cold beer, soda pop, and other items. The fridge, in fact, proved to be very handy as there was always something cold to drink when she worked up a thirst; and painting, she discovered, was thirsty business.

Emily could usually be found, on her days off, in her little studio with a paintbrush in her hand and a look of intense concentration on her face. Chris started calling her Rembrandt. And she would just give him a courtly little bow when he did and otherwise ignore his teasing. Before her accident, Faith had been fond of photographing nature. She had generally shied away from taking pictures of people. But Emily was discovering that she had a fondness for painting portraits. They weren't classic studio type portraits as she was hardly a *realist* when it came to her art. In fact, when she'd showed Chris the picture she'd painted of him his less-than-flattering response was, "You've got to be kidding!" But his reaction didn't bother her. Art was an expression and she was just expressing herself through her painting. If people liked it, fine. And if they didn't, so what. She stepped back and looked at the portrait she'd just finished of her mother. It was a haunting work on a large canvas in black, white, and grays. "Good grief, Mom," she whispered to the painting, "you look so lost. That's it!" She sighed in satisfaction. "I'm calling this one *Lost*."

When she showed it to her mother a few days later, Faith's reaction was stunned silence. "You don't like it?" Emily's voice sounded little girlish.

"Ohhhh, Emmmmey, no, I doooo liiike it. Ittt juuust stuunns me, hooow yoooou caaaaptured thhheee waaay I feeeeel. I dooo feeeeel sooooo looost so muuch offff theee tiiime. Annnd yoooour paaainting, looook aaat heeer. Sheeee issss soooo lost."

"I was going to ask if you wanted to hang it somewhere in the house. But maybe, it's too much of a reminder…" Emily's voice fell off.

"Ittt's a reeeeminder inn a gooood waaaay. Let's puuuut ittt innn myyy beeedroom.

And that's exactly where it went. Faith would often find herself standing in front of the painting, shaking her head at how Emily had reached into her psyche and pulled out exactly what she'd been feeling and living for such a long time. Her little girl had a talent. That was for darned sure.

***

One day, Faith realized a pattern had been established. When Emily left for work, she'd start to stress, and the stress would escalate until she couldn't stand it any longer. Then, the weeping would begin. One Saturday, when Clark was home, he was able to get out of her that she was so frightened that Emily would get into a car accident on the way to work or the way home that it was more than she could bear knowing her daughter was on the road. "And yoooou toooooo," she added. "When yoooou driiiive tooo the desert onnnn Mooondays and hoooome on Friiiiidays, I worry sooo much aboooooout acciiiidents."

To allay Faith's anxiety about their commutes, they started texting her when they had arrived safely or they'd text that they were on their way home and would be there soon. That way, at least the mid portion of her day wouldn't be stress-filled with wondering if either of them was stuck in a smashed up car on the freeway awaiting an ambulance. But while that did help to a degree, Faith still stressed during the actual commute times. Those hours were the worst times of the day for Faith.

One morning, Faith lay in bed. She had heard the front door close behind Emily and her car start. She took some deep breaths and waited. She looked at the clock. It was seven straight up. It would be at least an hour with the traffic and all before Emily got to work. She stared at the ceiling then looked at the clock again. When she realized her breath was starting to come faster, she sat up and reached for her log. And she wrote:

> What a long week. Been trying to live life, not dissect it. I have changed. So much slower. And, oh, the anger! Dang, I used to control. But when something is new or does not work I…just can't deal with it. The rage! After I am so humiliated. It is so far past embarrassment. I am cruel. Not just to whoever is in the room, but to myself.
>
> So how do I feel 2day? Well, it's 7:50 a.m. and until I hear from Emily, that she is safe at work and off the road, I sit in bed. I have my daily list of "to do" but do nothing until she is ok. Well, not true. I pray. & now I tear up. I hate what I have become. I don't want to pass my fears on to Em. I want her to fly into her future, but darn it, I'm frozen. 7:57 still 7:58. Text! "I'm here." I can breathe!

One day, when Emily left for work, on a day she normally had off, she explained to her mother that for the next few evenings she would be coming home later than usual because of some inventory situation. She hoped by giving her mom a head's up that it would preempt too much stress on her mother's part. That night, Faith just hit the wall and was weeping her heart out by the time Emily got home. The next day was Friday. Clark made it home from the desert when expected and all was well, at first. When Emily texted that she was on her way home, Faith flipped open her journal, hoping writing would keep her mind occupied.

> Emily just texted that she's leaving work. 7:48 I don't want a repeat of last night – I know I shouldn't cry – panic – worry – when she drives home. Clark keeps telling me to have faith and trust, etc. and part of me knows that, but…then there is the new (or broken) part of me that just takes over – the tears and fears I cannot control. So tonight I write. Now, to be fair, I tried last night to be busy. I polished copper. Something you do, well, once a year, or never. So I decided to polish thinking busy would help. NO! So tonight I write. There it is 8:10 and the anxiety is starting in pit of stomach – okay – I'm going to do yoga and stretch. 8:25 still stretching, trying to stay calm. More sit ups. 8:39 OUCH! 8:45 Clark called her. Emily answered, she's parking! So did it! I didn't cry once and maybe I'll sleep without leg pain from all that stretching. I did it!!!!!!!!!!!!!

CHAPTER 19

THINGS HAD FALLEN INTO A routine since Clark had been working in the desert and week flowed into week. Saturdays were catch-up days for Clark, and if he wasn't sleeping in, he was running a multitude of errands. Late one Saturday afternoon, he returned from Home Depot only to find Faith jogging in place in the family room like this was the most important thing in the world. He winced knowing just how his knees would feel if he were the one running in place. "What are you doing?"

Joooooggggging."

"Why?"

Panting, she slowed up a little and tried to explain. "I haaave to soooo I won't beee anxious."

It was like pulling teeth, but Clark finally got the explanation out of her. That her speech therapist had repeated to her, yet once again, to expend energy when she was anxious about Emmy being on the road so she wouldn't stress over the possibility of her daughter ending up in an accident, remote as that may be.

That night, Clark had a chat with Emily. "I went online today and saw that they have those mini trampolines at Target. So bring one home with you tomorrow. That way, when your mom has to jog her heart out until you get home, she can at least jog on something more forgiving than the family room floor."

Emily was nodding. "Okay, but I think her episodes of anxiety are becoming a bit more of an issue than they were. I think maybe we need to see if the doctor will give her something for this anxiety."

"Your mom hates taking pills."

"I know, but maybe it would be the lesser of two evils? At least for a while."

Clark acquiesced. "Okay. Let's see what the doctor has to say."

***

Autumn had arrived, kids were heading back to school and life was marching on. Faith was improving on some fronts but not on others. And while she did make considerable use of the mini trampoline when her stress levels spiked, it wasn't enough. She had started taking the prescribed medications but, if anything, the meds made her more anxious than before. When Clark arrived home late one Friday afternoon, he spied his jittery wife standing in front of the concrete wall in the backyard with a can of spray paint in one hand and a look of intense determination on her face. He skirted around the truck and instead of heading for his beer made his way down the driveway. "Whacha doin'?"

"Paaaainting the waaaall."

He glanced around at the discarded cans of paint that he could only surmise were empty because the concrete wall was, well, was almost completely covered with what he could only describe as graffiti. It looked like the Cripes and the Bloods were having it out. "Why?"

"Ittt was uggggly."

She began wildly shaking the can she was holding, then sprayed a swath of bronze arching above an arch of brown that had been sprayed above an arch of gold. Clark just shook his head. If that was a rainbow, it was kind of ugly. But not as ugly as the wall, apparently.

Leaving her to it, Clark had gone into the kitchen and found Emily cutting up vegetables for supper. "What's gotten into your mother? She seems a bit more hyper than usual."

"I'm thinking it's that medication, to help control her anxiety. I think it has the reverse effect on her. It's making her even more, as you said, hyper."

Clark popped the top off his beer and took a long swallow. "What are you saying, princess, the experiment failed? The meds aren't working?"

"They really aren't."

"So what should we do?"

She glanced at the clock. "It's too late to call the doctor now, but," drying her hands she reached for her phone anyway, "I'll just leave a message with his service if they are gone for the weekend. I think we need to have her stop those meds and we'll just deal with the anxiety as we have been. A day at a time."

"If I recall correctly it was you, not so very long ago, that suggested we get her on the meds."

"It was worth a try, but," she held up a finger then left a message for the doctor, "I don't think being wired all the time is doing her or any of us any good."

Clark was so grateful for his take-charge daughter. He took another long swig of beer then headed for his easy chair in the family room.

***

Clark's knees ached as he walked the site and made notes on his clipboard. The week was flying by and it would be Friday before he knew it. His thoughts turned toward Faith. Emily had texted that she was doing much better now that the doctor had pulled her off the meds. Thank goodness. He smirked at the irony: that the old Faith would never have agreed to take the meds in the first place. And she would have been right; they had been doing her more harm than good. Beyond that, he could tell that things were getting a little better. He knew she was working hard with the speech therapist; he could hear the improvement. But she was still exhausted most of the time, had a short concentration span, and he'd noticed that she was losing weight. Probably part of the depression that had descended. She claimed almost from the beginning that most food didn't taste as good as it should. He meant to ask Dr. Wellbrock about that taste thing last time they were there. Guess he'd have to start writing things down as Faith wasn't the only one with memory issues it seemed. Which reminded him; they had an appointment with the neurologist on Friday afternoon. He'd have to head for home early that day.

***

The doctor greeted them both warmly then they got down to business, discussing the results of the test she'd taken a few weeks before. "This wasn't something we scored per se. What it did was provide a baseline." He smiled at Faith then looked at Clark. "I'm going to have Faith take the MMPI2 test again in a few months. This one was kind of a trial run, getting her familiar with the test format and we wanted to see how long it took for her to complete it. Next time around, if she completes it in a shorter span of time, it will give us an indication of her degree of improvement."

Clark nodded while Faith said, "I'mmmm n-nooot looooking fooorward t-tooo thaaat agaaain."

"Well, let's hope it's easier the second time around. Once you take it for the second time, I think will have enough of a track record of your situation that you may be able to apply for disability and start collecting."

Clark looked surprised. "She's eligible for disability?"

"Can she work outside the home and bring home a paycheck?"

They both shook their heads at that. "Buuuut I'dd liiiike tooo, soooomeday. If I weeeere on diiiisability, woooould I ever beeeee abllle toooo work?"

"We can cross that bridge when we come to it. Let's wait until after a few more tests. We'll need that to convince the powers-that-be that you're eligible for disability in the first place. They don't just loosen their purse string if they can avoid it."

"So she'd be getting a monthly check?" Clark was already doing calculations in his head.

"Yes, if she gets it. And I'd say the chances of that are excellent." The doctor cleared his throat signaling a change of subject. "Now, Faith, you have been doing so well with your speech therapy sessions that I am going to suggest another type of therapy for you. Group therapy."

"Whaaaat doooo yooou meeean?"

"It's just what it sounds like—a group of people who all have TBI to one degree or another. They get together and share experiences, expectations, and ups and downs. And I see you shaking your head."

Faith pressed her hand to her heart. "I caaaan't taaalk abooout thiiis with oooothers. It's tooooo peeersonal tooooo meeee."

"These people have been where you are, Faith. They are all at different stages of recovery. I think it would be beneficial."

She was now hugging herself, rubbing both upper arms. "I, nooooo, I'mmmm noooot reaaady fooor thhhaaaat."

"Okay, I won't push it. But I will bring it up again later on."

"Before I forget," Clark jumped in, "I wanted to ask you about the fact that Faith seems to be losing weight. She's just not eating much since the accident and it has me worried."

"Faith?" The doctor turned to her. "Can you say why you aren't eating as much?"

"F-fooood isss juuust nooot thaaat gooooood. S-soooometimes sooomething taaastes gooood. Buuut m-mooostly nooot."

"What do you eat?"

"T-theee uussssual. B-buuuut mooostly craaackers. Thhheeey d-doooon't disssssapppoint."

"This isn't surprising. Sometimes, when a person suffers a brain injury, the taste buds are affected to the degree that food doesn't taste as it should. And so a person no longer eats for enjoyment but just to maintain the organism, so to speak." To Clark he said, "In time, I expect Faith will regain an enjoyment of food and then this weight loss will turn around." Then he turned to Faith and admonished, "But you need to eat a variety of things, not just crackers."

"III kkknnooooow. I'lll trrrryy."

"So like everything else, this is just a matter of time." Clark sounded resigned, drawing the doctor's attention directly to him.

"Now, let's talk about how you," he looked pointedly at Clark so he would know he was included in this discussion, "both of you, are doing."

"It's hard on both of us because I'm only home on weekends with my job out in Lancaster."

"Yes, I recall you've been out there for a while. How much longer will you be there?"

"At least another month or maybe even two."

The doctor was looking at Clark closely as he spoke, reading body language as well as listening to the words. "Do I sense some ambivalence about this job?"

"Ambivalence? No, it's more likely…guilt."

"Guilt?"

Clark sighed deeply not knowing if he should express what he'd been feeling, but Dr. Wellbrock was a good guy, so he dived in. "I feel guilty on Monday mornings because I'm so relieved that I'm taking off for the week." Looking over at Faith he whispered, "I'm sorry."

Faith reached out and touched the back of Clark's hand with her fingertips. Then told the doctor, "I c-caaan unnnderstand whaaaat hee's s-saaaying."

The doctor nodded in encouragement. "Tell him about that."

"Ittt's beeeecause," she looks at her husband, "I f-feeeeel reeeelieved wheeen yoooou gooo awaaay tooo."

Nodding at both of them, Dr. Wellbrock composed his thoughts then began. "Clark, Faith is no longer the same person you married. She is a new person. Some of the old is still there, but a lot of her is new—different. What's happening here is that you two are not exactly strangers to each other, but you no longer know each other. That is why you both feel relief when the other isn't around. When we are around someone new, we are on alert, and being on alert all the time is not comfortable. When we get away from this new person, we relax. So you both are more relaxed when you are alone than when you are together. Clark, you need to start to get to know this new person all over again. Faith, you need to become acquainted with your new developing self as well."

Clark and Faith just looked at each other. Then Clark asked the doctor, "How do we do all that?"

"Step one is to say goodbye to the old Faith. She's gone and you, both of you, really deep down, know that. We've talked before about the stages of a process a person goes through after a tragedy: the denial, the anger, the bargaining, the depression, etc. Grieving is part of that process. All the steps don't necessarily happen in order. They interconnect and they blend with one another. What we are talking about here is grief. Neither of you have grieved the old Faith's passing yet. You need to do that, then the path will be cleared for you to become acquainted and connect with the new Faith. Once you and Faith reconnect on that special intimate level once again, your feelings of guilt will evaporate.

Blinking away some wetness that dampened his eyes, Clark asked, "How do we say goodbye?"

"Perhaps one way would be to sit together and look at some old photos and say goodbye to that Faith together."

What the doctor had said to them made sense, but on the way home, they didn't talk about it. Then both put it away in the back of their minds. Life was rolling along if not smoothly, at least uneventfully. And they silently agreed to leave it alone for now. And another week rolled into another week.

***

Faith, bleary-eyed, poured a mug of coffee. One taste told her it had been sitting on the warmer for far too long. She didn't bother to look at the clock to see what time it was. She didn't care. Looking up at the white board she read:

Hope – call
Plants – water
Cat food
Laundry
Read book
Do math

That last one was what did it. She wrinkled up her nose and decided it was all too much. Placing her coffee mug on the counter, she turned on her heels and headed back up to bed.

Sitting on the bed, she closed her eyes and just let thoughts come to her. She thought about her accident, that ever-present *thing* that lived with her always. She thought about what she was supposed to be doing just to get from one day to the next. And she thought about Clark. What was going on with Clark? He was working so hard, such long hours and days. He was gone so much. She loved him. She missed him. And they barely talked anymore. She opened her log and wrote:

> Alone – came in – figure out – define – survive – heal – all alone – please define marriage.

***

When he pulled into the driveway early Friday evening, Clark was looking forward to being home, popping open a cold beer and just chilling. He sincerely hoped that nothing momentous had happened that he'd be hit with when he walked in the door. Emily hadn't sent a text about anything, so he figured that was a good sign.

"Hey, Chris," Clark greeted Emily's boyfriend when he entered the kitchen. "You on kitchen duty? What's for dinner tonight?" He pulled open the fridge and extracted the beer he'd been thinking about the entire drive home.

"We figured tri-tip on the grill would be nice. I'm just whipping up something to dip our veggies in. Got some carrots, celery, and jicama ready to go in the fridge. And potatoes baking in the oven."

Clark took a long, blessed swallow of his beer. "How did you become such a wiz in the kitchen?"

"Pretty much self-defense. My mom's a lousy cook, plus my allergies. I learned to fend for myself. And I like good food."

"Well, more power to you, kid." Clark saluted him with his beer then headed for his easy chair.

***

It was almost like old times. The four of them sat around the dinner table and filled each other in on their days.

"So, Dad," Emily decided to break the ice, "I assume you talked to the lawyer on your way home today. How did that go?"

"The guy seems to be okay and he was quite optimistic." Clark started ticking things off on his fingers. "One, he'll go for the maximum from that woman's insurance company. Two, he'll go after the car manufacture because Faith's airbag didn't inflate."

Chris jumped in. "That car didn't have a side airbag to begin with, and it was the side of her head that took the brunt of the banging."

"Even so, if the regular airbag was functioning properly, it would have prevented a lot of bouncing around. Anyway, to continue, he's also confident we can go after the construction company, the city of Burbank, and the state of California. He figures even with the conservative climate with juries today not agreeing to huge claims because of injuries that we'll still be entitled to something that will pay the bills."

"So he really sounds like he knows what he's talking about?"

"Oh, yeah. He immediately recognized my frustrations in dealing with the insurance companies. He said they can be one of the most exasperating and wearisome things because they are so expert at stonewalling even when they know they will eventually end up paying."

"I guess a lot of people just give up in time and that's what they are hoping for."

"Well, we're not giving up. We can't afford to give up."

Faith had been listening to Clark and Chris, turning her head from one to the other like she was watching a tennis match. "Won't heeee neeed t-toooo talk toooo meee?"

Clark reached over and rested his hand on top of hers. "Absolutely, sweetie. He asked me to bring you in tomorrow to depose you."

"T-toooo whhhhat?"

"Do what he called a preliminary deposition. Just ask you some questions. He usually doesn't work on Saturdays, but I told him I'd like to be there and weekends were all I had available for the next block of time."

"So, he's doing this pro bono?" Chris wanted to know.

"Well, he'll get a contingency fee of one third, and that's only if we receive a settlement."

Chris swallowed a bite of tri-tip then pointed his fork toward Clark. "I call that a pretty good incentive to get as much as possible."

"I asked him the odds. He's dealt with a lot of similar cases and he gets results. He did admit the results are varying, but he gets results nonetheless. He also told me to start documenting every conversation, every phone call, relating to the accident, to write down the date and time and a summary of each and every conversation. So it looks like we're getting ready to go to court sometime in the future."

***

Joe Lovitt, a tall man with thinning gray hair and ears a bit larger than average, looked over the top of his glasses and shook Faith's hand. "Pleasure to meet you, Faith. Clark, thanks for bringing her in." Looking back at Faith, he continued, "Today, I'll just be asking you some questions. Later, down the road, once the proceedings are more imminent, we'll be doing this again, but much more in depth."

"O-o-oookay."

"Is it all right with you if we record the deposition we're about to do?"

She nodded.

"I take your nod to be a yes?"

She nodded again.

"We lawyers like verbal responses, so once I get things rolling here, please answer my questions verbally."

"Sure, I c-caaaan d-doooo that."

"Great." He started the recording equipment then turned back to Faith. "So let's get started. One thing I want you to start getting used to is keeping your answer as short and to the point as possible. When we get to court, if the defendants' lawyer asks a 'yes' or 'no' question, answer only 'yes' or 'no.' Do not elaborate."

"Ooookay."

"And if the question requires more than just a 'yes' or 'no' response, give the shortest response possible."

"Ooookay."

"All right. Let's go over what happened the day of the accident."

***

The weekend went quickly. On Monday, when Hope drove Faith to her therapy session, Faith told her about the appointment with the attorney. "Thhiiis whooole idea of gooooing to cooourt is giiiiving meee the wiiiilllies."

"I can well imagine. Here's a thought, why don't you sit in on a couple of court sessions. Get a feel for them so it won't be completely new when you end up in court."

"Goood iiiidea. Wiilll yoooou cooome wiiiith meeeee?"

"Sure. But better yet, we should ask Cliff to do the honors. As a former cop, he's been in court before to testify on cases. I think he'd get a kick about going with you."

"Willl heee piiick meeee uppp in the Veeeette?"

Laughing Hope said, "You drive a hard bargain, sis. I'm sure he'd bring the Vette. We'll look in to this and figure out when. Okay?"

"Ooooookay."

CHAPTER 20

TIME FLOWED LIKE A RIVER as day blended into day, and before anyone knew it, Christmas had come and gone. While Emily thrived at her job, her mother was always foremost in her mind. Faith worked hard on the homework the speech therapist gave her, she slept hard, and when she'd had too much and hit the wall, she hit the wall hard. It broke Emily's heart to come home from work and hear her mom in her bedroom sobbing her heart out. That didn't happen every day, but enough days that she did worry about it. Emily's phone signaled a text. Hope was in the habit of letting her know when she'd dropped Faith back at home after therapy, and that's indeed what this text was about: *Hit library after therapy. All's well. F's napping. H.* Emily put her phone away and refocused on her job.

***

Faith rolled over in bed and looked out the bay window. Tree leaves were moving in a gentle dance so she surmised it must be breezy out. She got out of bed and opened the window. Perfect weather. This time of year, you never knew if you were going to be shivering and need a jacket or if it was going to be balmy. Today was balmy. She walked around the bedroom and noticed a laundry basket of folded clothes near the doorway. She guessed that Emily had placed it there, so in the manner of the old Faith, she started putting clothes in dresser drawers. Spying a couple pieces of jewelry on the dresser top, she picked them up. Did Clark give these to her? She wondered. She couldn't remember. She hated that she could rarely remember things. She looked at them long and hard, trying to get a glimmer of a memory. Nothing. On a sigh, she put them away in the jewelry armoire and then noticed the little framed saying on the wall above the armoire. She let her eyes scan the words slowly. Then she went back to the beginning and read them again. Then once again. On the third reading, she pretty much got the meaning.

Opening her log, Faith began to write:

> A framed picture with a saying hangs on my bedroom wall. *He who conforms to the course of the Tao, following the natural process of Heaven and Earth, finds it easy to manage the whole world.* I read those words again and again, pondering. I have trouble managing a day or even an afternoon, or even to prepare a simple meal – Rice Chex for breakfast or a cheese sandwich for lunch I can handle. But beyond that…forget it. How can it be easy to manage the whole world? And why did I think that saying was important enough to frame and put on the bedroom wall in the first place? I do remember my sister telling me about the old me and my beliefs and what she called *The Scriptures According to Faith*. I think this saying must be connected to my philosophies of life. I'll have to think about all that some more.

She reread the words she had written in her log and tried getting her mind around the questions she had asked. Then shrugging, she gave up and started flipping back through her log, focusing on some of the earlier entries.

One entry read:

> Such an illiterate pompous weenie!

She had no idea who she had been writing about.
Another entry read:

Nice thing about a con cuss ion – it screws up your life. So today I will try…to…go slowly – like the special ed student I have become. I don't have class this a.m. as I cancelled. My human body just can't take 2 stressful days in a row – so I will rely on my own – no machines to break down – just clean kitchen cabinets the old fashioned way. No machines – to break down – to ticked off triggers. Triggers! – anything that doesn't work from weed wacker (sp?) to returning defective bra.

She wondered what had broken down the day before that had upset her. Was it the weed whacker? She couldn't recall even writing that entry. Then an entry from November. It read:

Told I need to stretch my comfort zones. So went to Ralph's instead of Vons – really out of comfort zone! Something new. Well…didn't panic…but shopping there took forever – probably because of Thanksgiving shoppers. I should have thought of that before doing this experiment! Cried when I got home for joy of bed & rest. Needed to rest to get the energy to put the food away. So I did it, but too much. I'll stick with the store I know.

A lot of the entries were simply children's books she'd read and recorded there. *Hop on Pop*; *One Fish, Two Fish, Red Fish, Blue Fish*; *Cat in the Hat*; *A Fly Went By*; *The Cow in the Silo*; *Goodnight Moon*; and *A Story, A Story*. Now, that had been a hard one, a lot more words than the previous books, but she had made it through the book. She reread the entry she had written:

This book challenged me. But I got through it and do feel a sense of accomplishment. It's called *A Story, A Story*. It is an African fable of how stories came into the world. The Sky God gave three challenges to Ananse, the Spider man. Once the challenges were fulfilled, Ananse received a golden box of stories. When he opened the box all the stories scattered out to the world. After I finished it I thought about the idea of stories. I think that stories have always fascinated me, but I'm not 100% sure about that. It's more a feeling than a memory. But stories, yes something about stories.

Faith closed her logbook and spent some time thinking about that entry.

As she had been rereading it, a ping had gone off way back in her mind. It reminded her of something, that's what that ping was about, but what? She opened the log again and read that entry one more time. Then another time. Then she smiled as a feeling of excitement welled behind her breastbone! It was as if a light bulb had just been turned on in her head. Pandora's Box. Faith felt a glow of triumph inside her. That story reminded her of Pandora's Box! She remembered Pandora's Box! But what did she remember about it? She concentrated hard and it came upon her like a flower blooming instantaneously in fast-forward motion. She remembered something, something from long ago. It was a memory and it was hers! She remembered reading a book with Hope that their father had given Hope on her birthday one year, and in the book was the story of Pandora's Box. Faith sat still for the longest time as she held her memory to her, embracing it.

Setting her log aside and putting her hand on her stomach, she felt it—as well as heard it—growl. Yes, she was hungry, and as she didn't hear any activity downstairs, she figured Emily wasn't home from work yet. Maybe she should try to get dinner going for tonight. Wouldn't Emily be surprised? But what could she fix? Oh, my goodness! Her mouth dropped open in surprise. Another memory! She remembered one summer day so very long ago when Emily was a little girl and she was hungry. And she kept asking for ravioli. She had fixed her daughter ravioli. That's what she'd do. She'd fix Emily ravioli for dinner in celebration of her memories coming back.

***

When Emily got home from work, she stood in the kitchen doorway and simply stared in dismay at the mess. But she didn't spend too much time goggling at it; the things her mom did she had learned to take in stride. Her mother had all the canned goods pulled out of the cupboards and spread out on the counter. She was moving them all around in kind of a frantic motion like she was desperately looking something. "Mom? What are you doing?"

"Llloooking fffooor sooommething."

"I got that. What are you looking for?"

Faith stood back and literally pulled at her hair with both hands that were shaking with little tremors of anxiety. "A caaan of soooome-thing. Buttt I dooon't reeeemember whaaat. But I wiiill wheeen I fiiind it." There were tears starting in the mother's voice. "Buuut I wiiillll fiiind it. I wiiilll fiiind it." And she started moving cans around again. Then in frustration, Faith made two fists and shook them. "I caaaan't fiiiind it." If Emmy hadn't been there she'd have started throwing cans, but she pulled herself back and just cried out her frustration instead. And the tears started flowing.

Emily stepped up to her mother, gently took her two wrists, and then slowly rubbed the back of her hands until she uncurled them. Finally, she waited until Faith looked at her in the face. "It's okay, Mom. Calm down. We'll find what you are looking for." She pulled a Kleenex out of a box on the counter and handed it to her mom. "Now dry your eyes and blow you nose, then think, a can of what?" Emily reached over and picked up a can of artichoke hearts that her mom often liked cut up in a salad. "This?" She held up the can.

"Noooo.

"Well, let's backtrack. What did you do earlier today that might have brought you here to the kitchen?"

"I-doooon't reeemember."

"So let's look on the whiteboard and see if it will jog your memory of what you did today?"

They both looked at the board. It read:

Therapy – Hope
Mow lawn
Laundry
Matt – gift
Read
Math

"See, Hope came and took you to therapy. I suspect you napped this afternoon. What did you do after your nap?"

"Ohhhh, I wrooote sooomething in mmmmy loooog. Thaaaat's it!" Faith pressed her hands to her cheeks as the memory flooded her. "I wroote sooomething and-and-and…"

"Slow down, Mom."

"And, I had mmmmeeeemories. Of thiiings."

"What things?"

Ohhh. I reeeemembered raaavviioli."

"What?"

She gestured to all the cans scattered around on the kitchen counter. "Raaavviioli, liiike yooooou eaaat."

"Yuck, *Mom*! When did I ever eat ravioli out of a can?"

"Whhhen yooou weeere liiiitle."

"Oh, yuck! Do you mean that Chef Boyardee stuff you used to feed me when I was a kid? We haven't had any of that in the house for years. And, I might add, thank goodness for that."

Disappointment caved Faith in making her sag. "Yooou doon't liiike it?"

"Maybe when I was six. What were you going to do with a can of Chef Boyardee ravioli?"

Faith looked like the air was escaping out of all her tires, deflating them. "I waaas gggoooing toooo fixxx you diiiiner."

"Oh, Mom." Emily hugged her crestfallen mom then stepped back. "You are so sweet to want to fix me dinner. But a can of ravioli will never do. Hey," she was suddenly inspired, "if you want Italian, why don't we go out for dinner? We can at least celebrate the fact that you had a memory of fixing me ravioli when I was a kid."

"Whhheeeere ssshouuuld weeee gooo?"

"How about that Italian place near your old shop. It's got great food and great ambience. And rarely a long wait. What do you say?"

"I sssaaaay, I'm huuungry. Leeet's gooo eaat."

"After you wash your face and brush your hair. And while you do that, I'll text Chris and tell him to meet us there."

***

The restaurant had low lights, soft background music, and great garlic bread. Who could ask for more? The waiter dressed in black and white with a red kerchief peeking out of a pocket asked, "Would you like something to drink."

"Pppinot Grrigio," Faith said. Then she looked shocked. She looked at her daughter and said, "Doooo I drrriiink thhhaaat?"

Emily nodded. "Yes, you do, and it's been a while since you enjoyed a glass so go for it, Mom."

The waiter addressed Emily, "And you miss?"

"Just water for me, thanks."

Chris arrived and slid in next to Emily. "Water for me too, thanks."

When the waiter left to get the drinks, Emily grinned at her mom. "Hey, another memory! Your pinot grigio. Looks like you are on a roll today."

"Thhiiis reeeeally isss a ceeelebration." Faith looked at the menu but only briefly. She put it aside and asked, "Whhhaaat dooo I geeet whheeen weeee arre heeere?"

Emily opened the menu and pointed at something. "This thing with the peas."

"Ssssshhhooould I orrrder thaaat?"

"I guess. That or the ravioli as that's what started this whole adventure to begin with."

"Yeeesss. I waaant raaaavioli."

"You got it!"

"Raaavioli, Chhhris?"

"No, can't handle the cheese. I'll find something."

They placed their order and then sat back. Emily watched her mother sip the glass of wine. Faith savored that first sip then went back for a second one.

"You like?"

"Ummmmm." Faith's eyelids were lowered as if she were transported.

"Good?"

"Ummmmm."

Emily enjoyed her mom's enjoyment of the wine.

"So Disneyland!" Chris clapped his hands once for emphasis. "Emily and I decided you need to get out and have some fun. So we thought next week on one of her days off, we'd take you to Disneyland."

Faith swallowed the sip of wine that was in her mouth and then put her glass down. "Ohhhh, ohhhh, thaaank yoooou, buuut," she was shaking her head.

"But, what, Mom? You love Disneyland."

"Isn't it veeeerrry faaarrr awwway?"

"Well, kind of." Emily suddenly got where her mom was coming from.

"Too much, too soon?" Chris asked.

"I-I thhhhiiiink soooo."

"Mom, it's been months. I think it's time to start stretching the envelope."

"E-Emmy, I-I-I..."

"Mom, it's time to..."

Chris reached over and patted his girlfriend on the leg, his way of pulling back on the reins. "Why don't we start with a place that's a little closer to home for the first time out? What about Universal Studios?"

Emily looked from her mother to Chris and back again. Giving in, she said, "What do you say, Mom? Universal Studios my next day off?"

Faith considered it then nodded. "Oooookkkay."

"And we'll put Disneyland on the backburner for a month or two down the road."

When their food arrived, they all dug in with gusto. At one point, Emily looked over at her mother who was clearly relishing her meal. "I'm so glad you finally started eating again."

"Wwhhhaat doooo yooooou meeean? I eeeaat evvveeery daaay."

"You picked every day for months and months. You said things didn't taste good or tasted bland. You were starting to lose weight. I can admit now, I was a little worried about all that. But lately, you've gotten your appetite back, so I guess food is tasting good again?"

"Yeeees. Annnnd thhhiss. Thhhiis is veeerrry gooood."

Sated, they all sat back while Faith enjoyed the last few swallows of her wine. She looked around the restaurant and actually recalled a time or two when she had eaten here before. And there was that one December when they had the shop Christmas party here. And that brought her shop to mind.

She looked her daughter in the eye and asked, "Whhhy dooon't I haaaave thhhe shhhhop annny looonger?"

"What do you mean?"

"I juuussst waaant tooo knnnnooow whhhy I doon't haaave ittt annny looonger."

Emily took a deep breath. "Well, you and Dad never talked to me much about our money situation, but since your accident, Dad has kind of filled me in. I guess back then, with two businesses, and neither of them making a lot of money, well, it wasn't economically sensible to keep both of them. And as Dad's was more profitable, and yours…well, I guess it was sacrificed for the greater good."

Faith had listened carefully to Emily's explanation, trying not to get lost in the words. "I seee. I guueeesss hiiis business isss moooore impoooortant thaaan miiine?"

"He is the breadwinner, Mom. And, speaking of Dad's work, he's finally almost done in the desert."

Chris piped in. "Yeah, I thought he was going to be finished out there a lot sooner than this."

"Well, the client came up with another addition, another wing, actually. That just about doubled the time allotted for the job. So he's got a couple of months to go. But it all worked out and for the best because it almost doubled the dollars too. I think Dad will actually end up really pleased with the bottom line on this job. And he will be starting next door soon as he's done out there. So that's good."

"Your neighbor wasn't ticked off that his start date was pushed back?"

"No, Gregory and Dad have become pretty chummy. Dad invited him out to the desert one day to show him what he was doing and Gregory was really impressed. And Dad showed me the blueprints for Gregory's house and it's amazing. He's practically tearing down the old house over there and rebuilding from scratch, so that will take a while. And I think Gregory has friends who will like what they see and Dad might get some great referrals."

"Yeess thaaat's allll gooood. Buuut I still wiiish I haaad soooomething tooo."

"You will again someday, Mom. When you get better."

"Yoooou beeelieve thaaat?"

"I do. Especially now. Today, some more of your memory came back. So it's a good day!"

Faith started to say that there was still so much missing, but she didn't want to burst her daughter's optimistic bubble, so she kept her own counsel.

Emily smiled at her mom but noticed that while she had appeared happy for a while this evening, she was looking sadly introspective again. She held back a sigh, not wanting her mom to know that she was starting to feel a little melancholy too. Faith's brain injury was starting to wear on all of them. Thank goodness Hope, Cliff, and Chris were all around to help when necessary. If it was all on her and her dad to keep things floating at home, she didn't know how they would continue to manage.

That night, after Faith went to bed, Emily texted her dad: *Mom had little meltdown today. But okay now. Love, Princess.*

Clark answered: *Glad you are there for her. Be home for the weekend tomorrow night.*

CHAPTER 21

FAITH HAD GONE TO BED early but had been jerked awake from a horrible nightmare. She had dreamed of being trapped in a labyrinth. The tangled false paths that turned this way then that way only to be dead ends had panic closing her throat. She couldn't swallow, she could barely breathe as she started running down one path only to have to stop and then she'd backtrack and try another path. She was trapped with no way out and was on the verge of a scream of frustration and fear when her eyes had popped open. She sat up in bed, literally clutching the sheet to her chest, feeling her heart race against her fists. Taking slow deep breaths, she looked at the clock. Not even eleven o'clock. By the time she had fully calmed down from the dream, she was wide awake and no longer the least bit sleepy. So she got up, picked up her log, and headed downstairs. She curled up in her comfortable chair in the family room, and opening her log wrote:

> I don't often have bad dreams, but this one frightened me. I was lost in a maze and couldn't get out. Perhaps my subconscious mind is telling me my struggle with my brain injury is like being trapped in a place with no exit. But I do feel there is an exit! I do! I have been working so hard to find that exit. If my subconscious is telling me it's not there, then there is something wrong with my subconscious!

Putting her pencil down, she reread what she had written. Nodding once, she closed the log and started to put it aside, but something stopped her. She reopened it and began reviewing the journey she'd been on for the past several months. One entry read:

> Too much – Darn it! Lunch with Hope. No nap. Crowds & by 5 ocular migraine. Could feel the overwhelming (ness) happening. By now, all these months later, I should be able to spend the day with Hope or a friend. Guess that's why TBI's have to go to therapy! Just keep gardening. Calm – maybe grow own food to save money? Get therapy!

And then there was an entry where she was trying to describe what depression felt like.

> Depression is so, well, depressing. Today I'm not so depressed so I can try and explain it. Trying to find yourself and pull yourself out of it is so nearly impossible. It's like looking at a treasure map that is upside down. But you don't know it is upside down. X is you. The treasure is you. And you have to find the treasure to get out of the depression. But…when you are depressed deep down inside and you want out but you don't know the map is upside down, there is no way to find the treasure and get out. It's perspective.

Just reading it confused her now. She wondered if it had made sense to her when she wrote it. Another entry said:

> I yelled (really cursed yelled) at Clark last night cause I couldn't turn on the TV – a hello – could I be more pathetic?

After reading that particular entry she wrote underneath it:

> I'm really tired of being broken. Need to find a way to see the future – these journals show me I am a wreck.

Another entry gave her pause. It read:

> When I was in therapy today having a melt down about all the frustrations I face on a daily basis, Cheryl said, "This too shall pass." I surprised myself when I realized I had heard that saying before. I knew she was quoting something. "This too shall pass." And what a powerful quote it is. I thought about it all the way home and I am still thinking about it. "This too shall pass." All things pass. Someday this horror that I have been going through will pass. I look forward to that day.

***

Emily tiptoed into the house, glad that Lola didn't bark when it was her. She and Chris had gone to a late movie for their Valentine's date and she didn't want to wake her mom by making any noise, but it looked like her precautions were unnecessary. The light was on in the family room and, upon investigation, she saw her mom sitting up in her comfortable chair by the gas fireplace with a throw over her legs coloring in a book.

"Homework?" Emily asked.

"Allllways."

"Can't sleep?"

"Duuuuh."

"Wow, you're quite the conversationalist tonight."

Faith looked up and smiled at her daughter. "Gooooood movie?"

"Yep." Then they both laughed because Emily was mimicking her, answering in kind, with a truncated response. "Did Dad call today?"

"Heee diiiid. I also goooot theeee caard heeee seeent innnn thee maiiilll. And dooon't thhiiink I dooon't knooow whoooo rem-mmiiiinded himmmm of Vallllentttine's Day."

"Guilty." Suddenly Emily had an idea. "Head's up, Mom!" And she tossed her mother her car keys. Looking up, Faith's hand shot up and she caught the keys just before they hit her in the face. "Good reflexes. Come on."

"Whhaaat?"

"It's been, what, nearly a year since you've been behind the wheel of a car?"

"Ittt's noooot a yeeeaar!"

"Well, a few months shy of a year. It's time to start driving again. Come on, chop-chop."

Faith started shaking her head in panic. "I-I-I'm n-not geeeting beeeehind the w-wheel of a-a c-car."

"Stop it, Mom!" Emily's voice was firm. "Stop stuttering."

"Ittt's noot stttuttttering. It's caaallled spppeeeeech dyyyysfunction."

"Then stop panicking! There is no time like right now to give driving a whirl. It's just you and me and it's late, so there's no traffic to speak of. Remember when you taught me how to drive? We always went late at night, and you let me drive to the parking lot at the market where there were no cars this time of night and we practiced there? That's what you and I are going to do now. So, come on."

"E-Emmmmyy, nooooo. Itttt's toooo laaate."

"No, it' not. It's only five blocks to the store and no main streets. Well, you just have to cross that one main street. Come on." She took her mother by the arm and literally pulled her out of the chair. "It's just like falling off a horse, Mom. You got to get back on or it will never happen."

"What iiif it's alreeeady tooooo late?"

"Bullpucky."

"I'mmmm nnnoooot drrreeeessed."

"You're wearing sweats, Mom. That will work." And taking her mom's hand, she led her from the room and out into the night.

By the time they made it the five blocks to the market parking lot, the flop sweat sliding down Faith's back had reached the top of her butt. Once in the lot, she tipped the rearview mirror down and looked at herself. Yes, the reflection confirmed what she already knew. There were rings of wetness on her sweatshirt under her arms.

"T-taaalk about sweeeating like a piiig."

"Do pigs sweat?"

"Theeey must or wheeere diiid that saaaying come from?"

They spent the next twenty minutes driving around the empty parking lot, making turns, backing up, parking, and pulling out of parking spaces and just generally letting Faith reacquaint herself with the basics. "Okay, Mom, take us home now."

"Fiiinally."

"Oh, stop it. You did great and you know it."

"I doooo know it. I always was a goooood driver."

"We'll do this some more at night the first few times before we tackle daytime driving. But you're going to get back to driving, Mom. This is LA for cripe's sake! You gotta be able to drive."

***

Hope pulled up to the curb behind the city bus that was disgorging passengers. "You sure you don't need me to come in with you?"

"No. Dr. Wellbrock said the teeest would taaake at least twooo orrrr three hooours. Maybe more. Remember last tiiime when I took it. I was there allll day and had to fiiiinish the next daaaaay. Soooo, just gooo home. I'll callll when I've finished."

"Okay, then. Just remember what I told you last time you took it. Don't overthink the questions. Just go with your first instinct."

"I rrreeemember."

"Good." Hope chuckled.

"Whhhaatt's soooo fuunnny?"

"Do you think having you take the test on April Fool's Day has any significance?"

Faith just gave her sister a squinty-eyed look and stepped out of Hope's air-conditioned car into a blast of hot air and exhaust fumes. "Iffff it's ooonlly juuust Apppril, it shhhoulldn't beee soooo hooooot."

"Wait!" Hope hollered and held out a paper bag. "Don't forget your peanut butter sandwich."

Faith took the bag and also grabbed her bottle of water in the holder. "Thaaanks. I probably will get huuungry beefore I'm doooone."

Hope watched her go into the building and stayed put for a few more minutes. Faith had been making remarkable progress. But she also did a lot of backsliding. She'd be going along fine, then suddenly forget something she hadn't forgotten in weeks. For example, she hoped Faith didn't get confused when she got on the elevator. What if she got off on the wrong floor? She'd been there often enough. She should be fine. Shouldn't she? "Oh, phooey," Hope said to herself and then called the office. When the receptionist answered the call, Hope gave a little laugh. "Hi, this is Hope, Faith's sister. I just dropped Faith off at the curb and wanted to make sure she made it to the office."

"She sure did. We just got her settled in the room to take the test."

"Okay, sorry to bother you. I'm just a mother hen. Be sure to give me a head's up when she's finished."

"Will do, Hope, I've got your number right here."

That settled, Hope pulled away from the curb and headed to the mall to do some shopping.

Faith sat in the little room at Dr. Wellbrock's office taking the MMPI2 test for the second time. It was more taxing than hard. She knew she had taken the test before, but none of the sentences seemed familiar to her at all. It was like she was taking it for the first time. She had to read each sentence three or four times before really figuring out what the sentence actually said. Once she had that figured out, she had to determine if the sentence was true for her or false for her. "I like mechanic magazines," she read in her mind for the third time. Well, how would she know if she liked them? She never read them. So she guessed that was a false. Dutifully she marked an "F" by the sentence. The next sentence was also a false, in fact, definitely a false. She didn't even have to think about that answer. It said, "I wake up fresh and rested most mornings." Ha! It had been a long time since she had woken up fresh and rested. One question was, "I would like to be a singer." Well, she had been singing in the shower, when she knew nobody else was in the house, ever since Cheryl told her it would help with her speech. And wasn't that a kick? She didn't remember words to songs per se, but somehow, she'd just start singing and the words came out. But, back to the test question, did she want to be a singer? No, she did not. So, that was another false. And then, "I used to like drop-the-handkerchief." What the heck was drop-the-handkerchief? She hadn't a clue. So that was another false.

Looking back at what she had accomplished so far, she wondered if it was wrong to have so many false answers. Should she go back and read them again to be sure? No, she could hear Hope telling her to go with her first guess. *Just leave them be and soldier on*, she said to herself in her head. Next question, "Evil spirits possess me at times." Ah, no, another false.

She looked up at the clock and sighed. She wasn't even halfway through the test and so much time had passed. She got up, used the restroom and sat back down at the table. She took a swig from her water bottle then picked up her pencil. She'd be here all afternoon at this rate.

After finishing the test, she was shown in to Dr. Wellbrock's office. "Good afternoon, Faith. I know the test took a lot out of you, so we won't spend too much time chatting today. Just a few minutes. How do you think things went with the test?"

"Cooonfusing, sometimes. Do yooooou know it asks theeee same question different ways again aaand again?"

"Such as?"

She thought for a moment. "One question asssks, did yooooou like your father? Another question laaattter asks, did your father like yooouuu? Sheesh!"

Dr. Wellbrock applauded. "Bravo, Faith! Short-term memory seems to be making a come back."

Smiling, she reached over and patted herself on the shoulder.

"But, for the record, that's not exactly the same question."

"I know."

"Okay, shifting gears from the test, how are things going in general?"

Nooot bad. I'm sttiill seeing the speeech therapist thrree days a weeek."

"Yes, I can hear the improvement. There's still some hesitation there, but you are really coming along. Do you realize the improvement?"

"Yes. I've beeeen wooorking hard. Haaarder than I ever haave beefore in my liiiife."

"Indeed. I know it's hard work. And you are clearly dedicated. So for the time being, I think you should continue on with the therapy, but what do you say to dropping it down to two days a week?"

She thought a moment and started shaking her head. "Noooo…"

"Faith, you need to push the envelope here, move out of your comfort zone to get better. You are in a comfortable rut and it's time to shake things up. I think three days a week is too much at this point. It's time to challenge yourself in other ways."

"Wh-whaaaat ways? Hoooow?"

"Well, let's talk and see what we can come up with…stop looking so uncomfortable. You trust me, don't you?" She nodded. "Good, so let's talk."

"Oookkkay. Yoooou taaallk."

He chuckled. "Maybe it's time to start looking for a part-time job."

Faith, thoughtfully, considered what he just suggested. "I haaave beeeen thinking about getting out offfff the hoooouse and dooooing something."

"Good. Start thinking about that harder, and then maybe begin looking around to see what develops. Now, what about at home? How are things there?"

"I haaaave my rooooutine: I taaaake waaaalks, read chiiiildren's booooooks, keep nooootes in my looog, do gardening."

"Speaking of your log," Dr. Wellbrock picked it up off his desk and handed it back to her. "I read your entries while you were taking the test. I noticed every so often there are different variations on the same theme of *Who am I?*" He used his fingers to place quotes around the phrase.

Faith nodded. "Yeees. Sooometimes, especially when I fiiiirst waaaake up, I have an aaadjustment period, fiiiiiguring out where I am, who I am. Not asssss muuuch assss at firrrst. Buuttt itttt stttill haaappens on occcccasion. It's coooonfusing," was the only word she could think of. "I liiive in the laaaand of unceeertanity. A place whh-here anythiiiing caaaaan haaaappen." She smiled a sad smile. "I don't thhhhink I'm inn Kaaansas anymore."

"And I am very impressed!" The doctor once again applauded her.

"Why?"

"What did you mean when you said, 'I don't think I'm in Kansas anymore?'"

"It's liiiike Dooorothy in *The Wiiizard of Ozzzz*."

"Exactly. You remembered that all on your own. Things are coming back to you."

"Yes," she agreed. "Theeey are."

"When a person sustains a head injury, so many things happen, as you are well aware. There are physical, mental, emotional issues that all demand your attention. One thing in particular that happens is that the voice in your head—the I, your ego—becomes disengaged. This is not necessarily a bad thing. But it is a disorienting thing. You've been juggling all these issues, and slowly but surely, pulling yourself back to you."

"I know. Fooor sooo long siiiince the accident, my life seeemmed just two-dimensional, but now it's getting better. But I'm still not able toooo doooo what I used tooo do. I used too doo soo many thiiiings. And now I dooon't. I meeeean, I have gooood daaaays, but those baaad days. Sooome daaays, I stiiiiill just cry and cry and caaaaan't get out of beed."

"We've talked about this before, Faith. That depression is a very important part of the healing process. The trick is we don't want you to be stuck in this stage of recovery for too long."

"I knooow. But I caaaan't help it soooometimes. The anger and the bargaining! I'mmm still in thhhoose staaaages tooo."

"Tell me."

"Wellll, it's tied innnn with the anger. Yooou feel the anger coming and yooou don't know how to sttttoop it. You lose yourself, yooour faith and your hope. Yooou don't know whaaat tooo grab on tooo to save yourself. Oh, God! Yooou pray! It has nothing toooo doooo with putting a bench dooown and kneeling. Yooou pray to any entity goooood or baaaad. It is the moooost lonely place on earth!"

"You've expressed this very clearly, Faith. I think you realize that healing is a process of layers and layers of gaining courage and believing in yourself again."

"I doooo get that."

"I am wondering if you need to try some medication again to help keep you on a more even keel?"

Faith began shaking her head.

"When the body is constantly on the flight or fight alert, that's not good. Medicine helps force the muscles down, the blood pressure down, the adrenalin down…"

"Nooo, thhhhanks, Dr. Welllllbrock. No medicines, please."

"Are you still breaking crockery?"

"Nooot sooo much aaanymoooore. I'm stttillll angry, buuuutt, not soooo mmaaany ttteeeemmper tantrums."

"Have you ever considered forgiveness?"

"What doooo you mean?"

"Once you are able to forgive the woman who caused the accident, your healing process will leap forward."

"But? Hooow do I forgive?

"That is a question for the ages, isn't it? I think it is different for everyone. But regardless how it happens, it is something you need to start thinking about. It is very important, Faith, to get to that place of forgiveness."

"Whaaat she did tooo meee makes meee so angry. It burns right here." She pressed a fist to her breastbone. "It's liiike an ever-burning fiiire that juuust seems tooo get hotter each daaay. How dooo I fooorgive her for stealing myyyy life away frooom meeee? I *hate* her!"

"Figuring out how to do that will come to you in time. For right now, I think we need to backtrack a bit and talk some more about your depression."

"It's soooo easy just toooo dissolve into tears. It's hard on meee. Nooot just me. It's haaard on Clark too. I try not tooo let it haaaappen too often. But I doooon't have the cooontrol. Sometimes, it's just easier toooo stay in beeed and cry."

"But that you do eventually stop crying and get out of bed is what matters. Think about those things you used to do that you mentioned earlier. Maybe you need to try to start doing one or two of them again."

"Weeelll my shoooop is sold. Soooo I caaan't doooo that again." She paused to think. "I used toooo taaaake pictures."

"Photography?"

"Yes."

"I don't see why you shouldn't start taking pictures again. Get back into that. Doing things we enjoy in life is what keeps us interested and interesting. It might help you withstand the urge just to cry and stay in bed at times. Depression happens when we are stuck. We don't want you to be stuck. So next time that urge hits you to weep the day away, get your camera out and start taking pictures."

"Good iiiidea."

Faith was setting up her next appointment with the receptionist when the waiting room door swished open. Hope breezed in and said, "Oh, looks like perfect timing. You ready to roll?"

"Yes. Let's geeeet oooout of here. Noooo offense," she added for the receptionist's benefit.

"None taken." She waved to the women as they escaped out the door.

Hope started the engine and turned the air on full blast before giving Faith her full attention. "So, how was the test this time around?"

Faith just shook her head. "Itttt was drraaaining. I'm juuust glaaad it's over."

"Do you want to talk about it?"

"No. I juuust want tooo goooo hoomme."

"Then, let's go home."

Hope dropped Faith off and saw that she made it into the house amidst Lola's happy welcome home barks, then she took off.

Faith's first stop was the bookcase in the family room. She pulled the album off the shelf that held photographs she had taken on various trips here and there around the country. She sat on the couch, slowly turning pages and looking at each picture in turn. It was like becoming reacquainted with an old chum. Wow! She was a really good photographer. She could admit that to herself. And when a little ping of memory went off dealing with mixing chemicals in a darkroom, she found she could almost smell the smells of such rewarding work as developing her pictures.

After ascending the stairs to her room, Faith dug around in the closet until she found what she was looking for. She pulled out the camera case and her tripod and laid them both on the bed. She opened her case and took out a lens. She found she was caressing it the same way she caressed Crestline. The joy in her heart painted a smile on her face. She had something to look forward to again.

GRIEVING

Tears are the silent language of grief.
—Voltaire

CHAPTER 22

FAITH AWOKE TO THE SOUND of the demolition going on next door. It was a happy, productive sound, and it put a smile on her face. This was a part of the construction process that Clark loved. During this stage, he was just like a toddler who would belly-laugh with glee when he knocked a tower of blocks over with a chubby fist. Tearing down was just as much a part of construction as the actual erection of the building was. She thought Clark loved that first stage because it represented all the possibilities wrapped up in a new beginning: punching holes in walls, leveling this, flattening that, making space to rebuild something new and fresh.

She thought about the fact that you couldn't have the building up without the tearing down and a river of words poured into her head. Sitting up in bed, she reached for the nearby log and wrote the thoughts she'd been having because isn't that just what had happened to her since the accident? First, the tearing down, and then the building back up? She wrote:

> I feel like I am a house that suffered incredible damage in an earthquake. So much of the structure knocked down, support beams broken, roof caved in. But then, little by little, slowly but surely, I am being built back up again. Not exactly the same, but stronger and better than before. Yes, the tearing down and the building up of things, so very natural. Decay and rebirth. It's all in the cycle of life.

She put the log aside and lay back on the pillow, listening to the sounds that awakened those thoughts inside of her. Clark doing his thing. She remembered past jobs, past times, when Clark would come home so charged up from a day of demolition that they'd fall into bed giggling like a couple of kids who hadn't a care in the world—their lovemaking being silly and easy those times. She rolled over in bed, lying on her side, and ran her hand up and down the cool sheets on Clark's side of the bed. When was the last time they'd made love? She couldn't recall. Their marriage had become like a stagnant pool of water with nothing fresh flowing into it—just this ever-present painful coexistence since the accident. Both of them were so sad and unhappy by what had happened; and both were at a loss to know how to move forward from it. Lord, how she missed his hands caressing her flesh.

She recalled other lovemaking times, too, when that sharp edge of intensity accompanied their coming together—those times when their mating had been that of a male taking his mate in the most primal sense. The excitement of those experiences was literally primitive it was so deep and wide at once, so intense that it was the true cement that bonded them as husband and wife. And the night their daughter had been conceived. It had been one of those rare and beautiful perfect couplings. Even years later, when it was brought to their minds, they would do a fist bump in the air in celebratory memory of that most perfect of nights.

How long had it been, Faith wondered? How long since they had come together in passion or even just for closeness or comfort? She couldn't bring it to mind. She did, however, recall what Dr. Wellbrock had said about how she was a different person. Maybe Clark didn't like the new Faith. Maybe he was no longer attracted to her? Or maybe he was still so in love with the old Faith that the new Faith didn't have a chance. How does one compete against oneself or at least one's former self?

The word grief tiptoed into her head. The old Faith was gone, as dead as if she'd died in that car accident. She'd been struggling with her new self; Clark must surely be struggling with that as well. The doctor had said they needed to grieve the old Faith's passing.

She realized she had been doing just that, in her own way, when she was alone to shed tears and bemoan the loss of herself. She'd break dishes as anguish washed through her then clean up the mess before her family got home. Then, lately, chide herself and tell herself that she had to stop throwing things, breaking things. She had to get used to the fact that she was a whole new person. She had been saying goodbye to little pieces of herself for weeks now. During one teary afternoon, she had boxed up the novels on the two upper shelves in her walk-in closet that she had read in the past and hoped to read again sometime. Reading which had been such a pleasure for her had become a chore and was no longer a part of who she was. Suddenly realizing that she'd never again be the voracious reader who would curl up with a book on a rainy day, she knew it was time to say goodbye to those books. After her speech therapy one day, she'd had Hope drive her to The Salvation Army store to drop them off. She experienced a little shift inside her when she passed the box over to them. Was it relief she felt? She wasn't sure, but she did feel lighter as they had driven away.

She had also discovered in recent days she'd started turning to comfort food while she grieved. Things had tasted so bland for so long after the accident, and now they didn't. She'd stepped on the bathroom scale last night before bed and her eyebrows had flown up almost off her forehead at what she'd read. She wasn't fat by any means, but she had packed on some pounds. She'd given herself a long, hard look in the mirror, thanking her ancestors for the genes they had blessed her with, as she was a tall woman and could handle a little weight without looking too robust. *So,* she thought as she lay in bed listening to the job-site noises next door, *I grieve and comfort myself with food, and where is my husband in all this?*

Still lying on her side, her eyes focused out the bay window where she could see leaves trembling and the branches of the trees swaying in a gentle breeze. Things were warming up now that Easter was behind them and spring was here. Spring? Already? Didn't she have her accident in the spring? She turned back the pages of her mind and thought about that. Yes, it had been in May. The middle of May. And her whole summer and fall and winter had been taken up with the trauma and the drama of the car accident, her brain injury, and attempting to find some equilibrium again after the accident. Poof! Nearly a year gone in the blink of an eye. Time was moving on, and she and Clark had to find it within themselves to move on too. Move on together toward somewhere other than this place where they had landed. She wanted her husband back. And for that to happen, he had to join her in grieving the passing of the old Faith. Now that he was home from the desert, it was time to take that step. And still, she hesitated in asking him to share the grief with her. Grief seemed like such a personal thing. She was doing just fine wallowing in it all herself. She didn't really want company and, yet, grief shared is grief halved. She had read that somewhere and even written about it in her log.

Sitting up in bed with a resolve that it was time to do just that, share the experience with Clark and get him through his grief too, Faith started planning what to do. *A ritual*, she thought. On Sunday when Clark wouldn't have work as an excuse to escape from this other work that was not only necessary but vital to their marriage. They needed to get on with their grief if they were to move forward in their relationship as man and wife. Her phone dinged. The text from Emily. Faith flipped open her journal and wrote:

> Heard from Emily. Took her almost an hour to get to work, as usual. I'm getting better. Didn't have to jog this morning, but still was worried in back of my mind. Not like it was when I got so antsy and the fear so slowly and painfully crawled up the spine. I learned to deal with it and to exercise. But when I get the text, my relief is immediate! Even when, like today, I wasn't really aware I was stressing just a little. It is so unfair for Em. But she is safe, my day can start.

Over dinner that evening, Faith told Clark that on Sunday, she wanted him to go through some old photos with her and then when

214

they were done, she wanted him to dig a hole in the backyard where they could bury them.

Clark looked at her with suspicion written all over his face. "And why would we be doing that?"

"Don't yoou recall thaat Dr. Welllbrock said we neeed to bury the old Faith and grieve foor her and thennn we move on wiiith ourrr liiiives?"

Clark slid back in his chair as if removing himself from the conversation. "Oh, please." He reached for his beer and upended it draining the last half of the can in gulp after gulp.

Faith watched the muscles of his throat move with each swallow. "He did saay thaaat. Don't yoou remember?"

Heaving a sigh he nodded. "Yes, I remember. Doesn't mean we have to do everything that man says."

"Hee's helping mee, Clark."

On a softer sigh, Clark reached out and patted his wife's hand that she had reached out across the table toward him. "Yes, I know he is."

"Heee said grieving is a noormal proocess that relieves soorrow and heelps us to adjust."

"Okay, okay. If you want to do this silly thing, we'll do it. I don't know what good it will do, but we'll do it."

And so they had. Not much had changed between them since that day. But that step had been taken. And while Clark hadn't shed tears as she had when they'd gently shoveled the dirt over the photos of the long-gone Faith, she had noticed out of the corner of her eye that his chin had started to tremble and wobble and that he'd firmed it by clenching his teeth. So he had been touched. He had been moved. And maybe, just maybe, he would find some way to grieve some more.

***

Whenever Faith felt the world closing in on her, she would grab her camera and start walking. She never got lost anymore. Sometimes, she walked for miles, but she knew her landmarks and could orient herself. Hills to the north, freeway to the south. She slipped into the rhythm of the city as she walked the streets and avenues and boulevards. She would snap a picture of a crack in a sidewalk that had a wildflower growing out of it. She'd come across a bunch of wild parrots in a tree and got that on film. She'd spotted an artfully arranged flower bed with a cat curled up asleep under the leaves of a shrub and had taken a picture of that. She came to think of her city as being both complex and simple at the same time. She spent more and more time immersed in it. It was always in motion. Cars. People. Animals. Even at night, when stars winked on the city ebbed and flowed. She remembered the expression "The Cosmic Dance" from somewhere and she began to think of her time out in the city with her camera as her opportunity to record bits and pieces of that dance.

And while her ramblings were mostly a pleasant interlude in her day, on one occasion, she came face to face with the reality that her accident would always be with her. She was simply walking past a parked car when it happened. A woman sitting behind the wheel of her car was digging for something in her cavernous purse when her elbow hit the horn. The blast was loud and long, and it caused Faith's adrenalin to spike as the flight or fight instinct blasted into action. The woman had been startled as well by the sustained honking. She finally pulled her elbow away from the offending horn and looked around. Spying a shaken Faith, she gave a little shrug, making a gesture with open hands, and mouthed, "Sorry." Then she went back to looking for whatever it was in her purse.

The woman had managed to put the incident behind her that quickly. Faith on the other hand, stood rooted to the spot on the sidewalk and realized she was trembling from head to foot. She had been tossed back to the day of the accident. She stood there, reliving in her mind's eye every moment from looking up and seeing the car coming at her, to seeing the other driver looking so surprised, to being pulled back to consciousness with a worker in a hard hat calling, "Lady, hey lady. Are you okay?" As the woman in the car pulled away from where she'd been parked, Faith watched her go with tears streaming down her face. A nearby house had a thigh-high stonewall abutting the property. Faith sat on the wall and tried to regulate her breathing, which had accelerated along with the adrenalin. And while in a few moments she was able to slow her breathing, her tears continued to fall unchecked. It was then that a police car pulled up to the curb. An officer got out, and skirting around his car, walked up to Faith.

"Ma'am? Are you all right?"

Faith nodded. One hand pressed to her lips to keep her chin from wobbling. "Yeess."

"What happened? Were you assaulted?"

"Whhaaat? Noo. It's juuust…"

"Just what, ma'am?"

Faith cleared her throat and swiped the palms of her hands over her cheeks wiping off most of the moisture. "P-posttrrraaaumatic stttrrress." Then she gave a little laugh, and in her halting way, explained to the officer about her accident, her recovery process, and the blaring horn.

It turned out the officer knew Cliff. He'd been a rookie when Cliff had been riding a desk at the precinct. That established, he offered Faith a ride home. Still being shaky from the experience and getting close to a blood sugar crash, she took him up on his offer. She got home, made a toast, and slathered it with butter and peanut butter and wolfed it down. After a second piece of toast, she felt less shaky, more herself. The rest of that day was uneventful. But her experience that morning hung in her mind like a dark cloud. The accident wasn't in the past. It was in the ever-present now. It was never going to be over. She would always be just one short horn blast away from being tossed back to the moment of the accident. She'd gone upstairs to her bedroom and stood in front of the portrait that Emily had painted of her. *Lost*. She was no longer as lost as she had been in the months after the accident, but she now knew that post-traumatic stress could hit you when you least expected it. Knowing she had to learn to live with that too, that was the kicker. Days and weeks passed. She remembered the horn and the stress and the residual horror of it. But that didn't stop her from walking through her city and taking her pictures. It only made her more determined not to let herself be held back by what had happened to her all those months ago.

One afternoon, she spied a sign in a store window. Help wanted. She went in, inquired about the job, and filled out an application. Leaving the establishment, she knew she wouldn't be getting that job. When she got home she wrote in her log:

> So very embarrassed! After so long you'd think I'd be used to making so many mistakes – but damn it – a simple form – checked the wrong box! Just to remind you, I am supposed to find a job. If I can't be trusted to check the right box! DUH! No, I'm trying to get a job, - BUT I'm no longer trustworthy. Yes, I'm ethical, honest & smart; but now I make so many mistakes. What KRAP! Better get in the habit of taking applications home and having Clark checkmark everything. Oh God! Helpless! Helpless! A year later and it's still too much!

One day, during her rambles, a porcupine surprised her as it waddled out from under a bush, crossed the sidewalk, and then continued on its way across the street. Startled though she was, she was enough of a professional to bring up her camera and snap a series of pictures. Only after it had disappeared again on the other side of the street did she wonder where it had come from. She'd seen possum around here before but never a porcupine. Were they even indigenous to the area? Maybe it had snuck out of the LA Zoo, which wasn't all that far away. Regardless, she had proof that it had been there. She slung the strap of the camera over her shoulder and continued walking through her city.

Later that day, Faith wrote in her log:

> I saw a porcupine during my walk today so when I got home I looked it up in my animal *Medicine Cards* book. One thing a porcupine represents is faith! Ha, what a synchronicity! So I saw that as a pretty good sign that I am on

the right path with my struggles in dealing with my brain injury and my venture back into photography. And maybe the porcupine is my new totem animal as it is representative of my name, Faith. I certainly have needed the ability to move mountains to recover from my injury.

***

More days and weeks flew by. The anniversary of the accident came and went, and Faith felt that the milestones she'd achieved over the past year were all positive. And yet, she still struggled with speech, although less so. The biggest thing currently in the forefront of her mind was that she continued to feel the distance between Clark and herself, and she didn't know how to bridge that.

The house next door was metamorphosing into a huge thing that looked so out of place in the neighborhood it was almost laughable. But as Clark said, this guy had friends and cousins that were all buying up houses that they wanted renovated, so he was giving it his all. He'd already done bids on two more houses in Glendale and it looked like he'd landed them. And yet, while the business was starting to hold its own once again, life at home was, well, not much to write home about.

Faith thought back on the ritual she and Clark had shared weeks ago. Beyond that experience, they didn't talk about their respective grieving processes. But Faith wasn't about to give up. She was hatching a new plan to help them along with getting through and beyond the grief. She just didn't know how to broach the subject with her husband. *Give it time*, she told herself in her head. *An opening will arrive and all you have to do is take advantage of it when it does.*

Later that evening, before bed, Faith wrote in her log:

> Napped this afternoon. Re-energized. Walked to store for exercise. Planned nice dinner. Quiet evening. Feel accomplished for helping family.

CHAPTER 23

HOPE HAD GOTTEN INTO THE habit after her therapy sessions of letting Faith take the wheel and drive them home. They'd take detours through little neighborhoods and drive the city streets and avenues, giving Faith practice behind the wheel. After they had graduated to boulevards, Hope told her, "We'll try the freeway next."

"I don't thiiiink sooo."

"Oh yes, we will. You can't live in LA without dealing with freeways."

So today, after therapy, a cruise on the freeway was on the agenda. Faith got behind the wheel of Hope's nifty Honda Accord. She buckled her seatbelt and checked her rearview and side door mirrors.

"Come on, stop stalling. Let's get on the 134 and see where we end up."

Faith rested her hand on the gearshift but didn't drop it into drive.

"It's not even noon, sis, so there won't be any traffic."

"There's allllways trrrraffic."

"You know what I mean. None to speak of—no traffic jams, no gridlock. Let's do it and then we'll have lunch."

Turning onto the onramp and blending into the traffic heading toward Glendale gave Faith that déjà-vu-all-over-again feeling. She'd certainly been-there-done-that before. Things went smoothly for a few miles. "Let's get in that lane," Hope pointed, "and get on the 2 to the 210 and head up to La Cañada."

Faith pulled into the lane that Hope indicated and as the free-way ascended and curved up, up, up over the city, her heart acceler-ated. "Ohhhhh noooo. Oh no!" Panic had her by the throat; all she could think of was that they were going to fall, they were going to slide off this concrete bridge that arched so high, so terribly high, as it curved away from the nearby shrub-covered hills to the right and you could see the tops of palm trees down below on the left. "Ohhhhh God!" Her hands and arms began to shake as adrenalin pumped through her system.

"Faith, you're doing fine, calm down." Hope grabbed her sister's forearm to still the shaking of her arm. "Just concentrate on what you are doing. Get your foot back on the pedal. You're slowing down too fast. That's a hazard. Just keep going. You got this."

Hope's voice penetrated Faith's fear and cleared the fog that had started to descend over her eyes. She couldn't stop shaking, but they made it over the high, curved bend in the freeway, and once on the 2, she headed for the nearest off ramp. Getting off the freeway and pulling over to the side of the road, she slammed the car into park. "Ohhhh God! I-I-I never waaaant to driiive over that part of the frr-rrreeeway ever again!"

Now that they were stopped, Hope asked, "What happened? Why the panic attack?"

"I thhhought weee were going tooo fall off. The way the road was curving, it's tipped oooover almost on its side, and I thhhhought weee were going to fall off into the treeeetops I could see below."

Hope knew better than to use logic explaining that the engineers knew what they were doing when they built that overpass. Logic had no place in a conversation with a person who had just experienced panic. "Better now?" She asked. "No more panic?"

"Better?!?! Noooo I'm not bettttter! Paniiic is like a viiiice that grabbbbs you! And sends suuuuch a fear upppp your gut yoooou have nooo control…It's just frrrreekin' luuuuuuckkky we goooot off the freeway alive!"

"Then, let's just sit here a minute so you can acclimate."

After a few moments, Faith placed her hand on her abdomen. "I think myyyy blooood sugar is crrashing. That sooometimes happens when I panic. I neeeed food."

"See that stop light? Turn left there, go about a block, and another left into In and Out Burger."

Unbuckling her seatbelt and reaching for the door handle, Faith said, "Yoooou drive."

"Oh, no, you don't." Hope pulled her back. "You don't get off that easy. You drive."

"Noooo!"

"Yes!"

"Drive!? Try geeettting bloated, gassy, and irrrrritable and all that cooomes along wiiith all that paaanic. And with alllll that goooing on, *you* try driving!"

"I hear you. Now, drive to the light and turn left."

Needing food and knowing an argument would take too much time, Faith bumped the car out of park and into drive and complied.

Faith wolfed down her double-double and fries like it was the last meal she'd be eating. When her blood sugar crashed, she needed to get food into her stomach pronto. As she shoveled the burger in, her equilibrium started to return.

"Are you going to need more?"

Faith shook her head. "Nooo. I'm better noooow."

"You're still a little pale, but I think you'll survive."

Sitting back from the remains of her meal, Faith shook her head. "Thaaat was harrowing."

"But you did it! You made it. So look at it as an accomplishment."

"Just sooo you knoooow. I'll be taking siiiide streets from now on. No mooore freeway."

"That's what you think." But Hope didn't say those words out loud as she knew her sister wasn't ready to hear them. Instead, she said, "Don't let that little scare stop all the progress we've made with you behind the wheel. Cliff told me that he was going to let you take the Vette out next time you guys come over for dinner. You know, a little spin up into the hills."

"Really? He said he'd let me drive it?"

"That's what he said. So you guys better come over soon so we can hold him to that."

***

One July day, Faith stumbled across the desk drawer full of unpaid bills. She looked at them one at a time and tried doing the addition in her head. That didn't work. Never good at math to begin with, it was almost impossible now to add long columns of figures even with all the math homework Cheryl made her do. Another search through another drawer and she came up with a calculator, and after a few minutes ended up with a good idea of how deeply in debt they were.

Flipping through the rolodex, she found Joe Lovitt's number and called it. When the receptionist answered, she asked to be put through and was surprised when she was.

"Yes, Mr. Lovitt, this is Faith Kinnnncade. Yoou are representing mee in the car accident case?"

"Yes, of course, Faith. How can I help?"

She gave a little self-conscious laugh. "Yoou can help by getting us a big settlement. Hooow long is this process going to take?"

"Well, things do move slowly, but we have served the city, the state, and the construction company. We have also named the woman who was driving the other car as a defendant. Her insurance company has just gotten a hold of us, and told us that all they can be held liable for is the maximum allotted in her policy and that they are willing to pay the max if she and they are removed as defendants in the lawsuit. I had it on my calendar to call Clark and let him know this good news."

"When will wee bee getting the money?"

"First, we have to remove them as defendants. I would be remiss as your representative if I didn't let you know that the chances are you might actually be able to get a little more out of them than what the policy says, but it would entail a battle and, realistically, you might not get enough more to make it worth the while. I was going to suggest to Clark that he take the money and then we focus on the other defendants."

"Yes, yes. I'll talk tooo my husband and wee will let yoou know. Thank you so much."

"Of course, Faith. Is there anything else I can do for you at this point?"

"I, I don't think sooo. Again, thank you soo much."

"Not at all. But before we say goodbye, as long as I have you on the line, maybe we should set up an appointment for me to depose you again. This time, it will be a more thorough deposition as we are going to start gearing up for court."

"Okay. But not on my speech theeerapy days."

"Which are?"

"Monday and Friday."

"How about a week from Tuesday at 2:00 in the afternoon."

"Do you have a morning time? I'm better in the mooornings."

"A week from Thursday at 10:00?"

"Yes." Faith wrote it down on the desk pad and hoped she would remember to put it on the whiteboard.

After hanging up, Faith picked up two fistfuls of bills from the drawer. "Yes," she crowed. "Yes! Yes! Yes!" Jumping up she tossed them into the air, doing a happy dance that resembled no kind of formal dance anyone had ever seen.

"What's this all about?" Clark asked from the doorway. He was wearing a quizzical smile watching his wife, who was on her hands and knees, picking up the mess she had made.

"I just spoke with theeee lawyer. The insurance company iissss goooing to pay. So we can coooover some bills."

The weight of the bills tumbling off Clark's shoulders had him sagging against the doorframe. "Really?"

"Really!" She was still kneeling on the floor looking up at her husband with a glow on her face he had not seen in a long, long time.

***

Sunday found Clark sleeping in. It was a luxury he rarely indulged in during the week, but weekends were different. He rolled over and discovered he was alone in bed. That would explain the running water; Faith must be in the shower. Then he heard it. He sat up in bed with a grin that split his face nearly in two. Was she singing in the shower? Tossing the covers back he tiptoed to the bathroom door and stood outside of it with his ear all put pressed to the wood.

"The old folks say / That ya gotta end your date by ten / 'But if you're out on a date / Don't you bring her home late / Cuz it's a sin.' / You know there's no excuse / You know you're gonna lose / You never win / I'll say it again / And it's all because your mama don't dance / And your daddy don't rock 'n' roll / Your mama don't dance / And your daddy don't rock and roll…"

"Well, I'll be!" She remembers Kenny Loggins "Your Mama Don't Dance"? Clark couldn't believe his ears. "When she's singing, she doesn't stutter or have to stretch out her words. Hmm? Who knew? And," he looked at Crestline who was sitting prettily by her food dish, waiting for it to be filled, "I'm talking to myself." Then it hit him like a ton of bricks. This time deliberately addressing the cat, he said, "She remembers the words to the song?" He listened closely. Yeah, she didn't have a radio on and he sincerely doubted she had sheet music in the shower with her. She was singing a cappella. From memory! He pumped his fist in the air. Things were looking up. Today was going to be a good day, he just knew it.

Slipping out of the underwear he slept in, Clark entered the bathroom and stepped into the shower with his wife.

***

"You want to do what?" Clark almost exploded with surprise. And to say he was aghast would not have been a mistake.

"I think we neeed to re-affirm our vows."

"You mean get married again? Good grief, girl, it was stressful enough the first time around. Why do we have to do that all over again?"

"Because the girl you married nearly twenty-five yeeeears ago is gone. And I am here. I neeeed for you to marry me. The *me* who I am now."

Clark tossed the rumpled sheet away and got out of bed. What a *climax* to their Sunday morning lovemaking. He raked both hands through his mussed up hair, making it stand on end as he looked back toward his wife who lay on plumped pillows looking like a cat at the cream bowl. Well, he'd also felt like a cat at the cream bowl before she'd punctured his after-coitus high with ah, he guessed it was a marriage proposal! Thinking of cats, he looked at Crestline who was still sitting by her bowl. He upended a box of Friskies into it and looked back at his wife.

Unable to help herself, she started chuckling. "Guess I tooook you by surprise."

"Yeah. I guess you did."

"Well, think about it. It's not the worst iiidea I've ever had."

"But why?" was all Clark could think to ask.

"Because I'm a new person, Clark. I want you toooo want tooo be married to that new person."

"Can I have some time to just think about it?"

Feeling generous she said, "Sure. Taaake all the time you need."

CHAPTER 24

FAITH COULDN'T FIGURE OUT WHY the attorney appeared to be upset with her. She was keeping her answers short like she'd been told, she was doing everything right, and yet he seemed miffed. Finally, she confronted him. "Is something the matter? Yooou seem upset with me."

Dropping the pencil he held, he pushed the tablet he was writing on away and stood up. "I want you to watch something." He pulled down a projection screen, clicked a button, and there before her eyes she saw herself during their first deposition months ago. She watched in shock at how pale she was, how shaky. When the recording was over Joe said, "Now, that was convincing! That was a woman who is shaken, haggard, unable to speak coherently—obviously a victim who deserves recompense. What do I see in front of me now? What I see is a stunning woman, dressed to the nines, who hasn't one hair out of place, and with makeup that is so tastefully applied it takes away ten years without appearing to do so. That, my friend, will never do!"

Faith hadn't been scolded so severely since she was a child. "But-but, I've worked soooo hard toooo get to this place. For more than a year, I've struggled and fought for every inch of recovery I've made!"

"It's a place that won't convince a jury that you deserve any payout. For God's sake, try and get the stutter back at least. And maybe dress," he wiggled his hands in the air, "frumpy."

A thunderstruck Faith merely stared at the attorney. "Frumpy? Frumpy! I dress woooomen for a living. Or at leeeast I did. I'm not going to gooo out of my house looking frumpy! And I worked soooo hard on my speaking, I won't go back to-to that." She threw her hand out toward the projection screen. "I'm nooot going to pretend I am back there. It would be dishonest."

"Look, Faith, don't get me wrong here. I truly hope you do make a full and complete recovery. But as far as the jury, don't lose the speech impediment too soon. We do have the videos, both mine and your speech therapists, but the real thing speaks volumes in court. Do you want to be convincing to a jury or not? And just for the record, dressing like a fashion plate isn't going to cut it. Go for little brown wren, not gilded swan."

Leveling him with a look, Faith pointed out, "Look, the fact that the woman's insurance company paid us the max should cooonvince them the accident wasn't my fault."

"Exactly. What the defense will claim is that it does nothing but prove the accident was *all* her fault. They will claim they were just innocent bystanders."

Faith was unconsciously scratching the side of her head that had suffered all the damage in the accident. She spoke softly. "Maybe it was all her fault."

"Faith, stop shooting our case in the foot. Your husband took pictures of the construction zone. There's plenty of evidence that the woman's clear vision was blocked and that driving there was a hazard. The construction company should have had men or women with stop signs controlling traffic as opposed to letting the traffic lights do the work. Now," he stopped pacing, sat back down opposite her, and pulled the pad of paper in front of him, "are you ready to get back to work here?"

***

When Faith got home, she opened her log and wrote:

> I hate that I have to prove that I'm not faking it. Just because I'm not a drooling…whatever, I have to prove something! Joe is nothing but a bulldog, bully, bullying attorney! It's all about

him! It was never about me! I naively thought
he would protect Clark and me. But it's all about
him!

Closing her log, she sighed. That didn't really get her anger at
Joe off her chest, but it helped a little bit.

***

Faith was in the family room, standing in front of her bookcase and
reading the titles of the books when she heard Lola start barking, the
front door open, then Hope's friendly, "Shut up, Lola."

"I'm back here, Hope."

Hope crossed the family room and stood next to her sister who
was still looking at the spines of the books on the bookshelf. She
thought about how much Faith had loved to read and how now reading was such a struggle for her. Oh, she was doing okay with her
children's books that her speech therapist required her to read. She
had graduated from the little, little kids' books to grade school level.
But even after all this time, too many words on a page and Faith lost
herself in the verbiage. In the beginning, right after the accident, a
part of her suspected Faith didn't even realize that she'd been robbed
of the enjoyment of reading. But after she'd taken a box full of books
to The Salvation Army a few months back, she realized that Faith
was slowly coming to grips with her new limitations. She watched as
Faith reached out and caressed the spine of a book as her eyes travelled over the title.

Hope finally asked, "What are you doing, sis? Getting ready to
box these up too?"

Faith picked up a book and looked at the cover then put it back
and looked at another one. "History." Faith ran her hand along the
spine of several books on one shelf. "They are history books. I know I
wasn't a history teacher. Why do I have so many boooks on history?"

Hope looked at the shelf of books where Faith's eyes were
focused. The books lined up there all had to do with the William the
Conqueror and the Battle of Hastings in 1066. "No, you weren't a

teacher, but history was kind of your thing. You were an art history major in college, remember?"

Faith cocked her head and considered that bit of information. "Yes, I remember that. But why all these books on 1066? Is that art?"

"You did your master's thesis dissertation on the Bayeux Tapestry. Which is all about the Battle of Hastings in 1066." Hope made a sweeping gesture at all the books on that shelf. "We all thought it was really weird that you chose that particular piece of artwork to do your dissertation on as you were such a pacifist and the tapestry, in part, was depicting the horrors of war."

"Hmm. That does sound like a paradox. Did I ever say why?"

Hope thought back. "I recall something you said back then. It didn't really make sense to me. You said, 'When I study the tapestry, it brings me right to the verge of…something…a revelation of something. I don't know what, but, someday, I will.' That's what you said. As you never in the following decades revealed what that revelation was that you were on the verge of, I guess it never revealed itself."

"Hmm?" Again, Faith shook her head. I don't remember any of that at all." Running her finger along the books' spines, she randomly pulled one off the shelf. It was an oversized coffee table book full of photographs of the Bayeux Tapestry. She flipped through a few pages with a little frown on her face as she looked at the pictures. "This is what I studied?"

"Doesn't ring a bell looking at it?"

"Noooo. Not really."

"Come on, let's sit down and look at it together."

The sisters sat side by side on the couch, turning pages and looking at photographs of the tapestry. After a while, Faith made a little humming sound in her throat.

"What was that all about?"

"I-I've just been trying to figure out why I chose to write about the Bayeux Tapestry."

"I don't think simply looking at pictures of the tapestry will help you figure that out? Do you?"

"Maybe. I don't know."

"Here's an idea." Hope got up, went back to the bookcase, and ran her hands along the bookshelf until she found what she was looking for. "Here! Your dissertation."

Sitting back down next to Faith, she opened the book. "Read it and maybe you'll be able to figure out why you chose to study it and write about it."

Looking at the size of the dissertation, a snicker caught in her throat. Taking it from her sister, Faith flipped through the hardbound tome that ran almost sixty pages in length. "I can't read all this."

"I know. But let's just look at parts of it. Like the title and table of contents."

"Okay."

Hope opened the book and pointed to the title. "Read this. You can read kids' books, so a title shouldn't prove to be too much of a challenge."

"*The Bayeux Tapestry – History, Stooory, Art: Three Strands, One Braid.* Wow, thaaat sounds like an impressive title even to me, who supposedly wrote it."

"You did write it, silly. Now, let's look at the table of contents page. See, you've got all the blah-blah-blah stuff, approval page, abstract, dedication, and then what the paper is all about. Part I is the Introduction. Part II is the History. Part III is the Elements of Story: Protagonist and Antagonist. Part IV is the Elements of Story: Irony and Symbol. And Part V is Art as Truth."

Faith's eyes were shining.

"Here." Hope passed the book to her. "Try reading the abstract. It's not too long."

Faith's eyes traveled over the first line of words, then the second line. Then she went back and tried again. Finally, shaking her head she passed the book back to Hope.

"Did you get lost in it?"

"Yes. It's tooooo much."

"What if I read part of it to you?"

"Read it? Now?"

"Just the abstract. That gives an overview of the whole paper."

"Okay, why not?"

Hope cleared her throat and began: "'The Bayeux Tapestry depicts a historical event in a work of art that is nearly one thousand years old. During those thousand years, stone and mortar edifices have been built and have crumbled, and still the tapestry survives. There are many messages here; history is only one of them. The tapestry, which is a tapestry in name only, is in reality an embroidered piece of linen portraying a chain of events that changed the course of history. The word *history* has the word *story* built right into it. So we need to take a larger view of the tapestry and look at it not only as history but also as a story told in thread. This is a lovely irony because we do follow the thread of a story when we read a novel or watch a movie. So here in this extraordinary work of art we have the thread of the story embroidered in actual threads: symbolism that is tactile as well as intellectual.

"This story has both a protagonist and an antagonist as most stories do, but which character is which? Ironically, while for hundreds of years most viewers of the tapestry have agreed that it is from the Norman point of view, celebrating William the Conqueror's conquest, making him the hero of the story, in recent years, another view has come to light. I, like historian Andrew Bridgeford, contend that the tapestry was actually created in England across the channel from where it now resides in Bayeux, and that it shows the English perspective of events before, during, and after what is clearly an invasion.' There! The overview of the dissertation."

Eyes shining, Faith stammered, "I caaaan't believe I wrote that."

"You did. Says so right there. That's your name, if I'm not mistaken."

"Wow." She took the book from Hope and just caressed the front cover. "I was pretty insightttful. Wasn't I?"

"Yes, you were. But that was just the abstract. As I haven't read this before, I can't confirm that it was just as insightful all the way through."

Faith laughed as her sister's teasing. Handing the book back to her she asked, "Will you read some more?"

"Okay, let's read more. 'What makes this work of art even more fascinating is that it has endured for nearly a millennia. No other textile can make this claim. There are those who think The Shroud of Turin, a length of linen cloth believed to be the burial shroud of Jesus, is older. But science says no. The shroud has been radiocarbon dated to the medieval period. So while that still makes it a remarkable seven hundred years old, it is not the oldest surviving textile. The Bayeux Tapestry is a one-of-a-kind survivor.

"Keeping with my premise that we are dealing with a story here, let's consider stories. Most are told with words, but this one is told with pictures. Like a modern-day comic book, there are plates and each plate (picture) has an explanatory phrase, a caption, above it. But unlike a comic book that tells a story on pages that need to be turned, breaking up the sequence of events, this work of art shows the events on a flowing tapestry that is reminiscent of a river of time.'"

"Stop!" Faith held up one hand like a police officer directing traffic while the fingertips of her other hand rested on her lips. "Reeead that again." Her words came out almost in a whisper.

"Unlike a comic book that tells a story on pages that need to be turned, breaking up the sequence of events, this work of art shows the events on a flowing tapestry that is reminiscent of a river of time." Faith sat so still Hope wondered if she had turned to stone. "Faith?"

Faith held up a finger halting any more words from her sister. "Wait." She was thinking and her mind was whirling at about a thousand miles an hour. "Thaaat's it." Again, her words were almost a whisper as if she were in a sacred place. "Thaaat's it. The revelation thaaat I knew would come to me."

"What?" Hope couldn't contain her excitement. "Tell me! Tell me!"

Faith's hypothesis manifested itself as she spoke. "Just like the tapestry, only different. It's whaaat kept pulling at me but I wasn't able to grasp it."

"What?" Hope could feel Faith's excitement and yet marveled that she was also concurrently so calm.

"This is just like Cheryl said. She said that at some point, a window would open in my mind and I'd make a quantum leap through it. And that's whaaat just happened. I remember it all now. I remember the research, the writing, the trying to grasp something thaaat was just beyond me and now…I have it. I haaave it."

"Are you going to share?"

"It makes so much sense. It's sooo huge, and yet it really doesn't change anything at all. It just…is."

"Faith! Spill it!"

"All of eternity is a river of time. Like you just read. That's what triggered my revelation. All events already exist, now, outside of time. Just like this tapestry is all of a piece, so is all of history in eternity all of a piece. Everything exists and is happening now. Everything exists and happens simultaneously—like the tapestry exists all in one piece in the now. But when we incarnate, we leap into the river of time, and then that dimension, time, sweeps us along in the river of the tapestry of eternity until time ages us, we weaken, and eventually are pulled out of the river of time—out of the tapestry of eternity and back into the ever-present now. Then, we, as a spirit or an entity, taaake a look at the immense tapestry of eternity once again, and once again, make a new choice and leap into it again and swim in a different part of the river of time."

"Wow, Faith. You just bowled me over. I'm…flabbergasted. Flabbergasted because it actually sounds, and I'm not trying to condescend here or sound like an idiot, but it sounds right. For some reason, what you're talking about here reminds me of that Shakespearian passage about *All the world's a stage and all the people merely players.* You know, seeing your tapestry of eternity, like reading a script, and then jumping into the fray and acting out what you've just seen."

Still hypothesizing, Faith continued. "Yes. Yes. So, extrapolating further, what happens is meant to happen because it's already happened; it's already part of eternity's tapestry—for want of a better word."

"And this is where some brainiac philosopher will start a debate with you asking, where does that leave free will if all eternity already exists in a huge *now?*"

Shaking her finger in the air, Faith said, "Believe it or not, I just wrote something about that in my log." Never far from her, Faith flipped open her log. "Here." She handed it to Hope. Faith's entry read:

> I stumbled across this passage today when I was on my computer looking up something completely unrelated and I can't stop thinking about it. It's a saying by Carl Gustav Jung that says: *Free will is the ability to do gladly that which I must do.* I wonder what made him say that? It is almost a negation of the concept of free will, and yet, is it? I guess I'll have to put some more thought into this.

Hope set the log aside and looked at her sister. "Wow. To me, it looks like some kind of synchronicity is happening here. You coming across that passage, then your revelation based on the tapestry."

"And you see what is so interesting is that whether my revelation is a truth or not is immaterial. Life as we know it will go on the same way, and only once this life is over will we ever know if what just hit me is the way of the universe or not."

Hope waved the log under Faith's nose. "Regardless of whether the revelation is a truth or not, I think it is very much a part of *The Scriptures According to Faith*, and you need to write it all down here in your log before it fades and is lost."

"Good idea. I'll doooo that after you take off."

"Which has to be soon, but, hey, shifting gears here, I never asked how things went with the attorney."

Faith frowned. "I don't know. He isn't happy that I'm recovering so quickly. He says a jury will want to see me as a broken woman instead of a woman who is bouncing back from adversity."

"What!?"

Shaking her head, Faith brushed it all aside with one hand. "I don't know. Maybe he's just being a good attorney and doing his job. I haven't decided about that yet."

"Well, his office contacted Cliff and me. We are going to be deposed as character witnesses. So I guess this thing is really getting in gear. Court, here we come?"

"And on that note, Cliff and I never did arrange to go to court to see how a session goes. Remember we talked about that? I think we need to get on that before I have to take the stand to convince a jury that I'm entitled to recompense for my injury."

"You're right! I'll have him give you a call."

***

After Hope had gone home, Faith sat on the couch for a long time with her dissertation on one side of her and her log on the other side. She thought about her revelation, about the river of time flowing through the tapestry of eternity and the idea of fate vs. free will. And she thought about her accident and the woman who had smashed into her car, altering her life. Was all that meant to be? If it was, what about forgiveness? Did the inevitability of an occurrence make forgiveness moot? Or did it make it all the more necessary?

Faith picked up her journal and started writing:

> If someone steps on your toe and says, "Oh, forgive me." You'd say, "Sure, think nothing of it." Is that really forgiveness? No it's not. Forgiveness is only truly forgiveness when you can forgive the unforgivable. But understanding that intellectually and being able to actually forgive are two different things.

After reading what she had written, she picked up her laptop and typed *forgiveness* into the search engine. More than she could handle at a time always came up when she typed in a word or a phrase, but she'd pick and choose what she wanted to focus on. What she saw during this search was a quote by Mahatma Gandhi. She opened her log and wrote some more:

LOST

Mahatma Gandhi said: *The weak can never forgive. Forgiveness is the attribute of the strong.* So now I have to wonder about strength too. Am I strong enough to be able to forgive the person who did this to me? I don't know if I am.

Closing the log, Faith sat and pondered Gandhi's words for a long, long time.

CHAPTER 25

Faith kept fidgeting on the hard bench seat. It was hot, it was stuffy, and she was having a hard time concentrating on the proceedings and an even harder time breathing. The courtroom was not only airless, but there were no windows to open to let fresh air circulate. The voice of the judge, which has been droning on, was suddenly being drowned out by the buzzing that had started in her ears. Her breath caught high in her chest and the word *claustrophobia* tiptoed across her mind. Unexpectedly, it seemed as if the walls were starting to close in on her too. Cliff rested his hand on her knee and whispered, "Are you okay? You're starting to fidget and to breathe funny?"

Feeling pins and needles starting to race up her arms, she mumbled back, "Blood sugar crash," and stood up, brushing past his knees to get into the aisle. He was right behind her, reaching for her upper arm as she stumbled out of the courtroom door. He sat her down on a nearby bench. Blowing out her breath, she bent over at the waist, resting her forearms on her lap and tried to regulate her breathing.

"What do you need?"

"Food, something to eat. Not sweets. Crackers."

Cliff spied a vending machine and headed in that direction. There were some crackers with peanut butter in them, so he opted for those and got a bottle of water while he was at it. Then he watched her like a hawk while she wolfed the first two crackers then nibbled at a third, sipping the water as needed. She was as pale as he'd ever seen her. When she started breathing more normally, he asked her, "What the heck happened in there? It was more than just a blood sugar thing. It looked like a panic attack."

"I don't know, maybe claustrophobia. There were no windows. Everything seemed to be closing in on me. Great Scott, I'm a wreck!" She held out one hand and watched it tremble. "I didn't know I was claustrophobic." She took a few more nibbles on the cracker. "Hooow am I ever going to get though days and days of the upcoming trial when I can't even sit in a courtroom for ten minutes without freaking out?"

"It's early days yet. You have plenty of time, probably months, before your case comes to trial." He rubbed a comforting hand over her back. "That's why we're doing this now, to get you acclimated to the environment. So what can we do so this doesn't happen again?"

She held up the cracker, "I think food. It seems like the adrenalin that shoots into my blood when I start to panic acts as a catalyst, causing the blood sugar to crash. So if I have something to nibble on, that will prevent the crash. Theoretically."

"Good to know. I think they probably frown on food and drink in the courtroom, but we can smuggle something in. Stash it in your purse so you can nibble and no one will be any the wiser." He looked at her closely. "Do you want to go back in there now?"

She shook her head. "Nooot today."

A couple weeks later, they decided to give it another go. They stopped by Trader Joe's first and got a bag of sesame sticks. She transferred them from the cellophane bag that crinkled and made noise to a zip lock plastic bag and put it in her purse. The sesame sticks were small enough to conceal in her hand. She was good to go.

When they got to the courthouse, she used the restroom, drank some water, and took a few deep breaths.

"Ready?" Cliff asked her.

"Let's do it."

He held the door for her and she entered the courtroom once again. This time, things went more smoothly. She was now prepared for the fact that she'd be sitting in a windowless room, listening to whatever case was on the docket for the day. The bailiff announced the judge, everyone rose, the proceedings began, and time passed.

Faith sat in rapt attention; the case was fascinating. A woman was suing her ex-spouse for alimony payments. The kicker was she'd never had alimony, but she'd had child support until the youngest had gone off to college. It turned out both her sons were grown men, married with children, and with good paying jobs of their own. And her youngest child, the girl in college, well, the father was paying that portion of the tuition that wasn't covered by the girl's student loans. Faith was curious as to how this woman thought she was entitled to alimony now that child support was a nonissue? Her attorney had argued that she had spent her entire life raising this man's children and had no skills, so it was up to him to provide for her.

Early on, during the proceedings, Cliff had kept a sharp eye on Faith. But there had been no evidence that she was about to have another panic attack or blood sugar crash again. During the first half hour, she dipped into her purse and snuck out a sesame stick every now and then. But once she got into the trial, she hadn't needed that crutch.

When the court recessed for lunch Cliff asked Hope if she wanted to stay or to head on back home.

"It's like a soap opera, Cliff. I want to find out how this thing ends."

Over lunch, they discussed the difference between this case and the one she was involved in. Cliff pointed out, "You notice that this is not a jury trial. The judge is making the decision."

"I noticed that. But it's still giving me a sense of how a court session is run."

"On a different note, I hear you've been driving yourself to therapy sessions these days."

"Yes. That little beat-up car Clark got for me can get me there and back."

"But?"

"It's draining to drive alone. But I'm doing it…mostly. I canceled my session Monday because I didn't want to drive there."

"And Friday's session?"

"I'll go. I know I can't skip too many."

After lunch, they waited outside the courtroom until it was time to reconvene. And it turned out that the show was going on out there too. Faith had always had good hearing. Eavesdropping had been a hobby for as long as she could remember, so it was no hardship to listen in on the goings-on. The ex-husband's attorney approached the other attorney and the woman who was suing her ex. He said, "My client is willing to offer you $10,000 if you drop the suit now before the judge makes a pronouncement." The woman actually laughed at that and walked away, disappearing into the women's restroom. When she emerged the ex-husband's attorney approached her and her counsel once again. "Last offer before we reconvene. My client is willing to pay you $20,000 cash today, right now, if you drop the case before the judge reconvenes." Faith was interested to see the woman in a huddle with her attorney. They were whispering so she couldn't hear a thing that was being said. But if body language was any indicator, the woman wasn't impressed with the offer.

Faith, her water bottle in her purse notwithstanding, got up and headed to the water fountain that was in closer proximity to where the woman and her attorney huddled. She pretended to drink but the smell of the water that arched up when she pushed the button was enough to discourage anyone from drinking it. The woman was saying, "A mere $20,000! At the $2,000 a month I'm asking for, that's less than I'd get in a year. I want alimony for life! No way are we taking that offer." The woman's attorney advised her to reconsider. He pointed out that there was no way to know what the judge was going to decide. This offer was a sure thing and it was not to be taken lightly. The woman adamantly refused to deal. "They are negotiating because they know the judgment will be in my favor. They wouldn't be offering this if they thought they were going to win. No, no, and no!"

Back in the courtroom, Faith once again sat in rapt attention, waiting for the judgment. And it wasn't long in coming. The judge pointed out to the woman that her sons were raised, were out of school and had jobs. Then he pointed out that her daughter's education was being taken care of. Then he hit home the zinger that she was an able-bodied woman in the prime of her life and she had no need of any alimony whatsoever. Faith was not surprised by the judge's decision, but she watched the woman who sat in stunned silence. As soon as the gavel came down and court was dismissed, the woman made a beeline toward her ex, saying loud enough for everyone to hear, "Okay, I'll take the $20,000." The man laughed in her face and walked away.

Cliff dropped a pensive Faith off at home and sped off in his Vette. She entered the house to the joyful barks of Lola and suddenly remembered she had turned off her phone in the courtroom and had not turned it on again. Hitting the on button, she saw she had a text from her friend Susie B: *Coming down tomorrow to be deposed as a character witness for you. Lunch?*

Faith's fingers flew over the keys as she responded: *Yes! Lunch!*

***

The restaurant had an al fresco area and, as the weather wasn't too scorching with a slight breeze to make things feel even better, Susie B and Faith had opted for that rather than sitting inside. Each had a glass of white wine and they were sharing a plate of fresh veggies and dip for an appetizer.

"But how did you get there?" Faith wanted to know. "How did you get to that place of forgiveness? I mean, compared to what happened to you, that little bonk on my head is nothing, and yet, I can't do it. You've had umpteen surgeries since your accident and more to come over the years. Don't you just hate the guy?"

Susie crunched on a celery stick and thought about it. "Hate him? No. Am I still angry with him? Yes. A person can remain angry with someone or be angry about something and still forgive."

"Really? It seems counter...whatever."

"Forgiveness is simpler than most people realize. It's just a decision. You decide to let go of all the resentment, poof, let go and it's gone. It doesn't mean that what the other person did to you is okay. But what happens is this: you forgive the person, not what the person did to you. Does that make sense?"

Faith's full concentration had been on Susie. But she was still shaking her head. "I don't know. You make it sound easy, but this isn't easy for me at all. I guess I'm just carrying such a grudge against her. She altered my entire life. I am no longer the same person. And that's not fair. I mean, this one woman gets off work early because she is sick and it set off a chain reaction, just my freakin' luck and I ended up broken!"

Susie listened to her friend with a smile of compassion on her face that was almost beatific. "I understand. Believe me, I do. And the broken Faith would never be able to say that this woman never intended to get off work and screw up a life. But guess what? That woman never intended to get off work and screw up a life." She gave a little shrug and held both hand out, palms up. "I've been where you are. I know what it's like to be broken, literally. I had every bone in my body broken in that car crash. I suffered in ways that are almost beyond anything another human being could comprehend. I carried my grudge. I lived and breathed that grudge, and one day, I realized it had taken root. It had taken over my life and, at that point, with that realization, I made a conscious decision. My life is mine to live and I was not going to let someone else, something else take charge. I realized I was so wrapped up in what had happened to me that I was missing out on all the good stuff in my life. My husband, my kids. I needed to reclaim my life and to do that I had to forgive."

"How did you do it?"

"I took that first step. And that was to stop looking at myself as a victim. I came to accept what happened. And you can come to acceptance too. Come to acceptance and embrace the change that has been forced upon you. Look at us, Faith. Look at us! Here we are, two gorgeous women out for luncheon, sipping on expensive wine and living the high life. It's all good. Don't let that woman take any more from you than has already been taken. It's time to take it all back. And, at the same time, it's time to let it go. Forgive her and move on."

CHAPTER 26

Log Entries

Feb 10

Washing the kitchen floor I realize how my life has changed. I used to be too busy living to really clean the house. Now I live to clean. Darn it! That's not why I went to college!!!!!

March 16

Okay, Hope, here's another tunnel I need help arriving at the end. One of my math problems asked, "If school starts at 8:30, and it takes a half hour to get there, what time do you leave?" Now I know the correct answer is 8:00. But I reply, "You watch Hobo Kelley until 8:15, then run like hell and get to school on time and your parents aren't the wiser." So as I'm going down this path, I smile, remember how much you and I liked her (Hobo Kelley) and figured we're 4/5 or 5/6th grade? Can't quite grasp the year. And I don't recall the other sister (whose name we do not mention) being there when we run to school.

So…the last time I remember her walking to school with us is 1961 and the fire. I remember being told to stay, saw smoke, told to run, shut up – and the police showing up in class & the p. station on either Verdugo or Oceanview. Now I've jumped from '61 to '64 or '65. But that's the path of filing.

So after fire, did we always walk alone? What were the Hobo Kelley years? And what form of punishment did she whose name we do not speak get for being a junival (sp?) pyro?
WELCOME TO THE BRAIN!

Mar19

Tax time and trying to help Clark. Such a chore! So many papers are lost. I'm putting in an hour a day looking for stuff. Anymore than that I loose lose? focus on other stuff. I'll leave water running cause I was washing dishes, but get distracted and go clean fridge. Or (darn it) left fire on the stove again! Better to putter in garden peacefully than burn down the house.

Hard to focus with the loss of Meghan (although it's been months and months), but must get taxes done.
Focus
Focus
Focus
I can do this!

May 15

I drove to therapy yesterday. Driving is pure tension. I am unable to relax. Every muscle screams in pain. Driving used to be so relaxing

and adventurous. Now it is a form of torture.
Then Cheryl had me do math. Another form of
torture for me. She tells me I need to do it for
my brain. It will give me a sence (Good grief! I
know I spelled that wrong!) of accomplishment –
still can't spell! Know that word is wrong, but, oh
well! I hate being the slowest student. Being the
slow student is humbling. Noise is distracting. I
hate tearing up – sometimes I just cannot stop.
But I did it today! I drove and solved math problems this morning. Then drove home – oh, the
tension! I tear up as I write this. I am so fearful
& I hate it! Pre-accident I was cautious but still
went everywhere exploring. Now I don't. I can
find any excuse not to leave the house. When I
saw the dead dog on the road going to therapy
yesterday, it was so sad. It represented me. I don't
know why. Then coming home I saw another
dead animal. It's too hard. I spent the rest of the
day in bed recouping. Part of me knows I need
to do this to get better, part of me wants to hide.

May23

Taken time off to re-group. Not going to
therapy as stress of drive is too great. Why do I
feel stress today? Oh! It's the anniversary of the
accident. Wish I hadn't noticed that. My head is
starting to ache.

June13

Heard about a train wreck on the news –
sorrow I feel for the injured!

Today I do find purpose. To help my family. Be it new cooking menus, hanging curtains, or mowing the lawn.

I drove today but felt dizzy. Pulled over then continued on my way to therapy. Exhausted. I did it. But is it worth it?

June18

Hope and Cliff on a little trip. Other sister bailed a long time ago. Alone! & I'm not to get depressed.

If I don't over due it I'm good

Really tired of being broken

Need to find a way to see the future – better attitude – bee positive

How do I get the world to understand I'm good for 4 hours a day?

July8

Woke up 7 ish – think about CVS purchase. How am I to look for a job & keep a job when I "snap."

But Clark said, at least I recognize it. Sales clerk was really trying, but the $5 off coupon wouldn't ring up. She really was professional. I just couldn't function with phone number request. I tried to be polite, just cancel – to leave – never did it dawn on me to try Clark's cell. At least I didn't cry or yell.

I'd like the opportunity to explain to her. Trigger – DUH!

Aug3

Woke late, walked, but overloaded later

Aug16

Taking pride in what I do. NO matter what – when job looking gets me down, I take the dog for a walk & talk to strangers. I will find something! Thank goodness for my camera. Walking and taking pictures gives me…a purpose.

Aug30

Woke feeling alive, with my kitty purring – the start of a new day!

Pride – I am doing it. Is it time? Or just hard work? Or both? As I pet my kitty I reflect – she has seen me thru this every step of the way. I reflect to the sound of purring-

When you grow up the youngest in a family of brains, you have to find your way – your edge. Well, the oldest totally messed us up. So that made it harder & easier for us kids. Hope always in a book, that was her path. I found mine in physical strength and discipline. Cheerleading. The book learning came later. I worked. I practiced. I committed and I achieved. So – now fast forward 36 years. I walk. I take pictures. I do this daily. All else will follow – & now I walk Lola. I helped a lady with doing directions & yep! No hesitation or confusion. I did it! So – proud – keep the physical strength up – book & brain will follow OMG – I might even get a job yet! Keep on truckin'

Sept15

I think I am finally at acceptance. Taken more than a year to get here. I experiment daily. I can do this. Getting freedom with car. Open----- -stay open. Routine – focus – pattern – no more than 4 hours – focus & I can do anything!

Sept20

Accept
Accept
Accept!
I have brain injury
Even if I don't want
To
Accept it!
It
Happened –
Now make it a part of
You –
Can you tell I'm having trouble accepting the accident. I so wish it didn't happen.
I wish I didn't hit the wall so much
I wish, I wish, but
If wishes were horses…
Main plan – find my courage
Find my strength
Find my life.

Sept 21

Oh no! Just erased all the texts that I had saved over the years. Darn it all! When I'm tired, I do stupid things. Outward – I look ok, but – oh, the brain!

ACCEPTANCE

Life is a series of natural and spontaneous changes. Don't resist them; that only creates sorrow. Let reality be reality. Let things flow naturally forward in whatever way they like.
—Lao Tzu

CHAPTER 27

FAITH AND CLARK SAT IN Joe Lovitt's office as he went over the terms of the settlement that the city and state were offering for the case to be dropped. Faith realized she had literally moved to the edge of her seat as the attorney read from the document. "So this means that they are willing to pay us without going to court?"

"Well, what it actually means is that the door is now open for negotiations. What they are offering here, well, it really isn't much at all. But a first offer never is."

"But this means we won't have to go to court?" Faith's voice was whispery with hopefulness that that was the case.

"We're not going to throw the court case out the window yet. It's still on the docket and all systems are go for that. But let's talk about this. You have options. They've made an offer, paltry as it is. You can counteroffer, but I wouldn't advise that because that actually gives them the advantage."

"How does it do that?" Clark wanted to know.

"What if they are willing to go higher than your counteroffer asks for. They give you what you ask for and that's the end of the line. If they had budgeted to go higher than that, it leaves money in their pocket not yours. I think the better choice is to simply flat-out refuse the offer to settle. That gives the impression that we want to go to court, and well, as we do, that's all good. It says we have faith in our case and we are confident that the ruling will be in our favor. But what a refusal of their offer also does is this—it means that if they make another offer, it will be a lot more than it would have been if they had received a counteroffer from us."

"But what if we make a counteroffer way out there? What about that?"

"A crap shoot."

"So?" Clark was processing all this. "So we refuse this offer and maybe they'll counteroffer or maybe they won't. Maybe they'll be willing to take their chances in court."

"That's always a possibility. And if that's what happens, no worries. We are locked and loaded and ready to fire."

"So?" Clark was still processing. "This really is, to use your words, a crap shoot."

"It always has been. All life's a gamble, Clark. Either they counteroffer or we go to court, and regardless of which way the ball bounces, it's a win-win. Really, it is. Refusing to settle isn't going to hurt you or your case at all. It will only encourage them to come back with a much more realistic offer if they don't really want to go to court. That's all."

Clark looked at the jack-o-lantern sitting on the attorney's credenza along the wall. "So the door has been opened and someone has said, 'Trick or Treat,' and we have to figure out if what we choose will end up the Trick or the Treat."

"Not exactly," said Joe, "but 'tis the season, isn't it?"

Clark's frown lines had deepened as he processed. "So we go to court. What if the jury looks at Faith and says, 'She looks fine to us. So no dice. No dollars?'"

"I sincerely don't think that will be their decision."

Faith, who had been doing her own deep thinking, took a deep breath and plunged in. "Okay, then. We refuse the offer."

Clark looked over at her with a raised eyebrow that communicated, "we do?"

"Hey, it was my accident, my case, my decision." She nodded once at her husband and turned back to Joe. "We refuse the offer."

Smiling at her, he reached across the table and shook her hand. "Good decision, Faith. I'll let them know right away."

Sitting in the car, Clark looked over at his wife. "That was a lot of money you just turned down there."

"Well, yes, I agree, it was."

"Did you ever hear 'a bird in the hand is worth two in the bush?'"

"Clark, we both know I'm not very good at math, but Joe was going to get a third of that so the two thirds that would have been left for us wouldn't even have gotten us out of the woods with the medical bills that have been piling up. The money from the car insurance is long gone. We need more than what was offered there. We do."

"You're right. Of course, you're right. I wasn't even thinking about Joe's third. Dang." He gave his wife a penetrating look. "And you, sweetie, you realized that all on your own. You really and truly are getting better. It's been a long haul and a long struggle, but I am so proud of you."

Ducking her head in embarrassment, she felt a flush spread over her cheeks.

***

Thanksgiving, Christmas, and the New Year had come and gone and still no additional offer from the defendants. So they were heading to court in a few days, and, come what may, Faith felt equal to whatever happened. Meanwhile, it had been three months since her last appointment with Dr. Wellbrock.

Faith sat in the waiting room, flipping through a magazine. An article on a new restaurant called Gustatory that had opened up on Coronado Island in San Diego caught her attention. Apparently, a picture of Einstein was its logo and its motto was "Eat like a Genius." The article made the restaurant sound more than good; it sounded fabulous. Maybe she and Hope could take the train down soon and do a day on the island. She was starting to feel more and more like stepping out of her comfort zone of Burbank and trying something new. Emily and Chris had finally gotten her to go to Disneyland and that had been a success. So she was ready for another step toward reclaiming her freedom. She was halfway through the article before she realized she was reading it without the struggle that generally accompanied her reading. A smile slowly spread across her face. Yes, more evidence that she was getting better! And she seemed to be doing it not step-by-step anymore but by leaps. By the time she had finished the article, she was beginning to wonder what was taking so long. Dr. Wellbrock was one of those rare doctors who hardly ever kept a patient waiting.

The door swished open and a man entered the waiting room. He went up to the receptionist to let her know he was here for his appointment. Taking a seat on the other side of the room from Faith, he stared at the toes of his shoes, waiting for his turn with the doctor.

Faith, who had started another article, heard the ringing of a phone in the distance and then the receptionist's murmuring answer. After hanging up the phone, the receptionist entered the waiting room and spoke to both of them. "I'm so sorry. Dr. Wellbrock has been detained at the hospital on an emergency, and so it looks like we need to reschedule."

While Faith set up her new appointment with the receptionist, the man took out his phone and slowly texted someone a message. The receptionist asked Faith, "Do you need to call someone to come and get you?"

"No, I walked today."

As Faith waited for the elevator, the man exited the waiting room and stood beside her. She politely and sympathetically inquired, "Head injury?" He simply nodded and sighed. "Me too." She told him. Then asked, "How long ago?"

"T-t-two m-m-months."

She felt tears sheen her eyes as she listened to him struggling with language as she had not so very long ago. "Over a year for me, closer to a year and a half. I guess you've just joined a club, a club you'd have preferred not to be a part of. But like me, you weren't given a choice."

"N-no, I w-w-wasn't."

They rode down to the ground level in silence. When they got out of the elevator, Faith headed for the door then, glancing back, noticed the man look around as if unsure of himself before he sat down on the marble bench in the lobby. "Waiting for a ride?"

He made a gesture with the phone in his hand. "M-my f-f-fian-cée h-hasn't t-t-texted m-m-me b-b-back."

To Faith, the man looked like a little lost puppy dog. She knew well that feeling of confusion and of being overwhelmed by the smallest of things. On consideration, she wasn't about to leave him alone. "Look, there's a coffee shop just down the block here. Why don't we go have a cup of coffee while you wait for your ride? We can share our horror stories with one another."

It took him a moment to process the offer then he nodded. "S-sure. Th-that w-w-would b-b-be n-nice."

Thomas held the door for Faith as they entered the coffee shop. It was a quaint old-fashioned shop, none of that modern upscale coffee house stuff here. Spotting a booth, they headed in that direction passing a couple of men deep in conversation.

One of the men was saying, "So the car swerves way over to the left to avoid the guy on the bicycle and hits the pedestrian who was just out for a walk, facing oncoming traffic, I might add, and kills her on the spot. Probably never even knew what hit her."

"The other guy responded, "Danged drivers."

"Driver, heck," the other guy shot back. "If that bicycle hadn't been in the lane of traffic, hogging the space that woman would still be alive."

Faith and Thomas slid into their booth, both shaking their heads at what they'd just heard while the waitress bustled up to take their order.

It turned out Thomas had also been in a car accident suffering a concussion that resulted in traumatic brain injury. Because of his speech difficulties, he did more listening to Faith than talking. She, completely understanding, was simply sharing with him the benefit of her experience over the past nineteen-some-odd months.

"We Californians know what kind of damage a house can sustain in an earthquake. Well, I guess early on, I saw myself as a house that had been damaged in a quake. Slowly but surely I rebuilt. Fixed this, repaired that, tossed something else out completely, and started brand new. Today, I am a composite of the house before the quake and the one after the quake: the old me and the new me. I will never completely be the old me again."

He shook his head. "T-th-that's t-the p-part I'm h-having t-trouble with. I k-k-keep t-telling m-m-myself th-that in t-t-time, I'll b-b-be f-f-fine."

Faith kindly shook her head. "I do hope that's the case for you. That you do get your old self back. I waited for that to happen for a long time. It never did and it really shook me to the core. Not just me, but my husband too. Talk about the Slough of Despond, you know, from *Pilgrim's Progress*? But once I realized what my reality was, well, at that point, I was able to start climbing out of that slough and back up into the light."

"H-how d-did y-y-you d-d-do th-that?"

"It wasn't just one thing. That denial you are experiencing, I was there too, believe me. Denial is a fabulous place to visit while you heal, but you can't live there. But getting from denial to acceptance takes a long, long time. What you need to do first and foremost is develop a sense of humor—a quirkiness if you will—to get through the dark times."

He was listening hard and thinking hard. "Y-yes. Th-the d-d-dark times. It's l-like w-w-wading through d-dark m-matter."

"Yep. Dark matter because the gray matter is messed up. Sorry, couldn't help that. Remember what I just said about quirkiness and developing a sense of humor?"

"I-I re-remember."

"One thing I learned through all this: mind and brain are separate. Brain is an organ, mind is soul. It is my soul that helped me survive my brain injury. If you are not a person who can guffaw at life, you'll not make it. It's my soul that saved me and helped me to continue to survive. People with a lesser determined soul may not live. I feel blessed through this accident that I learned the difference between body—the brain—and soul."

"H-h-how?"

"Good question. I think the answer is different for everybody. But one thing I do know is that what you need to do is to acknowledge what happened to you, face it squarely, understand the reality and the permanence of your loss. When you do that, you'll be able to grieve and then move on. But it took me more than a year to get to that place. So all that might be too much too soon for you at this point."

"H-how d-d-did y-you d-do th-that? F-f-finally g-get to t-th-that pl-place t-to m-move on?"

"Well, I'm a work in progress. One thing I did was to commemorate the loss of my old self. My husband and I took some photographs of the old me and some mementos from the past and we literally buried them in our backyard. Then, not long ago, I put up a decorative concrete lawn ornament as a kind of quasi-headstone. I etched the dates on it, the whole enchilada. It was one thing that helped me to let go and face the future."

"I c-c-can s-see th-th-that you are w-way ahead of m-me in t-t-terms of ac-ac-acceptance. I'm s-s-still s-stuck b-back there. I k-k-keep reliving the ac-accident over and over again in m-m-my mind. You know, fl-fl-flashbacks."

"That's what they call posttraumatic stress disorder. Dr. Wellbrock will be able to help you with that. So be sure and emphasize that it really is an issue for you."

"I'm th-thinking of a-a-asking him f-for s-some m-medicine t-to h-help m-me d-deal w-with all t-the s-stress."

Faith reached out and rested her hand on his wrist. "Oh, Thomas, I hope you reconsider that. The human body is a marvel when it comes to healing itself. Humans have been around for millennia upon millennia, but those drugs you're talking about, those pharmaceuticals, they've been around what? Ten, twenty, thirty years. Some not even eighteen months. And all with lethal side effects. They really are killing people. Not saving lives but ruining them."

He was grinning at her.

"And I just went off on a tangent, didn't I? My sister and I have that in common. We can get on a soapbox and just go on and on. Sorry."

"D-don't b-be."

"Before we got sidetracked you were telling me about your issues?"

"M-my b-biggest issue is m-my f-f-fiancée."

"She doesn't get it, does she? What you're going through?"

He shook his head. "K-k-keeps s-saying th-this isn't w-wh-what s-she s-signed on f-for."

Faith could tell that was a hard admission for him. *And,* she thought to herself, *what a rotten thing to actually say to someone who was injured and trying to recover.* She knew Clark had had a heck of a time with her injury too, but he had never put any blame on her or made her feel that he wasn't going to go the distance with her.

With sympathy in her eyes she said, "My husband had a hard time throughout my recovery too. And, yet, at the same time, he was also my rock. But, the fact is, he had something taken away from him, too, and he struggled with that." Faith thought a moment then nodded to herself. "Why don't you and your fiancée have dinner with Clark and me some day? Like maybe some Saturday soon? Clark can share with both of you some of what he, as a significant other, went through. Your fiancée can hear firsthand what it's like to be the significant other of someone who has suffered a brain injury."

"Y-yes. I'd l-l-like th-that."

Faith tore a blank page from her log that she carried with her at all times, wrote down her address and phone number, and handed it to him.

"T-thanks."

"And," she held up her log, "this is another thing. My log really saved me."

"D-Dr. Well-Well-brock t-told m-m-me to k-keep a l-log, b-but I h-h-haven't d-done th-that yet."

"For me, amazingly, I discovered writing was so much easier than speaking. I guess because that part of my brain hadn't been injured. Who knows? It might be that way for you too. Won't hurt to give it a whirl."

***

One Friday afternoon toward the end of February, Faith and Clark were summoned to Joe Lovitt's office.

"We've received another settlement offer. Finally, I might add. It took them long enough as it's the eleventh hour before our trial begins. This one is for quite a bit more than the first one." He named a figure that had both his clients smiling. "Before we get too excited about this, I want to caution you about any hasty decisions. They are trying to settle because they know we have a good case and they want to preempt anything a judge or jury might say. So today, we discuss this. Then I want you two to go home and discuss this some more, and next week, we'll give them an answer."

"Okay." Clark rubbed his hands together. "Let's discuss."

"First point is that if a settlement is agreed upon, it will be in confidence. That means part of the agreement will be that you can never talk about it with anyone. You can never disclose what you received. It's all sealed. Do you understand that?"

"A? I guess so, but why?"

"They don't want others getting the idea they can sue, and so by sealing the records and demanding a gag order, it protects them."

"So we can't talk about it?" Faith was confused. "But you just told us to talk about it."

"With each other, Faith. But no one else. The three of us are the only ones who can discuss this."

"Oh. I get it. What else do we need to know?"

***

That night after supper, Faith and Clark took Lola for a walk with the additional goal to talk about the settlement offer. After a covering a block in silence, Faith slanted a look at her husband, then plunged in. "I think we should take it."

"I don't." Clark immediately countered. "I think Joe is right. They're running scared now. So while that money figure is pretty impressive—even after sharing a third with the attorney—we can probably hold out for more."

Faith didn't point out that he was singing a far different tune than he had been at the previous offer. Instead, she shared her rationale with him. She told him about the trial she and Cliff witnessed when he had taken her to court to help get her acclimated to the courtroom environment. She explained how the judge rejected the woman's claim that she deserved the money she was asking for. "The court wasn't sympathetic to her plight at all."

"Sounds like she was just a gold digger."

"Be that as it may, what if a jury thinks we are just gold diggers?"

"You suffered, honey. You were a victim and it has taken nearly two full years to get you to a place where you can talk again without stuttering or dragging out your words. And the bills, we are buried under bills."

"And the settlement will cover them and we will be fine. Look," she hurried on, "that woman at court. She was offered a settlement before the judgment came down and she refused it. She was offered cold, hard cash and she said no. She ended up with nothing."

"And you're afraid we'll end up with nothing if we don't take the settlement?"

"It could happen."

"But it won't. We have a legitimate case."

"And we are discussing a legitimate offer. It's a very good offer. You wanted to jump on the last one."

"I was behaving like a little kid who was being offered some candy. I've wised up since then."

"Yeah, now you want the pot of gold at the end of the rainbow."

"Faith…"

"Don't Faith me. There is no pot of gold, Clark. They waited until the last minute to make this offer. If we refuse it, they won't be making another offer. This will go to trial. And there, we take our chances. A solid offer versus a chance. I say we take the settlement, we pay off the bills, and we thank that universal energy that some identify as God that your business is turning around so we can keep on keeping on. Those McMansions…"

"Are hideous."

"But they are what your clients want and you know how to give your clients what they want." They walked in silence for a while. "Honey, like Joe kept pointing out, it would be a crap shoot if we went to court. But this is a sure thing. And even after Joe takes his third, we'll be able to breathe again. I say, we do it."

Clark turned toward his wife and reaching out, placed his hands on her shoulders and halted their walk. Cupping her cheek with one hand, he looked deeply into her eyes.

"What?" Faith asked.

"Just like old times. When we'd discussed aspects of the business, you always had good ideas. So you're right, let's do it. Let's take the settlement and move on."

Lola had been looking alternately at whoever was speaking during the entire conversation. When she realized they had come to some kind of conclusion, she gave a happy little yip.

"And on that note," Clark said, "let's head back home and see what's on TV tonight."

CHAPTER 28

As SHE GOT PLATES OUT of the cupboard to set the table, Faith filled Clark in on their dinner guests. "I really kind of put my foot in it when we were talking about being brain injured. I mean, I was telling him that this has been the most humbling experience of my life. God's own truth is that I had no idea of the meaning of the word *humility* until I went through this. And I was explaining how these arrogant people with their noses in the air all the time, how they have no idea what it's like to be slapped upside the head, *literally*, and get a taste of the rougher side of things. Well, right in the middle all that, his fiancée comes striding up to the table."

Hope paused to gather her thoughts and Clark prodded her, "And?"

"And, talk about one of those arrogant people with her nose in the air. She fits the bill, exactly. But I had made the offer for them to come over for dinner before I met her. Gloria. She's a real piece of work. Talk about haughty! She came bustling up to the table where we were having coffee and just projected an aura of 'hurry up I need to be somewhere else.' Anywhere else. Her arms were crossed across her body and she was literally tapping her toe waiting for Thomas to get himself together so they could take off. I'm actually surprised she agreed to this dinner."

"Well, then, this sounds like it's going to be fun."

"Yeah, so, like I said, I might have put my foot in it when I extended the invite, but it's only for a couple of hours."

"After having canceled twice, I'm surprised they are actually coming over."

"I think she probably had to be seriously persuaded. Oh, well. Just remember how it was for us when all this was new. It was hard. And if we'd had someone we could have talk to who had been through it, well, it might have helped."

"So are you going to set the table or just hold the plates?"

Faith looked out the window. The weather was unseasonably warm, thanks to the Santa Ana winds yesterday. "Why don't we set up outside at the patio table? You're grilling out there, anyway. I think it will be more relaxing, less formal."

"Whatever you think, honey. It's your party."

Patio table set, they were back in the kitchen. Clark dug some seasoning out of the cupboard when the doorbell rang, setting Lola off. Deserting the field, he told Faith, "You get it, I'm going to tend to the tri-tip and grab some beers out of the fridge in the garage."

Faith held the door wide and shushed Lola at the same time. "Welcome. I'm so glad you could come."

"T-thank y-you for h-having us."

"Yes. Absolutely. Looking forward to the evening." Gloria's smile seemed forced and her words didn't exactly ring true, but at least she'd said them. She was also looking at Lola with a leery expression grasping the bottle of wine she was holding as if she might have to club the dog with it. Then realizing the dog wasn't going to attack, she offered the bottle to Faith. "You might like this wine. It has a nice, crisp, citrusy appeal."

"Thank you. Come on in. Clark is out back doing his manly thing at the grill. Shall we go out and join him?"

After greetings, Clark told them that the tri-tip had a little while to go, but they could enjoy their beer and wine with the guacamole and chips while they got acquainted. It seemed that none of them had anything in common except for the head injuries. Thomas had been a tax attorney but was no longer able to concentrate long enough to grasp what had once-upon-a-time been so easy for him. He was on hiatus from his firm for now and for the foreseeable future. Gloria had an art gallery in Bel Air but didn't seem inclined to discuss it much.

***

Dinner was not exactly unpleasant, but conversation was stilted. And it seemed that all parties were looking forward for the evening to be over. The conversation naturally turned to both car accidents and the aftermath. Faith described her experience like falling down a rabbit hole when her whole world suddenly became topsy-turvy. Thomas likened his to being in an elevator when the bottom drops out. Faith found it interesting that they'd both kind of felt as if they'd fallen into a hole of sorts.

Thomas was saying, "I-I d-d-despair be-because I-I c-c-can't d-do any-anything any-anymore."

Gloria didn't even disguise her eye roll as she refilled her wine glass and muttered, "Here we go."

Faith, ignoring Gloria, focused on Thomas. "Tell me, did you get up and get dressed today?"

"He nods. "Of-of c-course."

"Well, you see! You did do something. Believe me, there were many days I didn't even do that. So whatever you do, it's all good. Not that it won't take time and patience. Patience! Oh, how I hate that word. But, well, it does take patience and people. So many people. The Dr. Wellbrocks and the speech therapists and the physical therapists and the occupational therapists and the whatever therapists and to, well, to quote Hillary, 'it takes a village' to give you enough hope and help to get you back to speed. It's all the baby steps that make you whole again, and getting out of bed is just one of those baby steps." Faith seemed to be swallowed up inside herself as she talked and her voice changed cadence. "You are gone in an instant and it's a so unfair and you fight the process. But…," she pulled herself back to the present moment, "but you manage to do what needs to be done and go on."

Thomas took a gulp of his wine and said, "Y-your r-right ab-about one th-thing. It s-s-sure is u-un-f-fair."

Realizing she might have gone overboard, Faith smiled at him and added, "I have to admit, Thomas, because of the accident and everything I have gone through, I am a better person for it. I appreciate life more. I appreciate friends. Am I glad it happened? *No!* Absolutely not. Do I appreciate my lessons. Yes, I do. I am a much kinder person. Why be mean? Life is short. In a nutshell, I'm a better person for my lessons."

In an attempt not to ignore her other guest, Faith turned to Gloria. "What a beautiful ring." She reached out. "May I?" Instead of extending her hand, Gloria took the ring off and handed it to Faith. Upon examining it, Faith turned to Thomas and asked, "Is it an heirloom?"

"M-m-my g-g-grand-m-mother's."

Faith smiled at Thomas then looked back to Gloria. "I can't but admire this craftsmanship. Not at all gaudy or ostentatious like these modern monstrosities you see. Very tasteful. Very elegant." She handed the ring back to Gloria.

"Thank you." That said she slipped the ring back on.

Faith wasn't about to give up. "Have you set the date yet?" And the minute the words were out of her mouth, she knew she'd stepped in it. The immediate vibe told her that there was definitely trouble in paradise. So much for the planned segue into telling her guests about her plans to renew her vows with her husband at some point in the following months. Best to change the subject.

When Gloria excused herself to use the little girl's room, Thomas offered apologies. "S-s-sorry th-that s-she's a-acting l-l-like a s-s-snob. S-she is really f-f-feeling put upon. N-not be-because of y-you. Be-because of m-m-my injury. I d-don't h-have a c-clue a-any-more how t-t-to r-relate t-to h-her."

Clark tried to be encouraging. "Well, she's wearing your grand-mother's ring, so all can't be lost."

Thomas was shaking his head. "T-t-too l-little t-t-too l-late, I f-f-fear."

"Why do you say that?"

"If I'd p-p-proposed when I s-s-should h-have, when s-she w-wanted m-me to m-more th-than a y-y-year a-ago, w-we'd be m-m-married by now. B-b-but I p-put it off and l-l-less th-than a w-w-week a-a-after our engagement, the a-a-accident."

Faith glanced over her shoulder looking at the door to the house. "She's been in there an awfully long time."

"P-probably ch-checking m-messages on h-her ph-phone."

Clark stood up. "How about I just go check on her and maybe have a little one-on-one chat with her? Do you think that might help?"

Thomas brushed his hand through the air, "H-have a-at it."

When Clark entered the house, he saw the bathroom door was open and nobody was in there, so he availed himself of the facilities then went in search of their guest. He found her in The Rogues' Gallery looking at one photo in particular. It was the pile of rocks in the fallow field with the pine tree and the lilac bush.

"One of Faith's," he told her.

"She's a photographer?"

"Yes, would you like to see some of her stuff?"

***

Thomas reminisced. "I h-had the j-job, the g-g-girl, the c-c-car. I h-had it all. W-w-well, the c-car's b-b-been t-totaled."

"Been there, done that."

"And the j-j-job's on h-h-hold."

"And the girl?"

"I d-d-don't know."

"Speaking of the girl," Faith got up from the patio table and glanced in through the sliding glass doors. She saw Clark and Gloria sitting on the couch looking at her photo albums. "Why don't we go in and see what they are up to?"

When they entered the room, Gloria was saying, "See right here. There's a fierce honesty in this one with the juxtaposition of decay on the one hand and rebirth on the other interwoven in unity."

"What are you talking about?" Faith wanted to know.

"Your photograph." Gloria, more animated than she had been all evening, gestured to the picture. "The one of the cracked sidewalk with the little wild violets or whatever they are growing out of it. It's, well, it's art."

Faith humbly responded, "It's just a picture."

Gloria flipped back to some other pages and said, "Here, look at these two. This one is actually primal. It resonates. By that, I mean you almost hear a sound, something more primordial than the croaking of this bullfrog here. Something fainter than the whispering of the hummingbird's wings in this picture, and yet, overall, it is clear as a bell tone. Each picture says: *Here! Look! Listen! Wonder!* Overall, from what I've seen here, you have a truly impressive body of work."

Faith looked confused. "Body? Of work?"

"Absolutely. Taken together, it is almost like some abstract mathematical formula that points a finger toward truth."

"Mathematical? I don't know math."

Hovering one spread hand over a photograph, Gloria expounded. "It's all geometry. See? With respect to the orientation in space." Seeing Faith's continued confusion, she added an explanatory phrase. "The usage of space. You have a genius when it comes to the usage of space in the photograph."

"I just…take the pictures. That's all. I don't put any mathematical thought into it."

"Well, that's because you are a natural." Gloria flipped through the album and focused on a lake picture. "Look at this state of perfect intermingling. The placid lake surface then seeing the trees and clouds reflected in the lake as if the lake itself contains those things. An interpenetration. And the one here," she flipped some more pages, gave up, and picked up another album that was next to her on the couch and flipped until she found what she was looking for. "Here! This porcupine, the irony of this plump woodland creature waddling across a city street. So out of place and yet so confident in that place." She shook her head in amazement at what she was seeing. "The elements of consistency from photograph to photograph, the flow from image to image. You can see what I am talking about here," she turned back to the first album, "with this series of these pictures of the island in the lake. Notice the flow of energy between these pictures. Clearly of the same place, clearly on different days, and yet the continuity is almost seamless while ironically snapshots of a seamless flow of time."

The breath caught in Faith's throat while Gloria went on and on. That phrase again. The one she had focused on when she and Hope had been looking at her dissertation a while back – *a seamless flow of time*. It grabbed at her again. Meanwhile, Gloria was still expounding.

"Or this one of the different stages of the healing bruise on…is that your inner thigh? Remarkable. Mix those up in a showing and we could label it 'Displacement in Time' or something like that." Gloria was on a roll and she just steamrolled on. "It's the subtle rearrangement of point-of-view. What I like about this series of bruises is that it reminds me of that first photo of the crack in the sidewalk with the flower – a growth-out-of-decay or healing-out-of-injury sort of theme. This body of work, and yes, I called it that again, is just dynamic, all movement, growth, change. It's like your scarf."

Faith put her hand up to her throat touching her scarf. "My scarf?"

"Even your scarf falls into a perfect waterfall flow, almost impossible to make it look so naturally, so perfectly casual."

"I just…drape it." She made a fumbling gesture, clearly embarrassed.

"My point is that you are an artist. Not only here," she pointed to the pictures in the album, "but even how you drape your scarf. Your photographs are something I want in my gallery."

Clark, grinning from ear to ear, looked over at his wife. "Who knew, huh? And I thought they were just pretty pictures. But I also always told you that you were a class act."

Barreling right on Gloria didn't miss a beat, "But not yet. We can't show your entire collection, not at first. We need to introduce it and then the big splash."

Faith continued to have a hard time keeping up. "A collection? I have a collection?"

"In a few weeks, there's going to be a little art show here in Burbank at that little community meeting room in the park just north of here. You know the place? Submissions have already closed, but I have some pull with the people over there. I don't usually bother with that rinky-dinky little showing they have a few times a year. But we need to get some publicity out there before the showing at my gallery, and that's the place to start you out." Gloria stood up and started pacing back and forth across the family room, eating up space with long, deliberate strides. "We'll get you a wall and put up a few, just a few. Not the really stellar stuff. Save that for my showing. Not a lot of really important people show up to those little showings in the park. But you get an art critic or two from a couple of the newspapers." At this point, Gloria was almost talking to herself calculating out loud, "It won't matter so much *who* comes as much as *how whoever* comes *responds* to your work. What we're looking for," she spun and clasped Faith's arm, "is a reaction—that will be the spark that launches you. We get that first review then set you up in my gallery for your first real showing. I'll simply provide the platform." Then almost as an afterthought she added, "And advertise it, of course."

Almost feeling like she had been hit by another car, Faith took a couple of deep breaths. "Aren't I a little old to be embarking on something like this?"

"Ever hear of Grandma Moses?"

"Considering that I'm an art history major, I'd have to answer yes to that question. Also," she continued in an undervoice, "I'm not *that* old!"

***

Faith linked her arm with Thomas's as she walked him down the driveway and out to Gloria's car. "I'm so sorry, Thomas. The plan kind of backfired here. I didn't mean to steal all the thunder. Tonight wasn't supposed to be about me."

Thomas patted her arm reassuringly. "A-ac-acctually, I th-think th-this is all f-f-for the v-very b-b-best. Your ph-photos have g-given her a new f-f-focus, a new p-p-project to get her t-t-teeth into. Th-that will t-t-take the sp-sp-spotlight off of m-me and m-my impediments f-for now, and th-that c-can only b-be g-g-good for us."

RESOLUTION

If you flee from the things you fear, there's no resolution.
—Chuck Palahniuk

CHAPTER 29

HOPPING OFF THE TRAIN THAT had pulled in to the station near the airport, Faith gave a little twirl. "I did it."

"That you did." Hope, right behind her, was grinning from ear to ear.

"I took a nice, long all-day-long daytrip and didn't get stressed out, didn't freak out, didn't have a meltdown. I did it!"

"And now that we know you can get as far as San Diego and back on the train and live to tell about it, what do you say we fly to Vegas soon, rent a car, and then go visit Susie B for a couple of days?"

"I think I'd love it. I've been so boxed in here for so long, it's time to spread my wings and fly, isn't it?"

"Yes! Fly, literally!" Hope impulsively pulled her sister into her arms. "God, it's good to have you back again!"

Faith started to say, she wasn't back, per se, because she was a new person, but decided she didn't need to say that.

***

Over time, Faith had come to realize that facing things head on was the way to deal with them. Because of her experiences in the aftermath of her accident and healing process, she *had* evolved into a new and different person. She was calmer than she used to be. Hadn't had a temper tantrum in almost a year. So that was progress. She was more open, more generous, and, well, she was trying to be more forgiving too. She was working on that one. At the beginning, right after the accident, she had forgotten so many things that she had to relearn

from scratch. And her missing memories: when they started returning slowly at first then faster and faster in waves, for a short period of
time, she was overwhelmed with not only all the memories but also
the emotions that accompanied them. She'd had to learn how to cope
with long-forgotten emotions and, yes, even resentments. She came
to realize that dealing with one memory at a time and addressing it
and the feelings manifested with it was more productive than trying
to absorb all the returning memories at once. She'd mentally set this
one aside over here and that one aside over there and then address the
one that was knocking most loudly on her memory door first; that
was the best way to go. But none of her memories, none of her past
experience prepared her for the whirlwind of Gloria. Her instincts
told her not to fight the tempest but just to go along with it and see
where she landed.

***

Faith hadn't been inside this city building on the park property
since Emily had been in Girl Scouts, and it hadn't changed one
iota. Concrete walls. Cement Floor. Windows that looked like they
belonged in a schoolroom. Long utility tables that would stand up
under all kinds of use. She marveled at the organized chaos she was
witnessing of artists hanging up their paintings or placing their
sculptures here and there. Gloria was pointing out to her helper how
to arrange on the wall the six photographs that had been chosen and
framed for this showing. That done, Gloria turned to Faith.

"Remember, none of these are for sale. No price tags. No selling. What we're looking for here in this *local* art show is not a big
showy splash. All we need is some publicity. I've arranged for a couple art critics I know to come do a look-see. The rest is up to your
work. If it speaks as loudly and clearly to them as it does to me, we're
off and running."

Faith and Clark walked over to the park after supper to see how
things were going, and it was a good thing they had walked. There
wasn't a parking spot to be found while a few cars drove up and
down the little lot, hoping someone would be backing out so they

could pull in. They entered the building and just wandered, looking at what the other artists were showing. Some of the paintings were amazing. Faith pointed to one telling Clark, "I wouldn't mind hanging that on the wall over our bed."

Clark stepped back and considered it. "Eeehh," was his less-than-subtle retort.

Snickering at his response, she took his arm and they continued wandering. They stopped at the refreshment table. Clark put some sweets on a little plate while Faith opted for a glass of white wine. Sipping the wine, her nose wrinkled slightly.

"Cheap wine?" Clark whispered in her ear.

"Pretty much." A few more sips and she inconspicuously set it in a nearby trash barrel.

They noticed that Emily and Chris had just arrived and were slowly wandering from exhibit to exhibit. "So no Hope and Cliff tonight?" Clark polished off the brownie.

"They had some other commitment tonight, but they said they will definitely make the next showing."

The occasion proved to be quite the social event. The Kincades bumped into several neighbors, some of Clark's former clients, and a handful of customers from the shop Faith used to own. Clark stayed close by Faith's side in case she went into overwhelm with all the activity, but she held her own nicely.

After making the circuit and chatting with the other artists as well as the art lovers who kept coming and going, they hung out by Faith's photographs. People walked by, looked, and moved on. Just as they themselves had done when looking at the other artists' work. No one ooohhh or ahhhed as Gloria had. And while Faith thought the show experience was interesting, she was pretty sure nothing would come of it. As far as Gloria's pronouncement not to sell anything, she didn't have to worry about that. No one asked.

Chris stood back giving Faith's photos a good looking over. "You know something, I never really noticed it before, but I think this Gloria is right. Your pictures do have a really special quality to them."

"Well, thank you, Chris." Faith gave him a quick hug. "That means a lot."

Emily moved in and gave her mom a hug as well. "Yeah, Mom, you really are an artist."

Faith punched her daughter lightly on the arm. "Don't sound so surprised."

"Speaking of artists, princess, maybe you should put some of your paintings in one of these shows. The guy we were talking to over there said they have shows here two or three times a year."

Emily considered that for a moment. "Well, thanks for the vote of confidence, Dad, but I don't think I'm ready for anything like this. Maybe someday."

"Something to think about."

"Sure. Okay, we're out of here. See you guys later." And off they went, hand in hand.

Walking home under a canopy of stars, Faith broke the comfortable silence with an observation. "Do you realize today is the anniversary of my accident? Two years ago today."

Clark stopped and turned toward his wife. "No, I didn't realize that. You've come a long way in two years, baby."

"I certainly have."

Pulling her into his arms, he gave her a long, sweet kiss. A car full of teenagers drove past and the sound of catcalls had them chuckling as they finally pulled apart.

"So," Clark asked her, "do you think the show was a success."

"I think it was an interesting experiment. But I feel it was a bit anticlimatic. I sincerely doubt Gloria will be impressed with whatever the outcome was. I also doubt we'll be doing this again."

But, to the contrary, the little blurb that appeared in Sunday's paper on page three of the entertainment section had Gloria calling Faith full of plans for what she called their *real* showing in Bel Air.

After she hung up, Faith opened the paper, found the right section and managed to read the little blurb without any trouble at all. It said:

Last night was the unveiling of a new sensation in the world of photography. Faith Kincade's extraordinary art work has not been officially launched; that will occur in July at Glorianna's Gallery (more commonly known as G G's) in Bel Air. In this sneak-preview at the Burbank show last evening, art lovers were tantalized with just a nibble of what is to come. No spoiler alert here – just a bit of information to let you know that when you see Kincade again at G G's expect to be treated to exceptional accomplishment. These pictures of nature in all Her glory bring to mind William Blakes's axiom of *life delighting in life*. Kincade's work slowly draws you in from the first glimpse of a photo which on the surface is so peaceful; then it sucks you further into the depths of the picture which conversely depicts a volcanic force of life. Keep your eye on this newcomer. Faith Kincade is about to make her mark and join in the ranks of other photo artists from Adams to Michals. Move over and make room for her.

Faith read it again. Flattered, she felt herself blushing and was glad no one was around to see.

Meanwhile, the flattery notwithstanding, she had bigger fish to fry. Clark had agreed to a tasteful little ceremony in their backyard where they would reaffirm their wedding vows that they had made a quarter of a century before. And she was fully focused on that. At first, she had wanted to wait until fall to renew their vows because, as she logically explained to her daughter, they were in the autumn of their lives. She liked the synchronicity of that. But Emily pointed out to her mother on the QT that while Dad had agreed to do this for her, to wait too long might give him time to reconsider. Agreeing with her daughter, she chose instead to do it on June 24, which would be their twenty-fifth wedding anniversary.

***

The day dawned hot, but as it progressed, the occasional breeze appeared and was more than welcomed. Faith's backyard was blooming yellows and pinks and blues and whites; in addition, a decorative archway woven with little climbing tea roses had been added for the occasion. Folding chairs had been set up on the grass and food had been prepared. Emily and Hope draped tulle in artful waves along the concrete wall that ran around the backyard, camouflaging the spray painting that Faith, for reasons of her own, refused to let them paint over.

Friends and family gathered, settled, and the ceremony began. It was tasteful and, in Clark's estimation, blessedly short. They renewed their vows, then the party commenced. Appetizers, cocktails, and mingling were on the agenda.

Thomas had arrived alone and was reading the little plaque on the lawn ornament commemorating the passing of the old Faith and the birth of the new Faith. Every now and then, he stabbed a toothpick into one of the sweet and sour meatballs on his plate and popped it in his mouth. Faith approached and, placing his plate on a nearby table, he gave her a little congratulatory peck on the cheek.

"I see you found my little headstone," she made finger quotes around the word *headstone*.

"V-very t-t-tastefully d-d-done. B-by the-w-way, G-Gloria c-couldn't c-c-come s-she had s-some-th-thing come up l-l-last m-minute. Or s-she'd b-b-be here."

"Yes. She did call and apologize for not being able to cut loose."

Glancing around the yard as she chatted with Thomas, Faith saw that Clark was deeply wrapped up in a discussion with Brian over near the garage. Clark was gesticulating in the way he did when he was feeling passionate about something. Usually, passionately upset. And it was rare indeed for him to get passionately upset. And today of all days? Hmm? She wondered what that was all about.

Clark was saying to his former neighbor, "No, I haven't told her yet. Don't want to burst her bubble so soon after depositing that settlement check. But that bill really blindsided me. I thought the arrangement with the attorney was that he got his third and we got two thirds. And that's the way it was *before* they sent us a bill. We did get two thirds of the settlement. But! *A bill?* We weren't expecting a bill. I thought his one third *was* his payment for all his work. But, no, it's not. For cryin' out loud, he not only added up all those months and months of billable hours, he also billed us for every phone call and every postage stamp. Not to mention for all the expert witnesses he'd lined up, but who never took the stand because we never went to trial. They still get paid! For whatever reason, I don't know! The shyster lawyer, pardon my French at my own wedding, will end up getting fully another third once we pay him off, ultimately giving him two thirds and us one third. Which means all *our* bills won't get paid after all! Which is what we based our decision on when we choose to settle! Sheesh! What a racket those lawyers have!"

"Clark, I had no idea that's the way lawyers worked. Really. Never having…"

"Forget it, Brian. It's not your fault. Any attorney would have done the same thing to us, I'm sure. But I'm going to buttonhole Thomas and tell him if he's planning to sue to get something in writing with his lawyer that everything is *literally* pro bono and that any settlement is *all* the attorney gets and not a penny more! Get that in writing, in blood and in stone!"

Dr. Wellbrock approached Faith and Thomas with his wife. She was an age-appropriate woman—no trophy wife for him. After a few minutes of introductions and chitchat, she excused herself and wandered over to mingle with Clark and Brain. Faith watched her cross the patio and thought to herself that there was a woman with style, grace, and elegance.

She turned to Dr. Wellbrock and said, "That's who I want to be when I grow up."

He smiled at the compliment. "She's probably a year or two younger than you are, Faith."

"But, wow, she sure knows how to pull it all together, doesn't she?"

"That she does. Now, first off, congratulations. You and Clark have chosen a wonderful way to reach some closure here as well as opening a doorway into your new beginning. I am so very proud of you."

"You know better than anyone, it wasn't an easy journey."

"No, it wasn't, but you pulled it off. Not always, I might add, following my advice."

"Oh?"

He looked over at Thomas. "And you aren't much better."

"Wh-wh-what d-did I-I d-do?"

"Neither one of you were willing to take my advice about joining group therapy. But look at the two of you! Somehow you found each other, and it appears to me like you've bonded and are helping each other just like they do in group therapy."

Thomas turned to Faith and asked, "D-did we j-j-just g-g-g-get a s-sp-spanking?"

"Perhaps." She turned to the doctor, smiled at him, and gave him a hug. "I may not always have followed your advice, but I always trusted that you were on my side."

Thomas waved adieu and wandered off to refill his plate with appetizers. Dr. Wellbrock watched Faith as she smiled after Thomas.

"Has Thomas become one of your strays, Faith?" When she looked at him surprised, he said, "I recall from our first meeting hearing about your strays. I think you have another one."

"Yes, I suppose I do. Clark always said I had too much mothering in me for just one child."

"By the way, I saw that little blurb in the paper a few weeks back about your photography. Congratulations. Looks like that art critic is a fan."

"That show was kind of my dress rehearsal. The bigger one is just around the corner. I simply can't believe the direction my life has taken and so unexpectedly. And none of it would have happened without you. I mean, I met Thomas in your office and it's his fiancée who discovered my...talent, I guess it is."

"Apparently it is a very prodigious talent. Do you recall, I mentioned to you during your last visit that your most recent MMPI2 test indicates that you are a visual genius? What's happening with your photography just goes hand in hand with that assessment. Can't wait to read more about you in the paper."

She laughed. "Glad you didn't say the funny papers."

"And that you can make those connections just goes to show how much your brain has healed from that brain injury."

"Yes!" She affirmed. "Yes, it has."

He gave her another little hug. "And on that note, I'll leave you to your guests and festivities. I've got to collect my wife and head on out to another engagement."

Hope approached her sister with open arms and the two of them hugged. The hug would have gone on longer, but Hope suddenly started and said, "What the heck?" She pulled back a little and pointed. Faith followed the finger and saw it too. A tortoise was at the back corner of the garage placidly eating a dandelion.

They approached slowly and looked down on the creature. "Look! Look, I think it's Ogden Nash." Faith looked closer. "See that unique marking on his head and where's Emily?" She started looking around for her daughter.

Emily had seen her mother and aunt head for the corner of the garage and, out of curiosity, was heading for them. When she saw what they were looking at, she stopped dead in her tracks.

Faith beckoned to her. "Honey, come see. I think it's Ogden Nash."

Emily knelt by the tortoise and placed her hand gently on the back of its shell. She looked over at her mom with tears in her eyes. "It is. I just know it is. He's been lost for so long, but he finally found his way back. He must have been on a heck of a journey to get back here. And all in one piece."

Reaching out Hope took her sister's hand. "Yeah. There's a lot of that going around."

***

Sipping some champagne, Faith let her eyes sweep over the crowd. Clark was still talking to Brian, which meant Meghan was around somewhere. At least Clark looked calmer than he had a little while ago.

When Faith turned around, Meghan was standing there with open arms. She almost fell into them; she was so happy to see her friend and former neighbor. The embrace went on and on. When they finally pulled back, both had to dig out handkerchiefs and dab at their eyes.

"Look at you!" Meghan stood back a step and looked Faith up and down. "Gorgeous as always, and when you were saying your vows and not a stutter to be heard, my heart just sang."

They both quoted Cheryl in unison: "We don't say stuttering, we call it dysfunctional speech." Then they laughed, not because it was funny but because they had shared so much those first few weeks of Faith's ordeal two years ago.

"It wasn't an easy couple of years, but as Clark said to me not too long ago, I've come a long way, haven't I?"

"You certainly have. And, I might add, I didn't doubt for a minute you'd pull through. But I do notice you are serving your champagne in plastic glasses. No crystal?"

"Is that your less-than-subtle way of asking if I am still breaking glass?"

"Maybe."

"I moved beyond the need for that means of expression."

"Bravo, Faith! I knew you'd pull through."

As the afternoon wore on and guests started to leave, Clark found himself by his wife's side. He took her hand and brought her fingers to his lips. Kissing them, he winked at her. "You pulled off a really nice party, honey."

"Thanks." She looked into her husband's eyes and asked, "What were you and Brian talking about?"

"You saw us, did you?"

"You looked upset."

"Not with you. Not about today. Let's just enjoy our party and our guests."

Looking closely at his face, she knew he wasn't going to reveal anything until he was ready to reveal it. So she nodded, "Good idea."

They both looked around at their friends, feeling content.

"Do you want me to get you some more of those yummy meatballs before they are all gone?"

She patted her tummy. "No, I think I need to start a little diet before the upcoming art show."

"Well, don't lose too much weight." He slipped his arm around her waist. "I have discovered in recent weeks that I like a woman with some curves."

"What a sweet way of saying I'm plump."

"Like I said, I like the curves." He gave her a little pinch.

They saw Emily and Chris over by the garage talking to Hope and Cliff. Chris looked up and caught their eyes. Excusing himself from the little group, he joined Faith and Clark.

"By the way Chris, thanks for all your help in setting up." Clark clapped Chris on the shoulder.

"Don't mention it. But, there's something I do want to mention." He suddenly looked a little uncomfortable.

"What is it?" Faith rested her hand on his arm.

"Well, today put an idea in my head. I am going to ask Emmy to marry me. But guess I'm old fashioned. I'd like to get your blessing before I do."

"Oh, Chris!" Tears had welled in Faith's eyes and, pressing her fingertips to her lips, she looked like she was getting ready to go in for a hug.

"Hey, don't give away the surprise." Chris stepped back a little. "If you start blubbering and hugging me, Emily will wonder what I'm talking about to you guys."

"Tonight?" Hope wanted to know.

"Oh, Heavens, no!" Chris looked aghast. "I mean, not tonight. Soon, I'm waiting for the perfect moment. I just wanted to know if I had your go-ahead."

"And you are babbling." Clark laughed at Chris's discomfort. "You have our blessing, son. Now, go, get the girl!"

Chris, flashing a smile that lit his whole face, gave them a nod and blended back into the crowd.

***

When the party was over and the guests had all gone home, Clark took Faith by the hand, pulled her down on the couch next to him, and told her about the bill from the attorney. He had planned on waiting until this day had passed. But she had gotten wind that something was up, so, as his father used to say, there was no time like the present to deal with it. When he finished talking, he sat back and waited. Faith sighed deeply and didn't say anything for the longest time. When she did speak, she uttered one word. "Fuck."

"My sentiments exactly."

CHAPTER 30

CLIFF AND HOPE PULLED UP in front of Faith's house in their spiffy Corvette just as Faith and Clark exited the front door.

"Oh, Faith!" Hope got out of the car and ran to her sister hugging her. "You look fabulous!" All dolled up in a slinky silver dress, cut low in both front and back, and strappy heels, Faith executed a little turn for the group and took a bow.

"Head's up!" Cliff tossed his car keys in her direction. Snatching the keys out of midair, Faith look both surprised and cautious at the same time. Cliff strode up to her and gave her a peck on the cheek. "Just thought you should go to the show in style."

"I...I can't drive your car."

"Sure you can. I know you can handle it based on the couple of times we've taken it out into the hills. I called Gloria and arranged for you to have a VIP parking spot right in front of the gallery. You're good to go. We'll follow you guys in your car. Do the kids want to ride with us?"

"No they went on ahead."

"Okay, let's get this show on the road."

**

The art show at G G's was something Faith couldn't have imagined in her wildest dreams. She stood on the sidewalk, just outside the doorway, looking through the plate glass windows at the throng of people inside. Emily and Chris were schmoozing with the other art lovers, completely at ease.

Faith slipped her hand into Clark's. "Aren't they a lovely couple?"

Clark squeezed the fingers he held in his hand. "As are we. Come on, looks like a full house. You ready?"

"Not yet. Just let me stand here a minute." She took in the gallery entrance and noticed a quote painted on the glass near the front door in neat gold script. It read:

Photography deals exquisitely with appearances, but nothing is what it appears to be.

Duane Michals

"Do you suppose that's true?"

Clark, noticing Hope and Cliff coming down the block from where they had parked, asked, "What's true?"

"That saying," she pointed to it just as her sister and brother-in-law arrived to join them. "Do you think that nothing is as it appears to be?"

Hope chuckled. "I think that's a discussion that should wait until we are sitting in front of your fireplace with a bottle of wine. Come on, let's go inside and get this party started."

Standing in the doorway that Cliff held open for her, Faith, seeing her photographs displayed, pressed one hand to her accelerating heart; her breathing had hiked up a notch too.

"Deep breaths," Clark cautioned her. "Slow your breathing down." He gave her fingers another little squeeze while she did just that. "Ready?"

She nodded and they walked through the doorway and into the gallery.

Gloria linked her arm with Faith's, pulling her along, and strode with her around the room. She plucked a flute of champagne off a tray a passing waiter held and put it in Faith's hand while Faith glanced around at this photo and that one almost appalled to see the prices Gloria had affixed to each. But more startling than that was that half of her photographs already had sold signs tastefully attached to the frames. Her eyes bugged for a moment then she went into a

Zen place where she just let what was happening happen and she went along with it for the ride.

Thomas came up to her and gave her a little hug. "Y-you-you're a h-hit."

"Am I? I think Gloria's the one who hit the homerun. She really appears to be in her *glory* tonight. Pun intended. There's quite a sparkle in her eye."

"Y-yes, b-but n-not j-j-just th-this." Thomas went on to tell her that he was half owner of a race horse that he had named Little Miss G G, and last night when they had been at the races, the horse had come in. "It w-was q-quite the l-l-long shot. S-she's p-p-pretty h-high-st-strung s-so the odds w-were q-quite high. B-but s-she f-fooled th-them and p-placed. Of-c-course, we-we'd p-put a ch-chunk of ch-change on her. S-so G-Gloria was p-pretty s-stoked a-about th-that. S-saw it as a-a g-good o-omen f-for to-tonight."

Faith patted his arm. "Maybe it was a good omen for a lot of things."

"M-may-b-be."

After her second glass of champagne she wandered over to Clark and told him he'd have to drive the Vette home because the bubbly was so good she intended to have some more. "Thanks for the warning," he told her. "I'll make this one my last."

She found herself conversing with a youngish, long-haired man who was gesturing to the photograph of the porcupine. "I'd love for you to explain that to me."

An almost imperceptible frown line appeared between her eyes. Explain it? What was there to explain? In confusion she stated, "It... it explains itself."

"Ahhhh," the young man nodded as if she had just dropped a philosophical pearl of wisdom. "So it does."

When a publisher told her he was interested in signing her for a coffee table book of her work, she convinced herself she was dreaming and that she'd soon wake up to find herself back home in bed.

When it was time to go home, Hope pulled a black fringed shawl out of her purse and placed it around Faith's shoulders. "Here. I noticed you didn't bring a wrap and as you'll want to go home with the top down now that the wind blowing in your hair isn't an issue, you'll want this." She gave her sister a kiss on the cheek. "We'll follow you and swap cars at your place."

***

Faith wrote in her journal:

> I woke up today feeling lighter than I have since my accident just over two years ago now. At first I didn't know what was different; I just knew something was. Then I realized what it was! I have forgiven that woman who caused the accident. She has been my nemesis for so long, and suddenly she no longer is. When I took a deep breath and didn't feel it stop at that blockage under my breastbone because the blockage was no longer there, I realized that I am finally free. And it's all because I found it within myself to forgive. I have finally been able to accept all that happened and all that I have undertaken to get from that day to this day. If all that hadn't happened, I wouldn't be in this place in my life now. And this is a pretty good place to be. You cannot really heal without forgiveness, because forgiveness dispels the anger. Forgiveness frees you to be whole again. The woman who caused the accident was just a woman who made a grave mistake. Without forgiveness, you cannot move on, you cannot have freedom. You can't love. Before forgiveness, the pain IS you. The pain is a mantel you hang on to at night – and it's always night! Once you forgive the world is amazingly beautiful. After all, the job (of life) is not to harm anyone else. And when you don't forgive someone it is harmful to all parties.

The life process, in its wisdom, doesn't often give us choices; it just carries us along. If we go along gladly and don't fight the inevitable, what a stress-free world this would be. Realistically, I know that will never happen. For some reason humans are preprogrammed to fight the flow, to resist the process, not to go with it. But if people would really look at life, really observe as well as participate in it, in time they would get to that place where they see that just going along with the unfolding process is the best way to live. I keep coming back to the mantra Cheryl gave me at the very beginning of my speech therapy sessions. She told me to keep saying to myself "trust the process, trust the process, trust the process." I believe this holds true for the process of living too. If we just trust the process, everything will turn out okay.

***

Clark and Faith were sitting out on the patio, looking up at the stars. They each sat in their own chairs, but were linked as they held hands and swung their joined hands between the chairs. A recently discarded medical insurance form rested on the patio table.

"So it looks like a pretty good policy," Faith was saying. "I mean it's not too much each month and then we can get your knees fixed. We've been putting that off for far too long."

"Let's sleep on it and readdress it in the morning."

Faith knew when to push and when to back off, so she agreed. "Sounds good to me."

They heard the gate clink and Lola jumped up and started barking and then stopped immediately.

"Must be Emily." Clark gave his wife's hand a little squeeze.

When Chris and Emily came around the corner of the house holding hands too, Faith felt that all was right with the world.

Without saying a word, Emily walked up to her parents and held out her left hand. The diamond on her ring finger winked, reflecting starlight from above.

"Oh, Emmy!" Faith flew out of her chair and hugged her daughter.

"We're thinking a destination wedding. What do you say, Mom? You up for a nice, long trip somewhere?"

ACKNOWLEDGMENTS

Every successful novel is the result of a group effort. My gratitude and thanks go to numerous individuals without whom this book would not be as rich or as many layered. Thank you all for your faith and support. Early readers, Dr. Larry and Margaret Jean Sanders who graciously made observations and editorial suggestions, and my colleague Temple Blackwood who kindly provided input not only with this novel but my previous novels as well—a heartfelt thanks to all of you. And thank you to Shannon Rajewski at Christian Faith Publishing, for all your expertise and help along the way.

An affectionate thank you to my niece, Autumn Cade, who allowed me to use, as the cover of the novel, the portrait of her mother that she painted when her mother was *lost* and suffering from a traumatic brain injury.

An especially huge thank you goes to my sister, Susan Cade, who suffered a TBI and whose recovery is still ongoing. Thank you, Susan, for helping me to understand my own novel and bring it to life. Susan gave generously in terms of time and experience so that Faith's experiences in the novel would be authentic. And she allowed me access to her most personal journals so I could get more than just a glimpse into the workings of the healing brain. Thanks so much for your permission to use portions of that journal (almost verbatim) in chapters thirteen and twenty-six. The inclusion added a richness to the novel it would not otherwise have had.

Susan was my inspiration and my best critic as I moved from draft to draft. Without her insight, assistance, and support that vastly improved this work, it would not be the book it is now.

I would also like to thank my parents, Douglas Gilman Blizzard and Mary Louise Page Blizzard, whose love of books and the written word continue to be a life-long inspiration to me. They have been gone for many years now but continue to be my muses.

Also, let us not forget the over two million individuals a year, in the United States alone, who suffer from traumatic brain injuries (TBI). This book is dedicated to the very, very many who have suffered that blow to the head. May Faith's success against all odds give you the strength to do what you must do to carry on, overcome, and heal from the injury.

READERS' GUIDE: QUESTIONS FOR BOOK CLUB DISCUSSIONS

1. What is the symbolism of Faith's name in the context of this novel?
2. Did anything about Dr. Wellbrock surprise you? What was it?
3. The woman who caused the accident is only mentioned a couple of times in the novel. Why do you think the author chose to keep her in the background?
4. The bill from the attorney took both Clark and Faith by complete surprise. Should they have been surprised?
5. Faith's nemesis—the singing woman who hits the high notes that trigger Faith's anxiety—symbolized what?
6. For a large part of the novel, Faith's daughter, Emily, takes on the role of mother as Faith descends into the role of child. Have you ever experienced such role reversal in your life?
7. Do you ever expect to experience such role reversal in your future?
8. Is there any comic relief in the story?
9. Have you ever known someone who suffered from traumatic brain injury (TBI)?
10. How did his or her experience differ from Faith's?
11. When Faith gardens, she experiences what she calls Zen time, "a time when she went to that place of no time." What do you do that could be defined as enjoying Zen time?
12. Being lost is a strong motif in this novel. Are there any other motifs you noticed?
13. The title of the book is *Lost*. Was Faith truly lost?
14. Discuss the contradiction of Faith's eventual forgiveness of the woman who caused the accident in light of her sister Charity.
15. What part of the novel will remain with you as time passes?

ABOUT THE AUTHOR

BORN AND RAISED IN CALIFORNIA, Priscilla Audette received her bachelor's degree from UCLA in 1976 and her master's degree in English literature from North Dakota State University in 1990. An award-winning writer, Priscilla's first novel, *Seismic Influences*, was published in summer 2012.

Seismic Influences was a NABE Pinnacle Book Achievement Award Winner in fall 2012. In addition, it won the Award of Excellence: Outstanding Achievement in Fiction: First Place in the Women's Category in the LuckyCinda Publishing Global Book Contest in 2013. *Seismic Influences* was also a semi-finalist for The Writer's Network award. Audette's second novel, *Court Appointed*, published in 2015, won one of the Beverly Hills Book Awards of 2016. Audette has also been recognized by the Austin Film Festival and the Eugene O'Neill Theater Center for her scripts and stage plays.

A gypsy at heart, Priscilla has lived in California, Minnesota, North Dakota, Wyoming, and Maine where she currently makes her home. Please visit her website at www.priscillaaudette.com

CPSIA information can be obtained
at www.ICGtesting.com
Printed in the USA
LVHW01s2026200218
567274LV00002B/509/P

9 781641 400145